JOURNEY
to the
HEART STONE

JOURNEY
to the
HEART STONE

A NOVEL

CATHERINE RAPHAEL

Published by SparkPress, a BookSparks imprint,
A division of SparkPoint Studio, LLC
Phoenix, Arizona, USA, 85007
www.gosparkpress.com

Published 2022
Printed in the United States of America
Print ISBN: 978-1-68463-167-4
E-ISBN: 978-1-68463-168-1
Library of Congress Control Number: 2022937105

Interior design by Tabitha Lahr

For my son. You remind me to keep
my mind and heart open.

And to my writing group, for your
support and encouragement.

As it was, in the time before time, the Goddess
danced the dance of creation among the stars.

With a graceful sweeping step, she scooped
starlight together into a sphere of energy and
fused it into a world—our world—alive with
forests, grasses, mountains, valleys, rivers,
and oceans.
With the flick of one wrist, two moons
appeared; with the flick of the other, a sun.

The Goddess was pleased. But it was just
the beginning.
She tossed her head and twirled around;
animals, fish, and birds appeared.

The Goddess was pleased. But her work was
not yet complete.
Breathing deeply, she kicked up her heels and
spun again.
The People came into being.

Life was full.

All beings were connected to the land, finding nourishment and pleasure wherever they went.

The Goddess was pleased. But she imagined even more.

She gently placed the Heart Stone in the center of the world.

Then, from her heart, she sang a note of pure joy.

From this sound, her daughter, Kameeth, appeared, fully grown,

First Mother of the People.

The Goddess was pleased. Her dance was complete. Under her loving eye, our dance began.

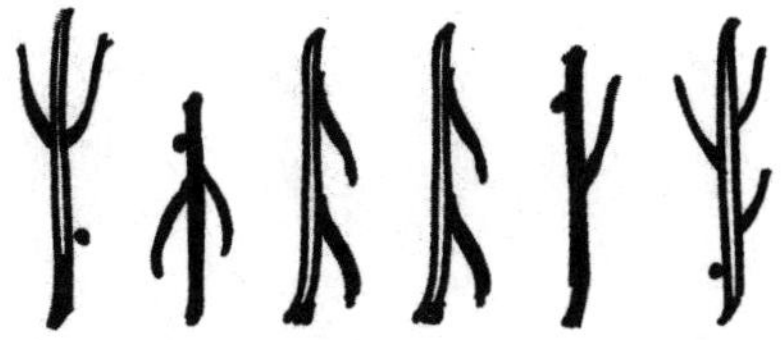

Chapter 1

The early morning sun chiseled through the mountain pass and illuminated an isolated dwelling on the far side of the valley, turning the gray stone walls rosy.

Rilda shuffled into the bedroom, depositing a mug of steaming tea on the bedside table. Cora feigned sleep. Tut-tutting, Rilda headed toward the windows. She was a tiny woman and had to stand on her tiptoes to reach them. With a sweep of her plump arms, she pulled the heavy curtains aside, letting in the light. It would take all day for the warmth to fully penetrate.

Rolling deeper into the covers, Cora mumbled, "I'm not getting up."

"Cora, dear, you've been in bed for days."

Cora curled into a tight ball and hugged herself for a long moment. Then, with a deep breath, she turned over and sat up.

"I dreamed of Kip again last night. He was so close, but I couldn't touch him."

Rilda slumped onto the bed. Tears filled her eyes, tears for her son.

Cora leaned her head on Rilda's shoulder.

Rilda pulled a handkerchief out of her apron pocket to dab her eyes. "Your brother is due back from the barn raising soon. And Dov is returning after his travels. They're coming to celebrate the Summer Solstice with *you*. You don't want them to find you in bed, do you?"

Cora drew her dark eyebrows together. "There's nothing to celebrate. Kip—"

"Kip gave his life for the Goddess," Rilda interjected. "We need to remember that and honor his sacrifice. Cora, dear, you are the Mother Minca."

"Ah, Rilda, still lecturing me," Cora said with a sigh.

Rilda stroked Cora's glossy brown curls before giving her a kiss on the cheek. "I guess I am."

Rilda stood up and started for the door, tucking tendrils of gray hair back into her chignon. "I could use some help in the kitchen. Don't start snoozing again." The door closed behind her.

Cora leaned back into her pillows. *Summer Solstice. What's the point anymore?*

She thought about her dream from the night before . . . and Kip. Her heart opened up to a cascade of memories.

Cora had been seven years old and Steff just a baby when their parents were assassinated and Vestor claimed power. Vestor had convinced the Mincans that the Carroo and Dute tribes were responsible for the killings. Tools used for farming, crafting, and hunting were turned into weapons. Vestor trained the Mincan men as fighters and relegated the women to subordinate roles. The war began soon after, the Carroos and Dutes caught unawares.

Vestor sent the siblings to Rilda's mountain home for caretaking, or more accurately, to be rid of them. Rilda, he assumed, was a simple country widow and would defer to his dominance.

Her son, Kip, a gap-toothed ten-year-old, had been the only one who could calm Cora's fears. Kip had welcomed her, encouraged her to play games with him, and helped her to laugh again. He and Cora had taught Steff how to ride. Dov, Mother Minca's Teller, had instructed all three of them in the fighting art of Rime. They honed their skills battling imaginary hordes of soldiers. Kip was the one who had come up with Vestor's nickname, Evil V.

Vestor forbade any sacred teachings, but Rilda believed in the Goddess. She risked Vestor's wrath to share Goddess stories and traditions. She taught Cora the women's Spirit Writing, the secret communication shared woman to woman over generations. Dov performed the Solstice and Equinox traditions and other rituals.

When Cora had her first menses, Rilda took her into the woods for three days of fasting, ritual bathing, and meditation. Suddenly, Kip was shy around her. In his eyes she had transformed into Mother Minca.

She teased and cajoled him to help him recognize she was still the same Cora, but it didn't work. Smiling to herself, she recalled when, frustrated, she surprised Kip in the stables, knocked him off his feet with a deft Rime maneuver, pinned him to the ground, and tickled him. Kip howled, then tickled her back. A warm flush spread through her body when she remembered how the tickling had turned to kissing, surprising them both. When they finally pulled apart, they looked at each other with new eyes.

A year later, Dov performed their marriage vows, unbeknownst to Evil V.

"Cora! I could use your help," Rilda called from the kitchen.

✾ ✾ ✾

RILDA TOOK A LOAF OF BREAD out of the oven, filling the air with a warm, yeasty aroma. Cora realized, for the first time in days, she was hungry.

Setting the bread on the counter, Rilda said, "Steff arrived a while ago, and Dov soon after. They're taking care of the horses. They'll be in shortly, dearest. You can prepare the apples for baking." She handed Cora an apron.

Cora cored four apples and placed them in a baking dish. She filled each hole with butter, spices, and a drizzle of honey. She had just finished prepping the apples and was licking a drip of honey from her finger when Dov and her brother came into the kitchen, Dov's lanky deerhound, Lali, following close behind.

Steff had curly brown hair like his sister but cut shorter, trimmed around the ears, and tousled on top. He had the same hazel eyes and easy smile. He was several inches taller, long and lean with broad shoulders. His brown tunic and leggings were somewhat worn and rumpled.

Dov's clothes, on the other hand, were clean and tailored. There were no embellishments beyond the Teller's pouches hanging from his belt. He had mellowed with age but maintained the refined appearance of Mother Minca's Teller. Now that he was in his mid-sixties, his walk had slowed a bit and his movements had grown more measured. His dark hair and beard were turning silver. He was a handsome man with gray eyes lined from both laughter and concern. He had a distinguished look, which he used to his advantage when traveling and telling his stories. Lali had been Dov's constant companion for many years. Her graying coat matched Dov's own head of hair.

"Hard to believe it's the Summer Solstice. There's still a chill in the air," Dov said as he gave Rilda and Cora each a quick kiss.

"Great to be home!" Steff said, picking Rilda up and swinging her around the room in a hug. Rilda swatted at him with her wooden spoon, laughing all the while. Gently putting Rilda back down, he put his arm around Cora's shoulder. "How are you doing, sis?"

Without answering, she turned into his embrace, hugging him close. "I'm glad you're home."

The table looked beautiful. Tiny clay birds, which Cora, Kip, and Steff had made when they were children, encircled a vase of summer flowers. The cerulean-blue ceramic dishes and crimson cider-filled goblets sparkled in the afternoon sun. During the cold winter, Cora and Rilda had embroidered new linens with chains of pink and yellow wildflowers for the Summer Solstice. Flatware, polished to a high sheen, sat by the dishes. A loaf of hearty brown bread was on the table, adjacent to a block of creamy butter and a tureen of spicy summer vegetable soup.

Cora and Steff sat on one side of the table, Rilda and Dov on the other. They held each other's hands. Cora, in her role of Mother Minca, gave the blessing.

We are grateful for the love and friendship
that brings us together.
We are grateful for the food and the nourishment
it provides.

We are grateful to Kameeth, Mother of us all.
May peace be with us on this Summer Solstice Eve.
Earth, air, fire, and water.
Blessed be.

When she finished, Cora served everyone a generous portion of soup. As she placed Dov's bowl in front of him, she saw the sadness in his eyes.

Cora sank back in her chair and asked, "Dov, is something wrong?"

"We can talk later, dear one."

"What is it?"

Dov glanced at Rilda before turning to Cora. "You asked me to find out about Kip. We will talk—"

"You know how he was killed? Tell me."

Dov took a deep breath and reached for her hand. "Kip and two others were rescuing a young boy, Ebru. This child was one of our best spies and a close friend of Kip's. It's a miracle Ebru and the others got away. Kip sacrificed himself to save them."

"I should have been there, Dov," Cora said, pulling her hand back. "Why did I listen to you and Rilda? I should have gone with him."

"Cora, when your parents were killed, you became Mother Minca. Rilda and I are honor bound to keep you safe," Dov said.

"But we've been in exile for almost thirty years."

"You're Mother Minca," Rilda reminded her.

"Exactly." Cora clenched her hands in her lap as she regarded Dov and Rilda.

"Dov, I can shoot a bow as well as you can. Rilda, you taught me to wield a knife. I can fight. I can think. It's time for me to use these skills for a better purpose. I am done with sitting around waiting. For what? By all rights, Evil V should have relinquished his leadership to me years ago, but he will not cede power. I should be fighting with the Resistance. Fighting for my place as Mother Minca. Fighting for my people."

"She's right," Steff agreed. "We should *both* be with the Resistance."

"Vestor is destroying our world and blamed the Carroos and Dutes for killing our parents."

"We know it was his doing," Steff said.

"Cora, please . . ." Rilda began.

"Enough," Dov said, running a hand through his hair. "We've talked about this bef—" Lali barked in the kitchen. They all froze at the clatter of horses arriving in the yard. Rilda jumped up and rushed to the kitchen window.

"It's your uncle!" Rilda called out.

Outside, Vestor and his companions dismounted. The youngest man took charge of the horses while Vestor and a second man came to the door. Vestor entered without knocking and aimed a kick at the growling dog. Nodding at Rilda, he entered the dining room and saw his young relations sitting at the table with Dov.

"Ah, Dov," Vestor drawled, "I thought you were dead."

Chapter 2

"Wishful thinking, Vestor," Dov said, standing up. Lali came to his side and glowered at the intruder. "I'm surprised to see you here. I would have thought the Solstice activities would keep you in the capital."

Upon his arrival, Cora and Steff had transformed into their vapid "Uncle Vestor personas." Steff lounged in his chair with his eyes half-closed, looking bored. Cora tittered slightly at Dov's remark. Vestor turned a stern eye upon her. Under his glare, Cora flushed and sat up straighter, her eyes downcast.

"It's you I've come to see, Cora dear," Vestor said, his voice brusque. "Stand up, now, and let me introduce you to General Fizor."

Cora glanced up at her uncle. Vestor towered over her chair. His chiseled features and severe expression held no warmth. His hair, the color of midnight, was pulled back and tied with a leather cord, accentuating his high cheekbones and pale-blue eyes. He was dressed in an immaculate royal-blue tunic with silver buttons at the neck. A black leather belt with an ornate silver buckle rested on his narrow hips. Tight black leggings were tucked into calf-high black leather boots trimmed in fur and silver buttons. Standing, Cora tugged at her tunic, both proud and self-conscious about the loose-fitting, overworn, mended material. Her leggings hung loosely and were worn at the knees. Her clothes were in the somber brown of mourning that she had worn since the death of her parents.

Looking past her uncle, she observed a lean man standing in the doorway. He appeared to be about seventy years old, with short, grizzled hair, cold gray eyes, and a ruddy complexion. He stood with military bearing, dressed in the black tunic and leggings of Vestor's Royal Guards. Colorful inserts ran from shoulder to cuff on his right sleeve, denoting his rank. His features were sharp as a hawk. As he leered at her, Cora felt like a morsel about to be devoured.

She rose slowly, fear clutching her stomach. "Welcome to our home, General," Cora said in a soft voice, extending her arm.

Rather than clasping wrist to wrist in the traditional greeting, Fizor took her hand and turned it over, exposing her wrist, a sign of dominance. Clicking his heels, he bowed slightly. Steff glanced at Dov and rose to greet the general.

"I'm Cora's brother, Steff," he said, offering a limp hand. The general clasped his wrist with more strength than necessary. Steff winced, retrieved his arm from the grasp, and slumped back into his chair.

"Oh, forgive me. I've forgotten my manners. Silly me." Cora spoke in a rush, her hands fluttering as she talked. "Please have a seat, gentlemen. Dov, would you get some chairs? Uncle, would you like some refreshments? General?

Our fare cannot compare to the food you're used to, I'm sure. We live a simple country life here. I haven't been to Merton since I was a child. I hardly remember it. I imagine it's a wonderful place, full of shops and entertainments. I'd love to go to parties. Do you remember Merton, Steff? You were so young when we left, I can't imagine that you do. Rilda, would you bring some more cider, please? I wonder what the town fashions are now. We're so behind the times and—"

"Sit!" Vestor commanded.

Cora sank to her chair, her head bowed and her hands in her lap.

There was a long, tense silence.

With a slight snarl, Vestor began. "Cora, it is time you were married. General Fizor is the man I've chosen for you. We're staying at the military base across the valley. I've brought a Teller with me to perform the ceremony. Tomorrow, you will—"

"No!" Cora cried.

Vestor took one step toward her. Cora felt a shiver of fear course through her body.

Rilda scurried behind Cora, putting her hands on Cora's shoulders reassuringly. "No, of course you couldn't possibly get married tomorrow, Cora, dear," she said in her calm, soothing voice. "Sir, what were you thinking? Cora's a sensitive girl. This is totally unexpected. She might like to get to know her fiancé before marriage. She needs time to sew a trousseau. I have yet to teach her all she will need to know about being a proper wife. No, she definitely couldn't get married tomorrow. Perhaps after the Winter Solstice."

Vestor stepped back, his arms folded across his chest. Eyeing Cora and Rilda, he considered the situation. No one moved as they waited for Vestor to speak.

"Perhaps you're right. She may need some time," he said with a sneer. "Can she be ready by the Winter Solstice? General Fizor can remain at the base and visit occasionally." He nodded toward the general. "Yes, now that I think upon it, a large, formal wedding may be a better idea. I shall return to town and start preparations. It will be a way to introduce Cora into proper society as well. I will give the bride away. After the wedding is consummated, Cora will return here to await her husband's visits.

"Mistress Rilda, I will have patterns and materials sent from town for wedding clothes. There's been enough of this brown mourning cloth." He gestured at Cora's clothing with a dismissive wave of his hand. "She must dress to suit my station. I will arrange a carriage before the Winter Solstice to escort Cora back to town. You as well, Steff. This will be a family occasion."

Steff grabbed Cora's knee under the table and gave it a sympathetic squeeze.

"Come, Fizor. We have stayed long enough."

General Fizor walked to Cora. Lifting her hand, he kissed the inside of her wrist with cold, moist lips. Cora barely resisted pulling her wrist away and wiping it on her tunic.

"I shall return after the Solstice, my dear. It will be a profound pleasure to get to know you better," he whispered in her ear.

Cora rose slowly. She gave a small curtsy to her uncle and General Fizor as they left. Steff remained in his chair and muttered a bland farewell. Dov hadn't moved a muscle since Vestor started speaking.

The friends remained motionless until the sound of the horses disappeared. Lali, voicing her opinion of Vestor, barked and broke the silence.

"He has some nerve barging in like that on the eve of the Summer Solstice," Steff said.

"Evil V always said he would find me a husband," Cora said. "I didn't want to believe him. I thought, with time, I could present Kip as my choice, and he would come to accept it. I never had the chance. Well, I won't marry that old man, or anyone else either!"

"You won't," Steff said. "Not if I have anything to do with it." He stood and paced the room.

"Rilda, I'm grateful you stopped me from spitting in his face," Cora said.

"Yes, at least Rilda has provided us with some time," Dov said, sitting back down.

"That's right, sweetest. We have time now to make our plans and avoid this wedding," Rilda explained. "You'll be safely away from your uncle and the general before the baby's due."

"Baby!" Dov and Steff exclaimed as one. Cora blushed at the shocked look on their faces. Being pregnant at thirty-seven years old was an unexpected blessing from the Goddess.

"I was going to tell you tonight," Cora said. "Kip was home for the Spring Equinox, you see, and . . . " she burst into tears, "now it's all wrong. Kip is dead. He didn't even know he was going to be a father."

"Oh, sis," Steff said, laying his hand on her shoulder.

"I was going to talk to you about it. I wanted your help planning what I should do and where I should go. And then Evil V turns up with that . . . that . . ."

"We knew this day would come," Dov said. "Your pregnancy makes it more complicated."

"He would kill me if he learns I'm pregnant," Cora stated, wiping her tears. "You know he would."

"Yes, he would," Dov agreed, looking Cora squarely in the eye.

"I have to leave. I'll join the Resistance."

"Cora," Rilda said. "In your condition and with Vestor searching for you, you would put them in jeopardy."

"Then I need to find a safe haven out of Vestor's reach. Dov, where can I go?"

"You can't go rushing off," Dov said. He took Cora's hand. "The general would raise a hue and cry. We need to come up with a workable plan."

"You may be right, Dov. But I am definitely not going to marry that—"

"That ancient general with the manners of a toad."

"Enough, Steff," Cora said with a rueful smile. "Yes, *that* man. I will not marry him."

"Of course you won't, dear," Rilda agreed. "We will figure something out."

"Let me think on this," Dov said. "The Goddess still has many friends in Minca. We will find you sanctuary."

❀ ❀ ❀

CORA TOSSED AND TURNED IN BED. Exasperated, she rose and pulled the mattress to the side of her bed, exposing a trapdoor. In the light of the full moons, she raised the door and descended the stairs into the darkness below.

The hidden room was bathed in warm light from a small oil lamp on the floor, an eternal flame honoring the Goddess. An altar on the far side of the space held objects representing the four elements—stones for earth, feathers for air, a candle for fire, and a beaker full of water. There was also a cameo that held her parents' likenesses. Next to the cameo was the talisman for the Mother Minca, a small orb made of lapis that was a gift from Kameeth to her daughter. On the wall behind the altar were four small, tattered tapestries said to have been stitched by Kameeth herself. They depicted an oak tree at the Winter and Summer Solstices and the Autumn and Spring Equinoxes. Stitched into the roots of each tree was a proverb in Spirit Writing.

Dov had created this room when Cora and Steff were first brought there to live. Aside from Dov and Rilda, only Cora, Steff, and Kip knew about it. This was their sacred space to perform the old traditions and dream of a better future.

Placing a pillow in front of the eternal flame, Cora sat down. She took several long, deep breaths. After a few moments, her chin trembled and tears ran down her cheeks. Suddenly, she sobbed, holding her sides, and rocked back and forth. Eventually, her sobs turned to sniffles. She wiped her face with her sleeve and closed her eyes.

"Mother, Kameeth, and Goddess, listen to my plea.

"Vestor has plans to marry me off. I don't want to marry anyone ever again. I want to go far away. I want to mourn Kip and raise my child. I want to live in peace. I *want* the life of an ordinary woman."

She inhaled deeply.

"If I can't have that—if I am to *be* Mother Minca— I need your help. Tell me what to do."

Chapter 3

"Dearest, you're smiling," Rilda said, handing Cora a bowl of porridge.

Cora was the last one to arrive for breakfast. She came into the room in a rush, eager to tell the others about her experience from the previous night. Dov sipped his tea. Steff eyed Cora while eating his porridge. Both men noticed the marked change in Cora's demeanor. Her eyes were alight with excitement.

Cora took a spoonful of porridge before putting her spoon down. She took a breath and began. "Late last night I went downstairs to meditate. I sat for the longest time and went into a deep trance. Suddenly, I was sitting in a warm, dark space. I think it was a cave or something. Spirit Writing covered the walls."

"Oh my," Rilda said, taking her seat.

"There was a small fire in front of me, and on the other side was an old, old woman."

There was a moment's pause before Dov said, "I've heard tales of Kameeth appearing in times of need. Did she communicate with you?"

"I didn't think so, but when I opened my eyes, it was there, right in front of me."

"What was it?" Rilda asked, putting her hand on Cora's arm.

"There was a beam of moonlight. It had come down through the trapdoor overhead and illuminated Kameeth's tapestry, the Summer Solstice tapestry.

"I got up and went over. The light drew me closer. Though it was tattered, I could see the delicate tree Kameeth had embroidered and could read the proverb. I knew it was important."

"So, what did it say?" Steff asked.

"The proverb said, 'There are stories that we tell ourselves, and there are stories that we tell each other; the most important stories are the stories we tell our children.'"

"That doesn't make any sense," Steff said, squirming in his chair.

"I'm sure it does," Cora said. "We have to reason it out."

They ate their meal in silence, contemplating the proverb.

Dov considered out loud, "If 'the stories we tell our children' is the clue, we just have to figure out which story Kameeth means."

"Children's stories?" Rilda said.

"What stories do we know?" Cora asked. "I always liked 'The Dog Who Thought He Was a Boy,' but I don't think that could be it. What about 'The Six Wicked Children?'"

"I doubt it," Steff replied. "It has a stupid ending. Maybe 'Two Wishes Plus One'? That worked out well in the end. And we could use some wishes about now."

"Maybe Kameeth meant 'The Love of Eyra and Pernell.' It's such a sweet story." Rilda sighed.

"Sweet, yes, but I don't think it has anything to do with our current situation," Cora said. "'Tura and the Evil Troll,' or 'Elvie and the Flying Horse'? What do you think, Dov?"

Dov sat back and pondered for a moment. "Well, there are lots of stories to choose from. But if we're looking for one that's an allegory for our times, 'Tura and the Evil Troll' comes pretty close, I think."

"Is that the story of the woman who married the troll?" Rilda asked as she went to the kitchen. Dov got up to help and Lali followed, hoping for some scraps.

"No!" Cora and Steff answered simultaneously, then burst out laughing.

With Rilda and Dov out of the room, Steff twisted in his chair to reach over to tickle his sister. "You're thinking of 'Tili and the Nasty Giant,'" he called out. 'Tura and the Evil Troll' is the story about the woman who was held captive by the troll."

Cora wriggled, laughing louder, and swatted at Steff's hand.

"I don't remember that one," Rilda called from the kitchen. "What's that noise? What's going on in there?"

Rilda returned from the kitchen holding a pear-and-nut cobbler. She gave her charges a stern look. "You're both much too old for that kind of horsing around. Let your sister be, Steff, and go get some bowls."

Steff let Cora go, but not without a final tickle.

Cora composed herself and tried her best to look serious. "Dov, you're our Teller. Why don't you tell Rilda the story?"

"I'd be delighted," Dov said as he sat back down with a fresh pot of tea. "Let's see, the original tale is about two hundred verses long and is usually told over several nights of feasting. Do we have that much food?" he asked, his gray eyes alight with humor. He smiled at Cora.

"Well, maybe you could give us an abbreviated version or talk very, *very* fast," Cora said, returning his smile.

Steff brought the bowls and dished out the cobbler with a dollop of heavy cream.

"I'll tell a shortened version, then. But let me have a bite of this first. That will sweeten the tale." Dov smiled and winked at Rilda. After a few spoonfuls, and a sigh of satisfaction, he began.

"Long ago and far away, an old woman sat on the top of a hill, weeping. She had been weeping for many days."

Dov's voice mellowed as he talked. He connected to each listener with his eyes and heart, drawing them into the story.

"She wept with pain and anguish, harder than you could even imagine. Her tears flowed like a river. They coursed over her aged face and withered body, soaked her tattered clothes, and seeped into the earth. The earth became saturated, rivulets of mud flowing down the hill."

Dov sipped his tea. "In the original version, there were five or six verses describing the quality and quantity of her tears. A waste of time, really." He returned to the story and momentarily transformed his voice into the high-pitched lament of the spiders.

"'Stop your weeping! Please stop.'"

Dov gave a shortened version of the next part of the tale. "In a nearby tree, three spiders sat on a branch. They had climbed up the hill from where they lived far below. The mudflow was washing away their webs and ruining their lives. They were a wee bit angry. Once they got her attention, they explained the problem. The old woman apologized and, wiping away the tears, introduced herself."

Modulating his voice into a falsetto, Dov began Tura's tale of woe.

"'My name is Tura. I am the mistress of these lands. I'm sorry about your homes. I understand, as my home is being destroyed as well. My gardens are rotting. My farm lies in ruin. My people are suffering. Although I am only three and twenty, I age years each day. I am under the spell of an evil troll, and my sorrow overwhelms me.

"'Last winter, there was a knocking on my door. On my doorstep I found a small urchin dressed in rags, curled in a tight ball, whimpering in the cold. Of course, I brought him in. I took him close to the fire, wrapped him in blankets, and brought him some food. I didn't realize the creature was a troll. He was so small and cold. Besides, I thought the stories of trolls were just fantasies meant to scare children in the dark of night.

"'When I bent over to hand him food, my back stiffened. I looked at my bejeweled tunic and thought the glitter had dimmed. Perhaps I should have realized right away and done something to save myself. But I didn't understand. By sunrise I was fully under his spell and couldn't stop what I was doing and what was happening. Every day of shelter, each morsel of food, brought more stress and ruin. The life force was being pulled from my farm, my people, and from myself while the troll grew larger, gaining strength and power.

"'Now I can only serve him. By next winter my home and my people will be destitute. I fear there is no stopping this path to destruction.' Tura commenced her weeping once more."

Dov grinned at Steff and Cora. "The descriptions of the pain and suffering Tura had endured is deliciously gory and goes on seemingly forever in the original. I will pass over it out of concern for Rilda's sensibilities."

Rilda blushed. "I'm not a child, but I would rather not hear anything too gruesome. Thank you, Dov. Please continue."

Clearing his throat, Dov returned to the high-pitched voice of the spiders.

"'Oh, sad lady. It's no wonder you weep. Although we are small spiders, perhaps we can help.'"

Again Dov summarized the rest of the tale. "Since they were such insignificant creatures, Tura didn't believe them. They convinced her to let them try. The spiders left her sitting there, sniffling. Crawling to the manor house, they climbed the wall and peered into the window.

"The evil troll lay on a chaise, sleeping by the fire. He had grown to a large hulk of a creature, taller than any human. Green hair sprouted out in tufts all over his head. His snores were loud and smelly, great puffs of acid breath, punctuated by a harsh grinding of teeth.

"The small spiders were terrified. Before they could reconsider, they climbed through the window and over to the troll. Slowly and gently, they wove a web starting at the troll's feet. Round and round they went, securing his feet to the chaise. The web was so fine and their steps so gentle, the troll slept undisturbed. Once his feet were wrapped in layers of web, they moved up his legs, over his belly and chest, and onto his neck, round and round and round."

Dov smiled. "There is a song and dance that goes along with the web-weaving part of the story. Little children really enjoy it, but I think we'll forgo that for this telling.

"Anyway, the troll woke up with a roar but was immobilized. There was strength in the tiny threads of the tiny spiders. Tura returned to her home, restored to her youthful beauty. Her people came running. They announced that a miracle had happened—what had been dying was coming back to life. The troll was carried off to a safe place where he could do no harm. And—"

"Balance was restored. All was well. Thus, there's no more story to tell!" Steff and Cora pronounced the traditional ending together with laughter and applause.

"So, if Cora is Tura and Evil V is the troll, are we the spiders?" asked Steff.

"I think it's bigger than that," Cora said. "I think Tura is our world, and the spiders are the three tribes: Carroos, Mincas, and Dutes. We need to bring the tribes together to restore balance."

"You may be right, love," Rilda said. "But that's an impossible task with the way things are right now."

"But we must try."

"I agree, Cora. And I don't think it's impossible," Dov said. "We'll make our plans and move swiftly. We will keep you and the baby safe."

"Where do we begin? I thought the Carroos were extinct."

"That's what they say, Steff," Dov replied. "I'm not so sure it's true. No one ventures beyond the Green Mountains anymore, but in my travels I've seen things, seen people. I think they're using their Mother-given gifts to keep themselves hidden and safe. We'll have to find out. Would you be willing to travel west to Carroo? There are some old trails you could follow. I will travel south to find Mother Dute."

"If I do find them, what should I do then? Tell them the story of 'Tura and the Evil Troll'? That's ridiculous," Steff said with a snort.

Smiling, Dov looked at his young friend. "That would be an interesting place to start. On the other hand, you could tell them about your sister's vision and what we've concluded. See if you can get someone, preferably a woman, to come back with you."

"Not back here, Dov," Cora said. "We should meet at the Heart Stone. That's Kameeth's place. I believe we are called to reunite the tribes there."

Suddenly, Rilda blurted out, "The bread!"

They looked at her, surprised by the seeming non sequitur.

Rilda smiled broadly. "Steff, do you remember what we sing when making the bread for the Summer Solstice? You know it, Dov? Cora?"

Minca, Carroo, and Dute,
Tribes of Three.
When braided together
all will be free.
This is the message
I have for thee.
The truth is in the Heart.

"I thought it was just a traditional chant with no particular significance, but under these circumstances, I think it may be an actual message!"

Cora squeezed Rilda's hand. "Yes. Kameeth has a message for us there 'in the Heart.' She is calling us there to find it."

Facing Dov, Cora asked, "Dov, how long do you think it would take you and Steff to find the Carroos and Dutes?"

"I imagine it would take us a long while to get there and find them," he answered. "With time to convince them and travel to the Heart Stone, we could meet there by the time of the Winter Solstice."

"That feels right," Cora said. "I will meet you there."

"But love, you can't travel to the Heart Stone. You'll be close to your due date. It wouldn't be safe," Rilda said.

"It's safer than staying here and being married off to that general! If I leave by the Autumn Equinox, I should be there in plenty of time. Don't worry, dearest Rilda, I shall be careful. You will have the hardest part. You'll have to convince Vestor and Fizor that I am still here preparing for my wedding day in a state of bliss. *That* will be difficult."

"No! I must go with you! What if something should happen? I would never forgive myself!"

"Rilda, you and Dov taught me how to take care of myself. I will be fine. Kameeth will guide me," Cora said with finality.

"So, it's settled," Dov said. "Steff and I should leave tomorrow. We'll meet at the Heart Stone at the Winter Solstice. With the help of Kameeth and the Goddess, we will accomplish our mission and arrive safely and on time with Vestor none the wiser. But," Dov smiled, "it is still the Summer Solstice. We have another story to tell and a pregnancy to bless."

The four companions finished their meal and tidied up. Rilda retrieved the braided bread that had been tucked away.

They went to Cora's bedroom, moved the mattress, lit lanterns, and opened the trapdoor. They went down the steps to the room below. Lali stayed behind and settled down protectively at the foot of the bed.

Dov arranged pillows in a semicircle around the eternal flame. Rilda placed the bread on an embroidered cloth next to the objects on the altar. Cora sat on her pillow, closed her eyes for a moment, and sent love to her parents and Kip. She silently called to the Goddess, Kameeth, and the four elements. She then opened her eyes and waited in silence.

Steff walked to the wall and, holding up his lantern, examined the tapestries. The Spirit Writing was unintelligible to him. Even knowing what the Summer Solstice proverb said, all he saw were what looked like embroidered sticks. As usual, when a man looked at them, the sticks moved and twisted, making themselves undecipherable. With a shrug, he took his place on a pillow.

Dov lit the candle on the altar and sat next to Cora. He removed a small vessel from his pouch containing red clay. Dipping his thumb into it, he smeared a bit onto his forehead to represent earth for the Summer Solstice.

When they were all seated, Dov sprinkled some Teller's Powder over the eternal flame. Rainbow sparks rose to the ceiling. Cora smiled at the effect of Dov's "magic dust." It took her back to the wonder she felt when she first saw the rainbow sparks as a child.

Dov began the Solstice story.

"As it was, in the time before time, the Goddess danced the dance of creation among the stars . . ."

Chapter 4

Following the Summer Solstice ritual, Cora grabbed the sleeve of her brother's tunic. "Come, let's put together a bit of supper."

Grabbing a basket, they strolled arm in arm through the cobblestone courtyard with Lali at their heels. Behind the stables was the sheltered spot for their garden. With careful planning and a lot of work, Rilda, Steff, and Cora managed to grow all the fruit and vegetables they could consume. Their deep, clear well provided them with plenty of water and kept perishables fresh. Steff and Cora were both good hunters, occasionally providing meat for their diet.

There were other farms across the valley. The isolated region created a sense of loyalty and community among the residents. The households traded for milk, flour, and other staples. Infrequent traders passing through the valley provided tools, fabric, and manufactured necessities. The families came together for celebrations, rituals, and to help each other with harvesting and other projects that needed many hands. Their life was simple but not uncomfortable.

Lali wandered off, her nose to the ground, exploring interesting smells. Cora and Steff knelt on the ground to gather lettuce into the basket. After a while, Cora sat back on her heels and observed her brother.

"I don't doubt your courage or abilities, Steff, but you haven't done anything like this before. Vestor will have you watched once you leave the valley and will try to stop you if he figures out where you're going."

"You won't talk me out of going," Steff said with a rare flash of anger.

Cora had tears in her eyes when she acceded. "No, I wouldn't even try. But please don't take any unnecessary risks, I beg you. If I were to lose you too, I don't know what I would do. My child will need you, especially since Kip is gone."

Steff hugged his sister. "Don't worry about me. Better you should worry about yourself. You'll have Fizor to contend with and a facade to maintain. Traveling will be difficult for you. Will you be able to do it? Are you sure you don't want Rilda to go with you?"

"No, she should stay here. She can keep up the wedding pretense. And I don't know if you've noticed," Cora said with a sigh, "but she's feeling her age more and more. A trip like that would be difficult for her to manage, regardless of what she says. I have Ty, my mountain pony. He's strong enough to pull a cart, so I should be fine. We've had many adventures together, as you know." Cora grinned.

Steff laughed. The sound brought Lali back to their sides, wanting to join in the fun. She jumped and barked until Steff threw a stick for her to fetch. They kept up their game until Cora had picked enough lettuce for their supper.

"Come on, children," she called. "It's time to go inside."

As they walked back, Cora regarded Steff lovingly. Grabbing his arm, she pulled him close. "I know you don't remember our father, Steff. He was kind, gentle, and smart. His loyalty and bravery were distinct traits. You remind me so much of him."

Taking the basket of lettuce from his sister, he kissed the top of her head.

❋ ❋ ❋

STEFF AND CORA PREPARED A light meal of salad, bread, and cheese for everyone. Over supper, they talked and joked. Steff described the barn raising and reported on the other families in the valley. Cora updated them on the beehives she was tending in the woods. They avoided anything to do with weddings and travels. Familiarity, humor, and love helped soothe their concerns for the future.

As they lingered over tea, the conversation turned to the morrow.

"Steff, I'll head out as if I'm on my usual travels. We could ride together until you need to head west," Dov said.

"I would like that. I haven't traveled beyond our borders. I would like to spend some time tonight studying the maps and figuring out a route. Where are you going?"

"I'm due in Tinton before the Autumn Equinox to officiate at cross-quarter weddings. I'll be stopping in villages along the way for my usual evenings of blessings and stories. I'll include 'Tura and the Evil Troll' on this journey, I think." Dov smiled wryly. "I'll keep moving south until I can slip across the border into Dute. Beyond Tinton, you should head west. You can avoid Merton altogether. I think some of the old trade routes to Carroo are still passable. Let's take a look at the maps after we clean up here."

"Don't worry about cleaning up," Rilda said. "I'll take care of that and start putting some provisions together for your trip. What time do you expect to leave in the morning?"

"The earlier the better, I think. Vestor won't be expecting us to depart so quickly after the Solstice," Dov said. "With luck we might be gone before it's noticed."

The friends talked a while longer, making plans. Eventually, Dov and Steff retired to the library to study maps and talk strategy.

Rilda cleaned up the dishes before preparing food for Steff and Dov's journey. Afterward, she went to the storeroom and pulled out Steff's bedroll and warm clothing, checking to see all was in order.

Cora returned to the ritual space and embroidered talismans for Steff and Dov to protect them on their travels. She then retrieved her mortar and pestle from a chest beneath the altar. She contemplated what to write to Mother Carroo and Mother Dute as she ground dried berries and salt with a bit of vinegar for her ink. With a stylus fashioned from an oak twig, she wrote on thin strips of fine linen. She described her uncle's tyrannical control and her exile. She went into great detail about the dire situation in Minca, the poor crops, and poverty. She asked for their understanding and forgiveness and requested their help in bringing the land back to balance by sending an emissary to the Heart Stone. When she finished, she folded the linen carefully and stitched the messages inside the talismans for safekeeping.

Her work complete, she went to bed and dreamed she struggled through a thick forest. Twigs and burrs caught at her tunic, trying to hold her back. In the far distance, she saw an old woman sitting by a fire, tears on her cheeks, a welcoming smile on her face.

❊ ❊ ❊

EARLY THE NEXT MORNING, RILDA and Cora prepared breakfast, thick slices of herb bread with cheese and sprouts slathered with Rilda's tomato relish. They brewed strong tea, adding honey and milk to each mug. It was a heavy meal to sustain them till the afternoon.

Cora carried the tray of food out to the stables where Dov and Steff were loading their packhorses. Rilda followed with a bowl full of nuts and dried fruit. Lali was already eating her breakfast in a sunny spot next to the barn. Sitting on bales of hay, the friends ate quickly and in silence, lost in their own thoughts.

When he was done, Steff stood and stretched. "We're packed and ready. We should saddle up and be on our way," he said.

Before they departed, Cora took the embroidered talismans out of her pocket. "Wear this next to your heart for safety," she said, slipping the cords around their necks. "I've stitched the message for the Mothers inside. Be safe." Smiling brightly, she held back her tears and gave each of them a long, hard hug. "The Goddess goes with you."

Rilda chattered on about how to prepare the dried food and the necessity of keeping warm and dry. Her hands were wringing her apron all the while. Dov and Steff smiled affectionately and kissed her goodbye. Whistling for Lali, Dov mounted and started out. With a final kiss for his sister, Steff followed, leading the packhorses. Lali brought up the rear.

Rilda and Cora held each other tightly and watched them ride out of the courtyard.

Returning inside, they set about doing their morning chores in silence. With the men gone, the house seemed unbearably empty.

❖ ❖ ❖

AFTER LEAVING THE COMPOUND, Dov and Steff rode their horses into the woods, hoping to avoid the prying eyes of the fort across the valley floor. They would travel east deeper into the Iron Mountains before turning south toward Tinton. The shade from the tall pines kept them and their horses cool and comfortable. The green undergrowth smelled like summer, rich and sweet. Lali kept pace with the horses, her senses alert for anything out of the ordinary. Birds chirped happily from the branches above. The woods were peaceful.

When the sun was past its apex, Dov stopped in a clearing by a mountain stream. Dismounting, he asked, "How about some lunch?" and took a satchel of food from his saddlebag.

"Great! I thought you'd never stop. I'm starving."

Steff jumped down from his horse. He led the horses to the water for a drink. Then he knelt down and stuck his own head in. Rearing back, he swung his wet head from side to side, whipping his hair in an arc, spraying Dov with water. "Krickers! That feels good. I wish we had time for a real swim."

"Watch what you're doing, boy. I've no wish to ride in wet clothes for the afternoon," Dov said.

Steff wiped the water from his eyes and didn't see Dov's mischievous gleam. He was caught off guard when Dov grabbed the front of his tunic and, with a sweep of his leg, sat Steff down in the stream with a splash. Steff was shocked for a split second, but then burst into laughter, collapsing back into the water with an even bigger splash. The horses rolled their eyes and wandered off to eat some grass.

Sitting back up, he extended his arm. "Come help me out, old man."

When Dov grabbed it, Steff pulled Dov off-balance and into the water with him. The two splashed, laughed, and drenched each other like a couple of children. Lali cocked her head at them questioningly, and then joined in. She ran rings around the men in the water, barking and jumping. When exhaustion overtook them, Steff and Dov collapsed into the shallow water, panting. Lali walked out of the stream and shook the water off. She barked at the men, encouraging them to do the same. Slowly, they rose and came to shore.

"I'm too old for this," Dov said.

"That was a pretty swift move. Think you could give me some pointers? It's been a while since I studied Rime."

"We can practice after we eat, if you like. We're not far from Tule, so we have some time."

The friends ate in amiable silence. Sitting on boulders near the stream, they chatted while the sun warmed them and dried their clothes. Lali found a comfortable spot in the warm grass and fell asleep. At last, Dov stood and stretched with a slight groan.

"Well, let's have a go."

Chapter 5

By early afternoon, Cora was restless. As she scrubbed the kitchen counter, her mind was on Steff and Dov, their journey, and the uncertain future. Rilda's laughter brought her back to the present.

"Love, you've been scrubbing that spot for quite some time now. You'll soon wear a hole in the granite. Why don't you sit down and let me make you a cup of tea?"

"I don't know if I *can* sit still," Cora said.

"Well, give it a try. You're making me jittery."

Rilda put the kettle on to boil, spooned tea leaves and calming herbs into the pot, and brought out a couple of mugs. Cora perched on the edge of a chair, plucking at the loose threads on the hem of her tunic.

"What has you worried? You know that Steff and Dov can take care of themselves. Steff has needed something to do. He's too old to be sitting in the middle of nowhere with his nanny and sister. He has been wanting to join the Resistance, you know. This will be good for him."

"In a way, I'm jealous of him. At least he's doing something. I'm just worried that I misinterpreted the signs and sent them on a fool's errand. If something happens to them, I'll blame myself." Cora burst into tears.

Rilda carefully filled their mugs and brought them to the table. She handed Cora a large handkerchief. Cora wiped her tears and blew her nose.

"I don't know what's the matter with me. I seem to cry all the time."

"Well, there's quite a bit to cry about, dearest. And you're pregnant. When I was pregnant with Kip, I cried a lot. Everything I cooked tasted salty from tears. And that was the happiest time of my life," Rilda said, smiling wistfully.

Rilda took Cora's hands, holding them gently in her own. With a slight squeeze, she said, "The work of the Goddess is often a mystery. On the other hand, I can't believe that our destiny is to live under the rule of Vestor and his henchmen. Balance must return if we are to survive. All Mincans, Carroos, and Dutes must come together. You have shown us this will happen. From the moment you told us about your vision, you had no uncertainty. It is only your fear that is causing doubt now."

Cora thought about that. "You're right. It is just fear. And I seem to have a lot of it," Cora said, blowing her nose into the handkerchief once again.

"Fear has a way of growing. That's why it's important to recognize it and let it go," Rilda responded, patting Cora on the knee.

They sat in silence for a few moments, sipping their tea. Eventually, Cora said, "I need to spend more time praying and meditating to the Goddess." Smiling over her tea mug, she added, "I'm really not in control here. She is."

The sound of a horse in the courtyard disrupted them. Cora glanced out the window and jumped up.

"Goddess, help me. It's the general. Tell him I'm out," Cora whispered.

"You might as well face him now, dear," Rilda whispered back. "The sooner you deal with him and send him back to Merton, the better. Put on your sweetest Vestor smile. It's time for your best performance."

She grabbed Cora's hand and led her to the door just as Fizor started to knock.

Cora took a deep breath. She made a face at Rilda before turning it into a smile and opening the door.

"Oh, General. It's you. We hadn't been expecting . . . I mean, what a delight. Or rather, won't you come in?" Cora said in her most simpering voice. She dropped her eyes and executed a shallow curtsy. Rilda followed suit.

Fizor stepped into the kitchen. Acting as if Rilda were invisible, he backed Cora up against the counter. "Miss Cora, I was wondering if you might like to go out for a ride this afternoon. Your uncle said you enjoyed riding. That's something we have in common," Fizor said.

"Why, I don't know. I should help Rilda with our chores."

"That's not a problem, Cora dear. Go on, saddle up. You've been cooped up all morning," Rilda said, waving Cora toward the door. "Remember what we were talking about earlier. You need some time to get to know the general."

"But . . . but . . ."

Fizor put an arm around Cora's waist and led her outside to the stable. With one withering glance back at Rilda, Cora accepted her fate.

Fizor insisted on saddling Cora's pony, Ty, and helped her to mount. He remounted his large military horse and leered down at Cora. Cora felt intimidated and apprehensive. *I suppose that's what he wants*, she thought. *Well, I'll show him!* Cora sat up straight, smiled sweetly up at Fizor, and urged her pony forward.

❀ ❀ ❀

WATCHING THEM FROM THE KITCHEN doorway, Rilda wondered about the wisdom of letting Cora ride off with him. He didn't seem very gullible. If Cora wasn't careful, he might see through her ruse. Rilda sent a little prayer to Kameeth that all should go well and went back to her chores.

It wasn't too long before Cora and Fizor rode back into the courtyard. Rilda, observing from the kitchen window, thought Fizor's jaw appeared even more rigid. Cora looked exhausted, slumped in her saddle. The general helped Cora to dismount and took her pony into the stable. Cora sat on a bale of hay, holding the reins of Fizor's horse until he returned to the courtyard. Standing, she offered him the reins. He took them, and her arm as well. Rilda watched Fizor kiss Cora's wrist before remounting and riding away.

After he left, Cora shuffled into the house. She shifted into her coy persona and gave a pert curtsy. In her most placid little voice she said, "What a delightful time I had. I shall tell you all about my fiancé after I've cleaned up." Reverting to her normal self, she added, "It was absolutely awful," and retreated to her room.

Rilda made a mug of warm milk. She went to Cora's door and knocked lightly before entering. Hearing the sound of water splashing in Cora's privy, she placed the drink on the bedside table and sat quietly in a chair. It was a long time before Cora came out wearing a robe, her hair wrapped in a towel. She took a sip of the milk before curling up on the bed.

"Thanks, Rilda. This is just what I need."

"I'm sorry it was awful, my sweet," Rilda said. "What happened?"

"We rode up the trail to the waterfall. He talked about himself the whole way, and I feigned interest. He's been in the army since the very beginning of the troubles and is, as he puts it, 'a natural leader of men.' He went on and on about the battles he's fought, the medals for bravery and his close friendship with Vestor.

"He obviously hasn't spent much time with women. He didn't seem to think I could even move without his help. At the waterfall clearing, he actually lifted me off Ty and set me down like I was a fragile teapot. How does he think I've managed all these years?

"Anyway, we sat down on the grass, and he continued to talk. He didn't even notice that I hadn't spoken one word since we left home. And then he grabbed me and started kissing me. Goddess, it was awful. I had no idea it was coming and was literally knocked over. He was lying on top of me, crushing me and slobbering all over me with his cold, clammy lips. It was disgusting," Cora said, burying her face in her hands.

"Blessed moons. Are you all right?" Rilda rushed to the bed and put her arms around Cora's shaking shoulders. "Did he hurt you? Oh, dear. Oh, dear. I'm so sorry. Don't cry, Cora, darling."

Cora looked up, and Rilda realized that Cora wasn't crying. She was shaking with silent laughter.

"Dear Goddess, you're hysterical!" Rilda blurted out, pulling Cora tightly to her bosom.

"No, I'm not. I'm fine," Cora said, pulling away. "I was ready to use my Rime defenses, general or not. One good knee jab, a twist, and a follow-up elbow to the jaw. I could have knocked him out and taken pleasure in it. Then I realized I couldn't. Not if I wanted to stay in character."

"Why are you laughing? What did you do?"

"I became a blithering idiot. I beat my little fists against his chest and cooed that he must cease at once. He stopped and listened to me. I told him his passion was too much for an innocent girl like me. I told him, 'I must wait for our wedding day.' And he believed me. Talk about an idiot."

"Clearly, the Goddess was watching over you."

"Probably," Cora said, laughing. "Well, anyway, once we sat up and straightened our clothes, I executed the final touch. I told him to return to Merton until our wedding day. I told him I must remain 'pure' and his being so close was too much of a temptation, him being so manly and all."

"And he believed all of this?"

"I told you he doesn't know anything about women. He muttered something about 'a man's needs,' then apologized. Profusely. Said he understood. Said he wouldn't pressure me. Said he would leave immediately."

"He's really gone?" Rilda asked.

"Yes. He gave me his promise. 'We will meet again in Merton, my precious jewel,' were his exact words. And he made me promise not to mention his clumsy overture to Vestor. As if I would!"

Cora and Rilda regarded each other solemnly for a moment. Then the tension broke. They both started to giggle, which soon became laughter. Finally, they collapsed on the bed, gasping for breath, tears running down their cheeks.

"You did it! You're a genius," Rilda said admiringly.

"I should have become a Teller," Cora said. "Thank the Goddess, it worked. We're rid of one problem. Now, onto the rest."

"Right you are. But let's celebrate this victory. Dinner is ready, and I picked some fresh berries for dessert. I'll even whip some cream."

"Berries and whipped cream? You know how to make a girl happy."

Chapter 6

Steff and Dov arrived at the outskirts of Tule at dusk. The setting sun created a soft chiaroscuro effect of light and shadow. The effect muted the appearance of rough stone and worn wood. The inn was still festooned with flowers from the Summer Solstice, adding brightness to an otherwise drab facade.

Children playing in the summer evening watched the newcomers approach and retreated into the shadows, wary of intrusion into their community. The village dogs recognized Dov and Lali and bounded out. When the children realized it was Dov, they gave a cry of delight and ran to greet him. The adults, hearing the excited children, came to the lane. They waved and called out greetings.

Steff had heard stories from Dov about the state of Minca, but this was his first opportunity to see the situation for himself. The buildings were in poor repair. The people were thin and dressed in ragged tunics. Yet their enthusiastic welcome was heartwarming.

A young woman took their horses to be stabled. The children pushed and pulled Dov into the inn, squealing with delight. They petted and stroked Lali and urged her inside as well. The adults followed, only slightly less effusive than the children. Steff brought up the rear, carrying their saddlebags.

The innkeeper was a big man with a full, graying beard and jovial manner. He greeted Dov with a bear hug. "You're here early this year, friend," he said.

"True, Rigar. We decided to leave Mother Minca's before anyone noticed. I doubt you've met Steff, Mother Minca's brother."

The entire village stared at Steff in silent awe. Unaccustomed to being seen with such scrutiny, Steff felt a flush rise up his neck and burn his cheeks.

After a moment, Rigar grabbed Steff's wrist in a strong grip. "Pleased to meet you. I remember your parents." Rigar gave Steff an appraising glance. "You've the look of your mother. Will you be staying for a while? We've not much to offer in the way of hospitality, but you're welcome here."

Steff turned to Dov, who answered for him. "No, Rigar, we're bound for Tinton. I've weddings to celebrate there."

"Ah, but you're here for tonight. We've got need of your talents too. Meli and Jib had a baby girl."

A young woman pushed her way to the front of the crowd and shyly handed her baby to Dov, who held her tenderly. "What's her name, Meli?" he asked.

"Rosi."

"Well, we'll have a blessing for Rosi tonight. What a perfect way to start the evening."

Suddenly, everyone talked and moved at once. Rigar maneuvered Dov and Steff through the crowd, down a hallway to a guest room in the back to leave their belongings and wash up.

When they returned, Steff was introduced to everyone. He knew he'd never remember all the names. Some people left to complete their evening chores. Others moved the tables and chairs to form a banquet table. Food was prepared and a table was set. Pitchers of cider and ale were brought out. A fiddler played lively tunes. Steff pulled out his tin pipe and joined in. The children jumped, danced, and got under everyone's feet. Lali retreated under a bench for safety.

The community was gathered, and the food was brought to the table. The villagers sat in silence as Dov thanked the Goddess for her bounty. The meal, a thin stew, was meager, but the bonhomie was rich. Sitting between Dov and Rigar, Steff glanced around the room. The friends and neighbors chatted quietly amongst themselves, occasionally peeking at him. Steff noticed that there were very few people his age in the room. He turned to Rigar and asked, "Where are Tule's young folk?"

"Some have joined the Resistance, but many of our young men have gone into Vestor's army. Some have been lured by talk of wealth and fame, while others were simply grabbed and put into uniform. The army takes most of our crops as well. They say it's a small price to pay for safety and security. Although we seemed safe enough before," Rigar answered bitterly.

"I didn't know," Steff said.

"Your uncle keeps us all in a tight fist. It's good you're traveling with Dov. You'll learn a lot about the ways of the world. Though I would caution you, Vestor has eyes in every part of Minca."

"Steff may not have traveled much, but he's not callow. I trust him with my life," Dov said.

Steff felt a surge of pride at Dov's words.

When the meal had ended and the dishes were being cleared, Steff felt a tug at his sleeve. A small boy, his face smudged with dirt, looked up at him.

"Please, sir. Will Mother Minca be coming?"

"What's your name, boy?"

"Triggi, sir."

"There is nothing that would please her more than to come to Tule and meet you, Triggi. For the moment she's back at our home and can't get away. I hope she'll be able to come soon."

"I'd like to meet her," the young boy said. "What's she like?"

Steff picked the youngster up and held him on his lap. "She looks exactly like me, Triggi, except she's a girl."

Triggi giggled.

The villagers stopped talking and listened to Steff's words.

"She's smart and can ride a pony and shoot arrows straight as anything. She likes to laugh and sing. She is true to the old ways. She's my favorite sister. Well, actually," Steff added with a laugh, "she's my only sister. She works toward being Mother Minca in the world, not in isolation." Steff addressed everyone in the room. "May the Goddess speed the day."

There was a murmur of approval from the crowd.

After a moment of silence, Dov stood up and spoke. "Thank you all for the welcome and the meal. Now it is time. Let's move the chairs for the blessing and stories."

Tables were quickly moved aside. The chairs were placed in a semicircle around the room for the adults while the children sat on the floor. Dov stood in front and motioned for Meli and Jib to come forward with Rosi.

Glowing with restrained excitement, the pair stood before their friends and family holding their small bundle. Dov stood behind them, his arms raised in an open embrace.

He closed his eyes and breathed deeply. Everyone focused on the Teller. Soon the entire room was breathing in the same rhythm. The energy was subdued and mellow. Dov opened his eyes and made visual contact with each person in the room, connecting their energy with his own. Then, using his deep, warm, singsong voice, Dov began the ritual.

We come together in celebration.
A birth. A new beginning.
Rosi.

We call upon the Goddess to be with us.
We call upon Kameeth to be with us.
And Minca, Mother of us all.

We invite the Nature Spirits to join us,
and the angels as well.

We honor the four directions and the four seasons.
We honor Meli, the mother, and Jib, the father,
And we share their joy.

Dov smiled broadly and lifted the baby out of her parents' arms. Holding her up for all to see, he continued:

Who will stand with Meli and Jib?
Who will love Rosi and teach her the ways of the world?
Who will teach her to honor her family,
her community, and all of nature?
Who will cherish this child in darkness and in light?

The entire community rose to their feet. Steff got up

too. He joined them as they called out, "We will! We will!" Dov continued the blessing:

In the eyes and heart of the Goddess, this child is truly blessed. She is bound by love to her parents and all who are gathered here.

Everyone joined in for the completion:

So be it. So be it. So be it.

Kissing her on the forehead, Dov returned Rosi to her parents' arms. A cheer went up around the room. Hugging and kissing ensued. The children of Tule jumped up and joined hands in a circle around Meli, Jib, and Rosi. They danced around the three, singing the "Blessing Song."

Welcome, welcome little one. We're very glad that you have come.

We're eagerly waiting for the day When you're big enough to come and play.

Dream sweet dreams when you go to sleep. Our love for you is very deep.

The commotion startled Rosi and she wailed. Her parents maneuvered through the children to sit in the back of the room, where it was quieter. The children collapsed in a heap on the floor, and Lali came out of her hiding place to join them. Dov sat down on the wooden floor amid the children.

"And now," Dov said softly, "it's time for stories."

The stories lasted long into the night. When the last parent carried the last sleeping child home from the inn, Steff helped Rigar put the furniture back in place. Dov sat in a corner talking quietly with one of the women from the village.

When the work was done, Steff bid Rigar goodnight. He went to the guest room and had a quick wash before collapsing into the bed that had been prepared for him. Thoughts of the day behind and the journey ahead kept him awake. As his eyes finally began to close, Steff heard Rigar's footsteps pass the door and climb the steps to his room upstairs. Dov remained in the front room, talking and laughing quietly with the woman.

Later that night, Dov and Lali entered the room. Steff jerked awake.

"Dov? Is that you?" he asked groggily.

"Go back to sleep, Steff. It's late."

"Where have you been?"

"Go to sleep, Steff."

"Who was that woman?"

"Sleep. We can talk tomorrow."

With a large yawn, Steff rolled over and went back to sleep.

Chapter 7

"So, the stories are true then?" Steff asked.

"What are you talking about?"

The friends had been riding in silence since they left Tule shortly after breakfast. Their journey had taken them back into the mountains, heading south.

"The stories about Tellers having a 'friend' in every town," Steff said.

Dov twisted in his saddle and regarded Steff with surprise. Facing forward again, he rode in silence. After a long time, he said, "It's almost midday. There's a grove ahead, near a small stream. Let's take a break and have a bite to eat."

Dov rode on to the grove, dismounted, and took down the pack that held their food.

Steff followed Dov to the trees and tethered the horses in range of food and water. Giving Lali a treat from his saddlebag, Steff left her in charge of the horses. Dov sat on a low boulder, their food spread on a cloth in front of him. His knees were drawn up with his arms wrapped around them, his long fingers interlaced. He gazed into the distance. Steff was curious why Dov hadn't answered his question and was anxious that he had breached some code of conduct. Was Dov angry?

Joining Dov, Steff found his own boulder to sit on. The sun was warm but not unpleasant. The grove was quiet except for the occasional call of birds. Dov seemed lost in thought. Steff remained silent and motionless, waiting for Dov to move or speak. When Dov's focus returned to the present moment, he smiled at Steff.

Standing and stretching, Dov said, "Get yourself some food. You must be hungry."

Steff reached for the bag of dried fruit and shoved some into his mouth. He picked up the knife and cut slices of bread, handing a couple to Dov. As they wrapped the bread around slices of cheese and dried meat, Dov spoke again.

"People have always had a respect and fascination for Tellers. The relationship that the Teller has with the Goddess, the training to do blessings, the talent to tell stories, make the Teller seem special, whether the Teller is a man or a woman."

Dov sat back down, took a bite of his food, and chewed thoughtfully before continuing.

"You saw how excited the people in Tule were when I arrived. It's like that for every traveling Teller. Since I'm connected with Mother Minca's family, it's even stronger. There are many people who would like to be close to a Teller, in the most intimate sense of the word. That's how those stories got started."

"It doesn't sound too bad," Steff remarked with a grin.

"You think so?" Dov looked at him closely. "When I was young and out on the road, it went to my head. I certainly took advantage of any opportunity that came along. I relished the attention.

"As I matured, I realized that most of the offers were made to 'Dov, the Teller,' not to 'Dov, the man.' The connections were sexual rather than loving, and it ceased to be so inviting. I started declining the offers. Nowadays I'm called upon to be a listener instead of a lover. That suits me fine, but the rumors persist."

Dov ate his meal and took a drink of water before he continued. "Sometimes I miss a deep connection with one person or having children of my own. But I have you and Cora, as dear to me as my own blood would be. I have friends in every part of Minca. My work is fulfilling. I have Lali for companionship. My life is very blessed. I have no complaints."

Steff looked at his friend with new clarity and said, "Sorry, Dov. We've never talked about this. Your life always seemed so adventurous and exciting, traveling around. I never thought you might get lonely sometimes. You've given up a lot for your calling. For Minca."

"Don't worry about me. As I said, I have no complaints," Dov replied. Smiling, he added, "It's probably why I'm so good at Rime. It's a good release for built-up energy."

Steff smiled.

"But what about you? Brother of Mother Minca and a personable fellow," Dov said, swatting Steff on the knee, "you must get your fair share of attention from the young women."

"Ha!" Steff laughed, grabbing another handful of dried fruit and tossing it into his mouth. Glancing up at Dov, he muttered, "I hardly leave the valley, so I don't know many girls. And honestly, I don't know how to talk to the ones I do know. They never talk to me. It's like I'm invisible. I feel like an idiot."

"Maybe they're just shy around you."

"I doubt it. I've known them all my life. I don't get it. Cora isn't like that."

"No. Cora isn't like that," Dov agreed. After a pause, he added, "I'm sure you'll meet others who are not like that either."

"Maybe," Steff replied, not sounding convinced.

Dov and Steff finished their meal in silent contemplation. As they packed away the food, Dov remarked, with a glint in his eye, "We've time to practice Rime before we move on. With your future as another longtime bachelor, you could use another session."

Steff sat stunned for just an instant before breaking into laughter. Standing, he grabbed Dov's hand and pulled him to his feet. With a sweep of his right leg, he plopped Dov back down on the ground. Landing with a grunt, Dov sprang back up. Once again, the two engaged in mock battle. Eventually, they collapsed on the ground in exhaustion. Steff gazed at the sky. "That felt good," he gasped.

Lali wandered over and licked Steff's cheek. A slight breeze moved the tree branches, cooling him off.

Dov sat, stretching and rotating his left shoulder. "Good? You must be kidding. I think you dislocated my shoulder with that last move."

"Ha! You had me from the very beginning. I never had the advantage."

"You've got a natural talent for Rime. A bit more practice and you'll best me easily. Just don't let your uncle know how good you are. Better he should continue thinking you're an incompetent fool."

"Right you are." Steff got up, brushed himself off, and went to get the horses. When he returned, he asked, "Where are we headed?"

"Next stop is Cordi, about six days' ride from here. There's a cave about halfway that we Tellers use. It has a natural hot spring. A long soak should feel pretty good after our travels."

The companions gathered up their food and belongings. Swinging into his saddle, Dov began singing the Mincan folk song "The Traveler's Lament." Laughing, Steff mounted his horse and joined in on the chorus.

My father was a traveling man,
To see the world was his life's plan.
By selling wares he traveled wide,
Then he met a girl; felt his heart divide.
His love for her was very deep,
And true love's promise he had to keep.
He pledged his troth; she was his bride.
He put his traveling life aside.

I knew quite well when I was three
That traveling was the life for me.
I'm older now and all I knew
Is melting in the morning dew.

Twas a happy life; few regrets had he.
She birthed him daughters numbering three.
When I was born, I was his pride.
He taught me 'bout the world outside.
Each day I grew, I had a plan
To see the world; be a traveling man.
To that end I did strive
And when I left, my family cried.

I knew quite well when I was three
That traveling was the life for me.

I'm older now and all I knew
Is melting in the morning dew.

I walked the world and sailed the sea.
The wonders all brought joy to me.
But sometimes in the dark I cried,
My heart empty, I missed a bride.
I never met my own true love
Whose life would fit mine like a glove.
The traveling life is all I've tried
And will be till the day I've died.

I knew quite well when I was three
That traveling was the life for me.
I'm older now and all I knew
Is melting in the morning dew.

Chapter 8

Steff was surprised and delighted by the Teller's cave. From the forest floor, a path led to a deep rocky fissure that had been turned into a corral. They settled the horses there. The path then wound up the cliff to a hot spring. The natural formation had been enhanced with boulders to make comfortable seating for three or four people. Farther up the path was the entrance to the cave. There was a large space with a cantilevered overhang to keep out rain and snow. A fire circle at the entrance ensured warmth in the winter and kept the bugs at bay in the summer. Wood was stacked alongside a box of cooking utensils and a pile of thick rugs and blankets. Several oil lamps were perched on rock ledges waiting to be lit.

After depositing their bags, the friends lit a small fire and heated some soup made from their dried meat and vegetables. They had brought some cider from Tule, which completed their meal.

"This is an amazing place, Dov."

"Isn't it? Tellers have used it for generations. There's a local man, Gré, who lives nearby. His family has maintained it since the beginning. He stocks food for the horses, fresh water, and enough wood for a few days of heat and also makes sure that rodents haven't taken over the bedding. There's another cave in the north of Minca and a small lodge out west for Tellers. They're a calm respite during our travels."

After her dinner, Lali settled near the saddlebags and fell asleep. When they were done eating and cleaning up, Dov and Steff stripped down to their under-breeches. Grabbing a couple blankets and lanterns, they walked back down to the hot spring.

Dusk was turning to night. The first stars were visible through the tree branches above. Steff and Dov sat up to their chins in the hot spring, soaking in the warmth. The lanterns cast their shadows onto the dark water.

The silence was broken by a female voice calling from below. "Is that you, Dov? It's been a long time, friend."

Dov sat up straighter in the water. "Blast," he whispered cautiously. "That sounds like Nikka. She's a Teller from the west of Minca, and she's no friend. Follow my lead here, Steff. You might want to slip into your Vestor-self."

Then he called out, "Indeed. Is that you, Nikka? What brings you here?"

A tall woman emerged out of the shadows. Soft light from her lantern glinted off the jet beads on her deep-crimson tunic and the gold stitching on the saddlebags she carried. Knee-high boots of black leather defined slender legs. Silk ribbons secured her lustrous auburn hair on top of her head, a few tendrils framing her beautiful face. She walked with assurance and grandeur. It was difficult for Steff to gauge her age, but she exuded palpable sexuality.

"I'm out on my summer rounds, same as you," she said, coming to the hot springs and perching gracefully on a rock. Although she talked to Dov, her attention concentrated on Steff, who found himself mesmerized by her green eyes.

"You don't usually come this far east," Dov said.

"Don't worry, I'm not here to claim your territory, but you're being extremely rude. You haven't introduced me to this delicious young man."

Steff felt a flush permeate his body, and it wasn't from the hot water.

"Nikka, this is Steff. Steff, Nikka," was all Dov offered by way of introduction.

"Steff? Not Vestor's nephew Steff, surely."

Dov grunted a confirmation.

"Why, how absolutely wonderful! So, you've come down from your mountain hideaway at last," she cooed, leaning toward him.

Steff couldn't move or speak. He just nodded and stared back at the extraordinary woman.

Dov broke the silence. "There's some soup up in the cave, if you like."

"No, thank you," she replied. "I'll take my pack up. Then I'll come join you, if you don't mind." She smiled enticingly at Steff as she rose and sauntered off.

"I don't mind at all," Steff called after her, his power of speech restored.

Alone again, Dov talked to Steff in a low voice. "Nikka is one of Vestor's agents. Being a Teller, she can come and go as she pleases. She has a good bit of Carroo blood in her and uses those talents to her advantage. That is how she gathers information. Be careful."

"Really? I thought she was rather sweet."

"Steff!" Dov said gravely. "You have to trust—"

Steff shoved Dov. "I was kidding! Actually, she gave me the creeps. I felt like a mouse being stalked by a cat. How do we handle this?"

"I'll be my most boring self. You play the incompetent buffoon. You do it so well," he added with a grin. "Avoid eye contact and remember your heart. If you stay connected to your heart, you will lessen the effect of her charms."

Dov had barely finished speaking when Steff jumped up in a panic, water dripping off his long limbs. "What about our packs?" he whispered hoarsely. "The messages from Cora! We should go back to the cave!"

"Don't worry. Lali won't let her get near our belongings. Sit down now and be quiet. Here she comes."

Steff sat back down as Nikka returned to the hot springs wrapped in one of the blankets from the cave. With a languid motion, she set her lantern on the rocks. Turning toward the men, she allowed the blanket to drop. Underneath the blanket she wore a filmy sheet alluringly wrapped and tied around her body. Steff leaned back in the water and feigned indifference.

"Mmm. This feels wonderful after a day of riding," she moaned, closing her eyes and slipping into the water. "Dov, you should do something about that dog of yours. She nearly bit my hand off."

"She's usually quite friendly. I don't know what may have gotten into her. Most sorry, Nikka."

After a few moments, Nikka stirred. Opening her eyes, she focused on Steff. "Doesn't this feel good, Steff?" she asked.

"Why, yes it does, Madame Teller."

"Oh, please, let's not be so formal. Call me Nikka," she said, reaching out and stroking his cheek.

"With pleasure," Steff replied.

"Easy on the boy, Nikka. He's not used to your feminine wiles," Dov said coldly.

She glared at Dov and then turned back to Steff. Softly, she asked, "So, tell me about yourself and why you are traveling with this old spoilsport. You'd have much more fun out on your own."

"There's not much to tell. My sister's getting married. She's involved in the wedding preparations, and I figured I'd hightail it out of there."

"Married!" Nikka exclaimed, sitting back. "Who is she marrying? When? And where?"

"My uncle arranged it. The groom is General Fizor. They're getting married in Merton at the Winter Solstice."

"General Fizor, you say. Now, that's interesting." Nikka pondered the new information.

Steff and Dov exchanged glances. "We're all so very pleased," Dov said.

"Oh, yes. He seems a fine fellow," Steff said. "I just can't abide all that wedding stuff, tunic patterns and all. I had to get away."

Nikka refocused on the two men. "Yes, he's a perfect match," she said with a satisfied smile. "I couldn't have chosen better myself. And, of course, you'd want to get away. Where are you going, exactly?" Nikka leaned closer to Steff.

"I'm going with Dov to Tinton. After that, I'm planning to do some hunting in the Eastern Mountains. I hear there's still a fair amount of game there."

"Will you be on your own?" Nikka asked coquettishly, moving even closer.

"Yes," he answered simply, unable to come up with another response.

"He has some distant cousins out that way," Dov said quickly. "He might visit them."

"I do?" Steff asked, genuinely surprised.

"Let me see now," Dov said, closing his eyes in thought. "Your great-great-great aunt Lorissa married and moved to the Eastern Mountains. She was the sister of Mother Minca Trini. Lorissa had seven children, if I remember correctly. The first, Shep, was born two days after the Autumn Equinox in the seventh year of Trini's Motherhood; the second, Tish, two years later during the waning moons following the autumnal cross-quarter . . ."

Dov continued reciting names and birth dates, marriages and deaths, covering several generations of these distant relatives, his voice modulated into a slow monotone. Steff stared in amazement at this litany. Nikka, on the other hand, was lulled to sleep. Her eyes closed and her head drooped. Dov winked at Steff and nodded toward the cave. Quietly, Steff got out of the hot spring and wrapped himself in a blanket. Smiling at Dov, he headed back up to the cave.

A short while later, Nikka awakened. Sitting bolt upright, she looked around. "What happened to me? Where's Steff?"

"I fear I bored you to sleep," Dov replied calmly. "Steff as well. He went back to the cave a while ago."

Nikka scrutinized Dov's face but could see no signs of duplicity. "Much as I enjoy your company, I think I shall turn in." She rose from the water with elegant grace. Dov averted his eyes, as her wet sheet was nearly transparent. She swirled the blanket around her body, picked up her lantern, and stalked off to the cave.

Dov sat for a while longer in the hot spring, massaging his aching shoulder muscles. Smiling to himself, he thought, *Now, there's a unique talent: boring people to sleep.*

When he got back to the cave, he saw Steff curled in a ball, sleeping soundly on a pile of rugs next to Lali. On the other side of the cave, Nikka tossed and turned, obviously awake and agitated. Lali kept a watchful eye on the woman but lowered her guard as Dov entered, her tail tapping the floor in greeting. Dov stroked her head before pulling on his leggings. Then, silently, he arranged some rugs and blankets for himself and stretched out to sleep.

Chapter 9

Early in the morning, Dov was awakened by Lali's low growl. Sitting up, he observed Nikka sitting with her back to the cave wall. She seemed to be in a light trance, her focus on Steff, who was still asleep. Quickly, Dov got up and called out in a loud, cheery voice, "Good day to you, Nikka."

"What time is it?" Steff asked groggily. "I was having such a strange dream." Sitting up, he, too, noticed Nikka.

Looking slightly flushed, Nikka stood up, straightening her tunic. "It's early, Steff," she said. "No need to be awake yet."

"Oh, I think it's time we broke our fast and got on the road," Dov said, nudging Steff with his foot. Steff, bewildered, nodded and got up. Pulling on his tunic, he went outside to relieve himself.

In the silence of the cave, Dov spoke. "Keep your charms to yourself, Nikka. He's a simple boy and of no use to you."

"He can't be *that* simple. He's of the Mother Minca line," she muttered, stuffing her belongings into her pack. "And traveling with such watchful companions does pique the curiosity," she said.

"He's like a son to me. I hope you appreciate that," Dov said simply.

She looked at Dov suspiciously.

Steff returned and Nikka glanced at the young man, considering the situation. With a shrug of her shoulders, she said, "Let's call a truce, Dov. While we're here together, no tricks from either of us."

Dov nodded in agreement. He walked from the cave. Nikka stirred the remains of the fire, added some more wood, and placed a pot of water on to boil.

"Would you like some tea, Steff?"

❉ ❉ ❉

ONCE THEY WERE WELL AWAY FROM the cave, Steff urged his horse up beside Dov's.

"What happened back there?" he asked.

"Nikka was hoping to search your dreams as you slept. Lali woke me up in time. I think she had just begun. The strange dream you said you were having? That would have been her consciousness trying to connect with yours."

"How could she do that?" Steff asked.

"I told you, she works for Vestor. She has no scruples. I doubt that—"

"No! I mean that literally. How could she *do* that?"

"Oh." Dov smiled at Steff. "I forgot you haven't known any Carroos. They can do a lot of interesting things. Probing dreams for information is one of them. I don't know for sure how they do it. I know it has to do with going into a trance and focusing on a sleeper, but I don't know any more than that. Nikka has a lot of Carroo blood, as I told you. She's honed that particular skill, it would seem.

"The Carroos I knew wouldn't probe a stranger to gain

information in the way Nikka was attempting, but any Goddess gift can be used for good or ill."

"But why would Nikka do that?" Steff asked. "She's a woman. Why isn't she aligned with the Goddess?"

Dov thought for several moments before answering. "I first met Nikka when she was four or five years old, a couple of years before the war started. Nikka's mother had died in childbirth. And her father sent her to apprentice at a very young age. I think he found raising a child on his own to be too difficult. At any rate, Nikka was very bright and talented, and Teller Parul took her on."

"Who's Parul? I never heard of him."

It took Dov so long to answer, Steff thought he hadn't heard the question.

"Dov?"

Dov sighed deeply. "That's a longer story. And a harder one."

Dov was silent again for long time. Then he said, "When I was a boy, I was sent to Merton to become a Teller. I was apprenticed to Breed, Mother Minca's Teller, the finest man who ever lived. Breed and I lived in Mother's compound in Merton, and I got to know Vestor. We became close friends. Very close."

"Friends? You and Evil V?"

"It's hard for me to talk about those times. I loved him like a brother. And he loved me, I am sure of it. Teller Parul became Vestor's tutor. He sought the position for nefarious reasons, I now believe. Vestor started to change, became broody. When Vestor became an adult, Parul remained Vestor's personal Teller and adviser.

"Vestor became jealous of his younger sister, your mother. He tried to convince me that the tradition of female leadership was misguided. I disagreed. We argued. Bitterly. He withdrew and cut me off.

"Parul supported Vestor, encouraged him in his darkest actions. I had no idea what they were plotting, but it eventually led to your parents' assassination and war."

"Oh my Goddess, Dov."

"I wish I had known. Maybe I could have done something to stop it," Dov whispered. He shook his head. "Now you know why I don't speak about the past."

Steff considered all he'd heard, then asked, "What happened to Parul?"

"He stayed at Vestor's side until he went into seclusion at the end of his life. Nikka grew up under Parul's influence. From what I understand, she was devoted to him. Now she serves Vestor faithfully."

They rode in silence for a long time.

Finally, Steff said, "But the Carroos. Growing up, I'd heard stories about them. They could fly, they could turn people into stones, they could disappear and reappear magically. You know the sort of things they are rumored to do. Maybe you should tell me the truth."

Dov nodded with a slight smile. "You're right." He took a deep breath. "Let's see. How should I begin?"

Dov closed his eyes and allowed his horse to determine the path they took. After meditating, he opened his eyes and asked, "Do you remember the story of Kameeth's daughters?"

"Of course I do."

"What do you remember about the daughters' gifts?"

"It goes something like this," Steff replied. "'Kameeth birthed three daughters, Carroo, Minca, and Dute, each with her own special gift. Dute's was the dance of body. Her connection with others enabled her to heal both bodies and minds. Minca's was the dance of the mind. Her skills as a craftswoman and inventor were strong. Carroo's was the dance of spirit. She could shift energy and perceptions and communicate with other creatures.' Am I right?"

"That's right, Steff. We all have a bit of those gifts of body, mind, and spirit, but each tribe has a stronger ability in one. The Carroos have developed their gift to be able to communicate with each other without words, conveying thoughts and feelings telepathically. They can also communicate with wild creatures, particularly birds, which is why they are vegetarians. They live in harmony with all creatures. They also have the gift of illusion. They can create an image that you would swear is real, but it isn't."

Dov laughed. "I had a Carroo friend years ago—one of their Tellers. He used to love tricking me. Sometimes he would buy me ale, but when I went to drink it, the mug would be empty. I could see the ale, feel the heft of the mug, even smell it, but it didn't exist.

"Your grandfather's grandfather was a full-blooded Carroo. I'm sure there are times when you seem to 'know' what Cora is thinking. The gift is there in a small way and could be expanded and developed. That's what Nikka has done. You can see how these kinds of gifts or skills could be used to enhance the life of the tribes. I think the Carroos, however many are left, are using their skills to stay hidden and safe.

"But it's also possible to see how the gifts could be used perversely and do great damage," Dov continued. "It's not just the Carroos. The Mincans' gift of the mind created wonderful machines for farming and craftwork. Now it has been twisted into creating weapons of war. The Dutes' gift of the body helped heal their wounded during the war. It was also used to ensure their enemies' wounds would *not* heal. The world's an interesting place."

"I was really enjoying our time together," Steff said. "But meeting Nikka and experiencing that . . . what did you call it . . . dream probing? Well, suddenly, it feels a lot more serious. I knew this was an important journey from Cora's vision, but now it seems more real—riskier or something." There was an uncharacteristic, apprehensive wavering in the young man's voice.

"Our mission is imperative and dangerous," Dov said. His tone was serious, but there was a twinkle in his eye. "We are traveling to distant places where we will be perceived as enemies. Our charge is to communicate a vision based on a child's folk tale. Your uncle's followers will stop us by any means necessary if he finds out about our plans. Your pregnant sister is planning to make the journey from her safe home to the Heart Stone alone. The balance of the world depends upon us. If you weren't feeling at least a little panicked, I'd be worried about you."

Steff's mouth was set in a hard, determined line. "I will do my best."

"I'm sure you will, but we should still have as much fun along the way as possible," Dov continued with an impish grin.

Steff looked shocked. "How can you say that?"

"Well, we don't know what's going to happen in the future. We should prepare for the possibilities as best we can, but worrying about them isn't going to help. We may as well make the best of each day. Enjoy our time together. I think that's what the Goddess would want."

Steff digested this philosophy. Then, in a serious voice, he said, "If you insist."

"I do," Dov replied, equally seriously.

Steff broke into a grin, pulled his tin pipe out of his saddlebag, and started playing a merry tune. Dov sighed with relief and rode on.

❄ ❄ ❄

TWO DAYS LATER, THE FRIENDS were enjoying their afternoon ride. The warm sun filtered through the leaves of the trees. The air was fresh and fragrant. Steff was entertaining Dov with an amusing story about the barn raising when Lali started barking furiously.

Lali had been making forays into the underbrush, chasing mostly imaginary rodents and birds. When her barking turned to howls, they jumped down, tied up their horses, and took off in the direction of her cries.

They ran as fast as they could, crashing through the bushes and swerving around trees. As they got closer, they caught the smell of rotting flesh. Lali frantically paced around a dark form in the dirt. She ran to Dov's side when he approached, whining pityingly. The lump on the ground was the remains of a human body, ripped apart and badly battered. Entrails spilled onto the ground, covered in flies and maggots. Steff pulled up short, turned quickly aside, and vomited his lunch in the bushes. Dov examined the remains. When he felt more composed, Steff joined him.

"I'd say this body has been here a while," Dov reported calmly. "He's been brutally attacked, tortured even, and left for the creatures and nature to dispose of." Bending closer, he studied the face. "Blessed moons. I think this poor soul is a Dute."

"How can you tell?" Steff leaned in for a better look.

"You can see that beneath the grime and blood his skin is a deep earth tone, and he is a very large man."

"What was he doing this far north?"

"Hard to say." Dov rose. "Let's take a look around. See if there's anything that could identify him or explain the situation."

"It looks like they dragged him through there," Steff said, pointing to some crumpled shrubs across the clearing. They searched in that direction and then around the clearing, before returning to the body.

Dov said with a sigh, "Let's prepare him for burial. That's the best we can do for him."

Steff went back to the horses and led them through the woods to the clearing. Dov searched through his pack for his trowel. He dug a shallow grave on the side of the clearing while Steff gathered up large stones to place on top. They lined the grave with leaves and berries gathered from the surrounding woods. Together the friends maneuvered the desecrated Dute into his resting place. They covered the body with more leaves before replacing the dirt. Finally, they placed the stones on top while repeating the blessing chant of burial: "Mother, Goddess, receive this child back to the womb of the earth."

When all the stones were piled onto the grave, Dov said, "Goddess, we do not know this man's name. We do not know his heart. But he is one of your children, and we ask that you receive him and bring him peace."

Steff, still shaken from the experience, added, "Goddess bless."

Dov put his arm around Steff, pulling him into a tight embrace. "Time to go. We can do no more here. And I have something to show you."

Respectfully and quietly, they untied their horses and led them back to the trail. Lali, standing beside the grave, gave a mournful howl before following.

They rode for a long stretch before Dov stopped and signaled Steff to pull close. Reaching into his pocket, he pulled something out and handed it to Steff. It was a piece of hammered bronze about the size of Dov's thumbnail sewn to a scrap of fabric, the same fabric as the shredded tunic the Dute had been wearing. The design looked familiar, figures from the Spirit Writing, which seemed to shift and change when Steff examined it.

"Where did you get this?"

"In the undergrowth near the clearing."

"What do you think it is?" Steff asked.

"I'm not sure. It looks like a talisman, probably for a safe journey, similar to the ones that Cora gave us to wear."

"It didn't do him much good."

"No," Dov said, taking the bronze piece back and replacing it in his pocket. They rode on. A while later, he said, "I wonder if he was trying to reach Mother Minca? Maybe Cora wasn't the only person to have a vision. I think I'll take it with me to Dute. Perhaps I can learn the truth about this man and his journey."

Their minds were filled with unanswered questions and speculations as they rode on to the next village. They arrived well after dark. A summer rain pelted down, adding to their somber mood.

❊ ❊ ❊

A FEW DAYS LATER, THEY REALIZED they were being followed. The trackers were good. Lali noticed first, emitting a warning growl. Dov silenced her quickly. There were no obvious signs, but both Dov and Steff felt their presence. Riding side by side, they conferred in whispers. They agreed to keep up the pretense of two friends on a journey, laughing and singing. Any meaningful conversation would be whispered. They ceased their Rime practice and kept their weapons at the ready.

The trackers did not attempt to intercept them or interfere in any way. They observed from a distance. And so it was, traveling from village to village, as they made their way to Tinton.

Chapter 10

Not long after Vestor's visit, Rilda looked out the kitchen window and saw a wagon pulling into the courtyard. She put down the bowl she was washing, dried her hands on her apron, and went out the back door, followed by the fragrant smell of her baking bread.

Outside two men lowered a large trunk onto the ground.

"And what, may I ask, do we have here?" she queried, tapping the trunk with her foot.

"A delivery from Merton, Mistress, for Mother Minca," the taller one replied with a small bow.

"Well then, bring it along inside, please," Rilda said, holding the door open.

They maneuvered the trunk into the library. "I have the key for Mother Minca. Is that you, Mistress?"

"No," Rilda replied, laughing. "I'm the housekeeper. She's out in the garden. I imagine she'll be back shortly. Would you like to wait? We're about to have lunch. Are you hungry?"

"We shouldn't impose on Mother Minca," the second man said.

"I'm sure she'll be delighted," Rilda said with a smile. "Living way out here, we don't get very many visitors. It'll be a treat."

"You're sure it won't be a problem for Mother Minca to eat with us?"

"With you? Why?" Rilda asked, looking at them closely.

"We're common workers. Back in Merton, we wouldn't even be allowed in the presence of Regent Vestor."

"Obviously things have changed in Merton," Rilda said with a sniff. "In my day, we were all equals, and that's how it should be. Of course, you can eat with us. We'll be grateful for the company. Now, you can settle your horse out in the barn. There's a water trough out there where you can wash up. I want to see clean hands at the table."

"You sound like my mother," the taller one said with a smile.

"Well, that's all right then," Rilda said, patting the large man on the arm. "What are your names?"

"I'm Ferka and he's Brun," the tall man responded. They both smiled at Rilda as they walked back to the door. Stepping outside, they nearly collided with Cora, carrying a basket full of vegetables from the garden.

"Sorry, Miss," said Ferka, grabbing the basket to keep it from spilling.

"No problem," she said with an inquiring glance at Rilda.

Rilda stepped up and took the basket. "Cora, dear, this is Ferka and that's Brun. They've come from Merton to deliver a trunk to you."

Ferka and Brun's shock and disappointment at meeting Mother Minca was obvious. She wasn't at all regal in her scruffy tunic and muddied boots. With her curls askew, she looked to be in her teens rather than in her thirties.

Cora smiled and extended her arm. "Forgive my appearance. I've been working in the garden all morning."

Ferka and Brun clasped her wrist in turn, serious expressions on their faces.

"Cora, you need to go in and wash up. These fellows will be joining us for lunch. It will be ready by the time you get back. We'll gather in the kitchen when you're ready." She dismissed the men with a wave of her hand.

Rilda took Cora by the arm and walked her through the door. "I think they were expecting the Goddess herself. You're a distinct disappointment," she whispered.

"Well, I'll go clean up a bit and see if I can make a better impression," Cora whispered back with a smile.

"Just be a clean version of yourself, my love. That's good enough for anyone."

❊ ❊ ❊

CORA TOOK CARE WITH HER washing and made sure there were no twigs or leaves in her hair. She exchanged her muddy tunic and leggings for clean ones and swapped sandals for her boots. After a moment's thought, she selected a silver-and-lapis brooch that had belonged to her mother, pinning it to her tunic. Glancing in the mirror, she saw a bit of her mother in her own reflection, the hazel eyes and the curve of her chin. *A definite improvement*, she thought, *but still not very regal.*

Ferka and Brun stood up from their seats when she entered the kitchen. Smiling at them, she said, "Please be seated. There's no need for formality here. You're with friends."

"Yes, Mother Minca," Brun said, executing a slight bow.

"I may be Mother Minca, but my friends call me Cora."

"Yes . . . Cora," Ferka said, blushing.

Cora inhaled deeply and then blessed the food. Rilda served her freshly baked bread, warm from the oven, along with thick summer vegetable stew and a fruit salad. Cool water with mint leaves quenched their thirst. Ferka and Brun ate as if they hadn't eaten in a very long time. Cora sat watching, her spoon halfway to her mouth, until Rilda kicked her ankle under the table to remind her of her manners.

"This is the best meal we've had since we left Merton," Ferka said, wiping his mouth with the back of his hand.

"Aye," Brun agreed.

"So, tell us about your trip, boys. Are you from Merton?" Rilda refilled their bowls with stew. "Pass them the bread, Cora."

The conversation flowed cordially. After the meal, Ferka gave Cora a large iron key for the trunk. The men hitched the horse up to the wagon and prepared to go. Rilda insisted they take a basket of food. "You never know where your next meal is coming from."

Cora intoned a blessing for their journey and clasped their wrists.

On the road again, Ferka and Brun concurred that Rilda was the best cook in Minca, and Cora the most agreeable Mother Minca there could ever be. They savored their memories of the afternoon and shared the story with everyone they met on their journey.

❁ ❁ ❁

IN THE EVENING, CORA TOOK the large iron key and opened the trunk. There was an envelope addressed to Cora on top of several bolts of beautiful material. Putting the envelope aside, the women lifted out the cloth, touching and exclaiming over the textures and colors. First there was a bolt of deep-royal-blue wool, the color Vestor favored for his personal clothes. Next was a brocade of lavender, muted greens, and sky blue with a pattern of spirals outlined in gold thread. The third bolt was sheer pale-blue cotton, the traditional color for wedding tunics. An almost transparent pattern of butterflies was woven into the fabric. At the bottom of the trunk were two pieces of fine leather. One was sturdy and black and the other blue suede.

"I didn't know there was still such fine fabric in Merton." Rilda stroked the brocade.

"I doubt that it's available to many people. I wonder what Vestor has in mind." Cora picked up the envelope and ripped it open. "Listen to this."

Niece,

I have sent you materials for a traveling tunic, wedding tunic, evening coat, boots, and wedding slippers. You will also find current patterns from Merton.

I will send a carriage to bring you to Merton. I will send a dresser as well, to help with your toiletry and arrange your hair in a stylish mode.

I expect you to dress appropriately. Do not embarrass me with your country ways and dreary mourning colors.
Vestor

"What arrogance," Cora said. Discarding the letter, she picked up the patterns and gasped. "Krickers! This is unbelievable! Surely, this isn't the style in Merton. I can't wear clothes like this. Look at this traveling tunic," she said, passing the pattern to Rilda. "I could hardly walk in that, much less ride a horse."

The pattern showed a formfitting, calf-length tunic.

"I think that's the point, dearest," Rilda said, studying the pattern. "Let's see the rest."

The pattern for the brocade coat wasn't as bad. It was full-length and tight across the shoulders with a standing collar.

The wedding tunic wasn't really a tunic. It appeared to be a floor-length sleeveless sheath with a neckline that plunged almost to the waist. It was tight enough to question mobility altogether. Close examination of the pattern revealed a slit in the back about eight inches in length that, along with the wedding slippers with wedged heels, would make only mincing steps possible.

"This wedding tunic is obscene," Cora said.

"Things are worse than we thought, Cora. Let us hope your message and this mission have come in time," Rilda said, laying the patterns aside.

Cora sighed. "I wish I could see more clearly how this will evolve. I put on a positive front for Steff, but I don't have any idea how I'm going to get to the Heart Stone by the Winter Solstice."

"Hmm. Yes, I've been giving it a lot of thought as well."

"You're not coming with me."

"I understand your reasoning, dear, though I don't agree. But I do have another idea."

"What is it?"

"Do you remember my cousin Shree? She's stopped by here on her travels a few times over the years."

"Of course, I remember her," Cora said. "What about her?"

"She travels throughout Minca working as an herbalist and selling odds and ends, as you know. She also works for the Resistance."

"I've wondered about that. Kip seemed to have a special bond with her."

"Yes. Well, I think we could ask her for help in this situation. Her father was a Carroo. She has many of their gifts. You would be safe in her charge."

"Can you contact her?" Cora asked. "How soon do you think she could get here? The Autumn Equinox isn't that far off."

"I'll do my best, sweetest."

"What would I do without you?" Cora hugged Rilda and kissed her on the cheek.

Rilda hugged her back. "You would do just fine, my love. The Goddess guides you. For now, let's put this fabric away and not worry about the future."

Cora sat back and put her hands on her slightly bulging belly. Her eyes opened wide as she felt little kicks. "Rilda, give me your hand."

Cora pressed Rilda's hand to her belly. "Ah, blessed baby," Rilda said.

The women sat together in silence, feeling the stirrings of their hopes and dreams for the future.

Chapter 11

Riding through the mountain pass, Steff saw Tinton in the valley below. It was a city almost as large as Merton, but from that height it looked like a child's model of a town. The green of summer faded into a haze over the buildings.

"Well, we've made it this far," Dov said as he urged his horse toward the trail down the mountain.

Steff slumped over his saddle, lethargic and flushed. "I don't think I've ever seen an uglier place. Why would anyone choose to live there?"

"It was beautiful in your mother's time. A cheerful, welcoming place. War and poverty have reduced it to this sad state, but there are many friends in Tinton, loyal to your sister."

They rode down the mountain in silence. A dreary rain started to fall. With each step, Steff sank lower in his saddle. By the time they reached Tinton, he was nearly lying on his horse's back, feeling very ill. Dov seemed to be leading him through a never-ending maze of streets. Movement was agony.

It was midafternoon, but Tinton was in darkness. It was silent except for the rain and the plodding of their horses' hooves. A pungent smell of garbage and human waste mixed with the smoke of cooking fires. People scurried past their horses, their cloaks pulled tight.

When they arrived at the inn, Dov dismounted and went to the door and called for the innkeeper. "Sig, it's me, Dov. I need your help."

Sig rushed to the door as Dov assisted Steff down from his horse. Sig grabbed the horses' reins, calling to her sons, who took the horses to the stable. With Sig's assistance, Dov half walked, half carried Steff inside.

"My companion seems to be running a fever. Could you help me get him to a room and send for Adja?"

"I will go myself," Sig said.

Sig helped them down the hall to a small, cozy room with two beds beneath a tiny window. A chair and washstand stood next to a small wood stove, a chest of drawers on the other side. A door opposite led to the privy. The room was more comfortable than the inn at Tule but could not be considered plush. Sig helped Dov get Steff into the chair before rushing off.

Dov helped Steff out of his wet cloak and into a warm bed where he curled into a ball, shivering. Dov closed the curtains and lit the fire while Lali settled down near the warm stove. He sat on the bed next to Steff's trembling form.

"Lie still," he said, patting him gently on the shoulder.

Soon Sig returned with Adja, the herbalist. Taking one look at the patient, Adja said, "This could be serious. Let no one enter the room until the fever has passed. For now, please bring some boiled water and fresh towels. Some broth might be good as well. Just knock on the door and leave it outside. Be sure to keep your boys away."

Sig regarded Steff gravely. His face glistened with sweat, and his low moans were distressing. She nodded to Adja and left the room.

Adja put his box of herbal medicine down on the washstand and removed his hat and cloak. Nodding to Dov, he stepped close to the bed and laid his hand on Steff's forehead. After touching the glands in Steff's neck, he pulled the chair up next to the bed and sat down. Casually crossing his long legs, he smiled at Dov, folded his hands over his paunch, and relaxed. "Nice job. Very convincing. I knew that brew would come in handy someday. What's going on? Who's your friend?" Adja asked.

Dov grinned back. "This is Steff, Mother Minca's brother."

Adja sat up straight and looked closely at his patient.

"Steff, this is Adja, Tinton's herbalist and a good friend."

Steff looked at Adja and groaned, "I'm going to be sick."

Dov grabbed the washbasin from the stand, and Steff promptly emptied the contents of his stomach into it.

"That's all right then. The toxins are passing through quickly. You'll be feeling better now," Adja stated, taking the basin from Dov and putting it outside the door. "So tell me, why the ruse?"

Dov answered in hushed tones, "Mother Minca had a vision. It's a long story that I'll tell you another time. The gist of it is that Steff and I are to contact the Carroos and Dutes."

"You're serious?"

"Very. I have weddings to perform here at the cross-quarter, so we traveled together. We've been followed for the last twenty days or so. We need your help to get Steff out of town and on the old trail to Carroo. Unobserved, of course."

"Not an easy task, friend," Adja said.

"No, but worth the risk."

There was a knock on the door. When Adja opened it, he found the basin gone and the requested supplies along with Steff and Dov's saddlebags in its place. Adja and Dov brought the items in. From his saddlebag, Dov retrieved some food for Lali, who jumped up, wagging her tail. Adja gave Steff a quick wash and helped him put on a fresh tunic and sit up.

"Pleased to meet you, Steff. Welcome to Tinton. Not an easy introduction to our fair town."

"I wish I could say it was a pleasure, Adja, but if it was you who created that concoction, I have my reservations," Steff said with a lopsided grin.

"Sorry about that. You really will feel better by morning."

Looking back at Dov, Adja said, "So, do you have any thoughts on how to accomplish this feat?"

"Actually, I do," Dov said, serving them each a mug of broth.

They talked and made plans as they sipped their broth. Steff soon grew tired and drifted off to sleep.

Dov and Lali walked Adja to the front door of the inn. As Lali took off for a quick run, Adja whispered, "This rain is supposed to hold for several days. That should help immensely." Then in his normal voice he said, "He will need the medications twice a day until the fever breaks. Keep him sequestered and quiet. I shall return tomorrow to see how he's doing. Meanwhile, send one of Sig's boys if he takes a turn for the worse."

The men clasped wrists and Adja departed. Dov remained on the porch, watching Adja walk up the street in the rain. Dov sensed furtive movements in the shadows between the buildings across the way, evil closing in.

❊ ❊ ❊

ADJA RODE UP TO THE INN LATE IN the afternoon of the following day. He took his saddlebags down before handing the reins to Sig's oldest son. Shaking off the rainwater and wiping his feet, he walked into the inn. He paused to greet the men drinking ale by the fire. Sig was wiping down tables preparing for the evening rush of customers.

"How's the patient doing, Sig?" he asked.

She stopped her cleaning and shook her head solemnly. "I don't think the fever's broken yet. Dov hasn't let anyone near him. The young gentleman's been able to eat a bit of broth and drink some tea, but nothing else. Dov hasn't succumbed, thank the Goddess. His appetite's been excellent. He did an evening of tales for the neighbors after you left last night."

"I'll go along in then," Adja said with a nod of his head.

Steff sat on the floor with Lali, quietly playing tug-of-war with an old sock. Dov sat off to the side reading. All three froze when they heard a knock at the door. Dov opened it cautiously, but eyeing Adja, he smiled and bid him to enter.

"You seem to have improved considerably since last I saw you," Adja remarked as he put down his saddlebags and hung up his cloak.

"Yes, thanks," Steff said, getting up to clasp Adja's wrist.

"It's been hard to keep him confined to the room for even one day. That's youth for you," Dov said with a wink.

"You know I've been *totally* cooperative. I haven't even complained about the meager portions of food you've been able to sneak in for me. I'm weak from hunger," Steff said, dramatically collapsing to the floor. Lali jumped on his chest and licked his face. Steff gave her a hug before sitting back up.

Dov laughed. "I know, I know. You're a shadow of your former self after one day."

"Well, I feel like it," Steff said, gently shoving Dov's knee.

"I can see you're barely able to stand," Adja said, joining in the teasing banter.

"Yes, well, it was your potion that poisoned me."

"Just a *little* bit," Adja said. "I've brought plenty of food in my saddlebags, including some of Burto's ginger biscuits. Help yourself."

"Burto?" Steff asked.

"Burto is Adja's lifemate and a wonderful baker," Dov explained. "Why don't you make some tea to go along with the biscuits, Steff?"

Turning back to Adja, Dov asked, "How is Burto? Well, I hope."

"He is well. He sends his regards. He is concerned about our plans but willing to help, if needed."

Steff busied himself with the kettle on the wood stove, adding tea leaves to the pot.

"I've brought the map and the other items you requested," Adja said. "We have a bit of time yet. Perhaps you could tell me about Mother Minca's vision and your travels so far."

"Have a seat, Adja. There's plenty to tell."

Settled comfortably with their tea and biscuits, Dov told the story of their quest. Adja listened with grave interest.

❊ ❊ ❊

BY TEN O'CLOCK, THE INN WAS BUSY. The crowd in the lounge was boisterous, bellies full and ale plentiful. Sig and her sons were busy serving. Dov walked his friend to the door, nodding to Sig as they passed. They were both bundled up against the rain. When one of her sons moved toward them, Dov smiled and waved him off. "Don't bother yourself. We'll get his horse. You've plenty to do here."

In the dim light, the men silently saddled up Adja's horse and one of the packhorses. They hugged goodbye, pounding each other's backs heartily. Dov watched as his friend mounted and rode off into the night. "May the Goddess be with you," he said under his breath.

Traveling the twisting streets, the rider checked to see if he was being followed. Seeing no movement behind him, he made his way out of town and onto the road traveling back toward the mountains. Far from town, he took another road, this one heading west.

He made his way cautiously through the rain, wary of the road in the darkness, wary of watchers. At last he came to a fork in the road. A small cabin stood to the right sheltered under tall pines. Dismounting, he tied up the horses and knocked on the door.

After a long time, the door opened a crack. Stepping forward into the dim light, the rider took off his hat. "Adja sent me. He sends greetings from the Mother."

With those words, the door opened wide, and Steff stepped inside.

Chapter 12

For the next several days, Adja stayed at the inn and took over Steff's role as the sick patient. When Sig delivered food or laundry to the room, she could see a body sleeping in the bed. Dov assured her the patient was improving and would be moving on soon. When they decided it was time, Adja dressed in Steff's clothes and slipped out of the inn and into the night. In the morning, Dov joined Sig at the kitchen table for a cup of tea.

"My friend left last night. He asked me to thank you for all your kindness and help."

"I'm glad he felt well enough to travel," Sig said, shifting uneasily. "I would help you in any way I could. I hope, after all these years, you know you can trust me."

"I do trust you," Dov said, clasping Sig's hand. "You're a longtime friend and ally. I knew my companion could find his strength here; you and your sons took good care of us."

"I didn't even learn the young man's name."

Dov quickly changed the subject. "The main reason I came to Tinton is for the cross-quarter weddings. I understand your son Ivo is one of the young men getting married. We have much to discuss."

Dov was pleased to see Sig smile. "I'm not usually so easily distracted, Dov, but you've touched upon a bit of brightness in this bleak world. The young folks are excited and have been making many plans. The wedding tunics have been sewn. We parents have been planning the wedding feast," she said, glowing with the telling.

They arranged for the three couples to meet with Dov and discuss the ceremony. By the time their tea was finished, both Dov and Sig felt content.

Dov performed his duties. He blessed new babies, mediated minor disputes, told stories, and honored the deceased. Adja hadn't stopped by, but Dov wasn't concerned. Adja had planned to ride toward the Eastern Mountains to continue the deception and give Steff more time. It was on the morning of the cross-quarter that Burto arrived at the inn.

The day was unusually clear for Tinton, which was taken as a good omen for the weddings. The three couples had been busy since early morning. As was tradition, the brides sat together braiding garlands of flowers. Their young men hung the garlands both inside and outside the inn and moved tables and chairs into the back garden for the wedding feast. Friends and family members helped, some with the furniture and decorating, others in the kitchen preparing food with Sig. Lali patiently waited under the kitchen table for the occasional morsel of food to fall to the floor. The group sang songs, laughed, and told stories while they worked.

From the top of a ladder, garland in his hand, Dov saw Burto in the doorway, a dark shadow encroaching on the activities. The man had been crying. Dropping the flowers, Dov climbed down and led Burto back to his room. Once inside, Burto's tears started in earnest.

"He's gone, Dov. He's gone," he said, clinging to Dov for support.

"Adja? What happened?" Dov asked, encircling him with his arms.

"I don't know," he wept into Dov's shoulder. "Last night I was awakened by a tapping at the door. When I went to see, I found my dearest Adja lying there, bloody, battered, and bruised. He had been dumped there. I almost didn't recognize him."

"Dear Goddess," Dov said. He helped Burto to the chair and knelt beside him, his arm around Burto's shoulder. When his tears subsided, Dov prodded. "Tell me."

"I brought him inside. I had to drag him. He couldn't even walk. I tried to leave him, to get some bandages, but he clutched my arm and wouldn't let me go. It took all his strength."

Burto stared into the emptiness with a haunted look on his face. After a long moment, his body shuddered, and his eyes came back into focus. "His eyes opened, and he told me to tell you he was sorry. He said he had held out as long as he could, but that they had broken him in the end.

"He told me he loved me, that our life together was his greatest joy." He was silent for another minute before he continued. "Then he smiled, actually smiled, and said, 'Tell Dov I have seen the Goddess.' His eyes closed and . . . he was gone."

Dov held Burto close, tears running down his own cheeks. "I am so sorry. Adja has served the Goddess and all of us well. I am sure he is by Her side."

"I trust that is true. We both knew what he was doing was dangerous but worth the risk. I called the neighbors.

They helped me clean him and lay him out on a trestle in our home. I anointed him with cassia oil and gathered evergreen boughs to cover him. There he will lie for the three days."

"I will let Sig and the others know tonight, after the weddings."

Burto looked at Dov pleadingly and asked, "Will you do his honoring?"

"Of course, I will."

They sat together in silence: Burto, wringing his hands and thinking about his years with Adja, and Dov, grieving his part in the death of his dear friend.

With a deep sigh, Dov stood. "Let me walk you home. I would like to pay my respects."

❀ ❀ ❀

GOLDEN HUES BRIGHTENED the usual dreariness of the city as the sun set over Tinton. It was the perfect evening for the weddings. Friends and families encircled the main room of the inn, each person wearing flowers and ribbons over their drab, everyday attire. Musicians played softly in the background as they awaited the arrival of the wedding couples.

Dov entered from the kitchen with the three couples following. The crowd clapped slowly at first before increasing in intensity. The musicians played faster and louder as Dov led the couples in a circle around the room.

Each couple was dressed in matching pale-blue tunics the grooms had colored using vegetable dyes and sewn by hand. The brides had embroidered the hemlines with Spirit Writing, sewing their love, hopes, and dreams into their wedding clothes. The couples were adorned with crowns of flowers, but their feet were bare, their footsteps on the wooden floor matching the rhythm of the clapping and music.

After three revolutions, Dov stopped. Instantly, there was silence, but the vibration from the footsteps and clapping lingered. Dov walked to the center of the room, and the couples moved to stand in a line in front of him. They looked excited and scared, flushed from the movement. Dov smiled. Then he said, "We call in the four directions." He raised his arms in supplication. As one, the crowd turned to face east.

"We invite the Mother of the East to join us tonight. The Mother of Spring, of new awakenings, you are welcome."

The group turned to the south. Dov continued, "We invite the Mother of the South to join us tonight. The Mother of Summer, of heat and passion, you are welcome."

As one, they turned to the west. "We invite the Mother of the West to join us tonight. The Mother of Autumn, of growing to fullness, you are welcome."

And then they turned north. "We invite the Mother of the North to join us tonight. The Mother of Winter, of contemplation and stillness, you are welcome."

As they returned to their original positions, Dov finished the invocation. "Goddess, we stand in your presence, grateful for your love that created our world. Mother Minca, we are your children and blessed to be so." He lowered his arms.

The drum began a soft, steady beat, the rhythm of a heart. The crowd around the room clasped hands and walked in a slow, steady pace.

Addressing the three couples, Dov recited the following:

We come into this world naked, to begin our lives.
Today you stand before me, your feet bare, representing
your entry into a new world: your life together.
May it be long and full of joy.
May you be blessed with abiding friendship and love.

May wisdom and humor guide your path.
May you find comfort in each other and in
our community."

Dov moved to the first couple and leaned close. The bride and groom whispered their vows to each other as he listened. Then they kissed. In one movement, Dov reached up and lifted the flower crowns from each of their heads. Crossing his arms above them, he said, "Vows are given, and vows are received," and then lowered the swapped crowns of flowers onto their heads.

Smiling, the couple joined hands, her right, his left, and extended their arms toward Dov. He pulled a ribbon out of his pouch and tied it around their wrists along with a twig of rosemary, symbolizing the eternal essence of love and marriage.

Moving to the second and third couple, he repeated the crown and wrist-tying rituals.

Their wrists would remain bound until they retired that night. This would require them to help each other to accomplish every task, emphasizing their new, permanent connection of mutual support.

Stepping back, Dov said, "Friends, these couples are united in love, united in marriage. I ask you to acknowledge this bonding."

The crowd stopped moving. They roared their approval, clapping, whistling, and stomping their feet. The brides and grooms kissed again before turning to the other couples to offer them congratulations. The wedding guests pressed forward to offer their best wishes.

The musicians began playing the wedding song. The crowd joined in.

Oh, joy of joys.
True love is found.
The vows are made; their wrists are bound.

Let's celebrate.
Gather all around.
The vows are made; their hearts are bound.

Goddess blessings.
The two are crowned.
The vows are made; their lives are bound.

The three couples were then lifted up and carried to the back garden for the wedding feast. Dov remained behind. Sinking into a chair, he collapsed, his head in his hands. Lali padded out from the kitchen. Sensing Dov's despair, she nuzzled his shoulder. He smiled and scratched her behind the ears and said, "Don't worry, Lali. I'm just a little sad. We'll go out in a minute and join the festivities." Lali licked his face. "Yes, girl, I like weddings too." He hugged her around the neck before standing up. Straightening his shoulders and tossing his hair back, he went to join the others, Lali at his side.

❀ ❀ ❀

THREE DAYS LATER, A LIGHT RAIN fell as Dov performed the final blessing for Adja. After the ritual, he walked back to the inn with Sig. When they reached the front steps, Dov spoke. "I'll be leaving in the morning, Sig."

"I thought you would be leaving soon. Where will you go from here?"

With only a slight hesitation, Dov answered, "To Merton, with stops along the way."

"Well, I'll pack some food for you and Lali tonight," Sig said. "Thank you for coming. The wedding was beautiful. I'm sorry that your time in Tinton ended so sorrowfully. We will all miss Adja."

"Yes. He was a good man."

"You needn't worry about Burto. We will watch over him. He is as loved as Adja was."

"I know."

They walked inside in companionable silence.

In the morning, Dov rode out of town, Lali trotting alongside him. They took the north road toward Merton. When he was sure they were not being followed, Dov rode through the woods toward an old southern trade road to Dute. It had been plowed over during the wars and was now overgrown, but Dov had old maps to keep him on track to the Minca River.

From there, he followed the river to Kameeth Falls, the rushing torrent that marked the border crossing between Minca and Dute. In the morning he would navigate the long switchback trail down the steep cliffside to the valley floor that was Dute proper.

In the gathering darkness, Dov erected a lean-to and gathered wood for a fire. Lali seemed restless, pacing around the campsite, disturbing the horses.

"Lali! Come here, girl," Dov called. She came to his side, whimpering. "What is it, Lali? Is someone out there?" Dov whispered, glancing around. She yelped in agreement. He scratched her ears, assessing the situation. The sound of the river must have covered the intruder's approach. There was very little protection on the riverbank, and it was a good distance back to the woods where the horses were tethered.

"Forgive me, Lali," he said softly. "I fear I was too

confident. If we have been followed, we will have to make a run for the trail. We'll leave the horses and trust the Goddess. Let us hope that it's dark enough to ensure our escape." He gave her another pat and stood.

Without warning, a volley of arrows shot out of the woods. Lali didn't have a chance to cry out before an arrow pierced her throat. Dov saw her fall to the ground just a moment before another arrow struck him in the back. "Lali!" he cried out, before falling forward into the river. His body was swept over the falls, down to the rocks far below.

Chapter 13

High on a plateau above the fast-running Minca River, Merton demonstrated Vestor's power, precision, and attention to detail. Vestor's stronghold, a citadel built out of dark stone, stood prominently in the center of the city. Turrets serving as watchtowers faced north, south, east, and west along the high wall. From the citadel, streets radiated out like spokes on a wheel. The small cluster of homes and businesses closest to the citadel were those of Vestor's friends and allies, each decorated with intricately carved wood, stained glass, and touches of gilt.

The rest of Merton was mired in poverty. The buildings were poorly maintained, their inhabitants struggling to eke out a living. On the edge of the plateau were a series of cogs, wheels, and weights activating cable cars that carried goods from the city to the docks along the riverbank. Large water-wheels moved machinery and mill wheels, providing power for craft workers and millers.

The northern turret of the citadel, Vestor's tower, rose above the others. Each level housed his administration, ascending in power with every step upward. The clerks worked on the lowest level, with generals and advisers on the higher floors. The top floor was Vestor's retreat, a large, circular room surrounded by windows. The furniture consisted of a solitary desk and chair. Papers covered the desk in neat stacks, held in place with paperweights of iron. No one entered this space without invitation. It was a private place, his lair.

From this vantage point it was Vestor's pleasure to survey the activities of the town, occasionally issuing orders and commands to his underlings in the rooms below. This day, however, he wasn't interested in Merton. He watched a lone figure riding toward the city. Vestor recognized Nikka immediately, her crimson robes and auburn hair blowing in the wind. His lips twitched in anticipation, a gleam in his dark eye.

Walking to the stairway, he called, "See that a room is prepared for Teller Nikka. Make sure she is comfortable. Let her know that I will join her in the Great Hall for a glass of wine before dinner."

The sound of scurrying feet assured him that his orders were being carried out, and Vestor returned to his desk. With renewed determination, he settled back down to his work, calculations for another incursion into Dute.

❊ ❊ ❊

As the sun set, Nikka was ushered into the Great Hall. As the door closed behind her, she sighed quietly. She was alone. She strolled around the room admiring the craftsmanship of the furnishings. She had been in Vestor's residence a few times before, but only in the office tower, never in the Great Hall. It took her breath away. There was nothing like it anywhere else in Merton—or in the world.

Several hundred people could mingle comfortably in the hall and yet, through the careful arrangement of furniture, it offered intimacy. The domed ceiling was high overhead with carved arches framing stained glass windows around the circumference. The fading light sent rose, turquoise, and gold hues cascading down the walls. Hundreds of oil candles lit tapestries depicting Vestor victorious in battles, preening in glory and lord of the land. There were several seating areas for conversation. A fire burned in a marble fireplace large enough for Nikka to stand in. She strolled around the room touching the fine materials, admiring the ornaments, and appreciating the elegance.

"Nikka, my dear, how lovely to see you," Vestor said as he strode into the hall. He extended his arm to her. Although he was reserved, as usual, his slight smile was warm.

A good sign, thought Nikka.

Approaching quickly, she took his wrist and executed a deep curtsy, her eyes downcast. "The pleasure is mine, my Lord."

"Shall we sit by the fire?" Vestor asked, leading her to a comfortable chair. "And a glass of wine?" Sauntering to the sideboard, he poured golden liquid into a crystal goblet and handed it to her. After filling his own glass, he sat in an elegant chair on the opposite side of the hearth.

Nikka observed him over the rim of her goblet, conscious of the disparity between them. He was seated on a chair that resembled a throne, while she was perched on an ordinary chair, comfortable but lower to the ground. They sat in silence. Mildly apprehensive, she sipped her wine.

"So, what brings you to Merton at this time of year? I assumed you were out on your travels."

"And so I was, my Lord. A very interesting trip indeed."

Nikka waited for Vestor to inquire. He said nothing, revealing no curiosity. He simply regarded her intently. Before she squirmed under his gaze, she said, "I met your nephew."

"Yes? How interesting. Where and when was that encounter?" Vestor asked nonchalantly. A tightening in his jaw was the only change in his impassive face, but Nikka sensed his agitation.

"He was with Dov at the Teller's cave. They said they were traveling to Tinton."

This remark was followed by another long silence as Vestor stared into the distance, lost in thought.

She waited a moment before adding, "Steff told me about his sister's upcoming wedding. He said he was going hunting in the Eastern Mountains to avoid the wedding preparations. Dov mentioned some distant relatives he might visit. It seemed plausible but unlikely."

She let Vestor digest this information. Again he seemed impassive, but Nikka knew the inner turmoil she had created with this information.

Vestor regarded her with intensity. "I regret I cannot stay for dinner. There's some pressing business to which I must attend. You will be well looked after. Perhaps we can resume our conversation tomorrow. Now, if you will excuse me," he said, standing.

"My Lord," Nikka said, rising from her chair and touching his arm.

He looked down at her hand before turning to face her, his eyes as cold as ice. "Madame," he said in a withering voice.

Nikka paled before his stare but stood firm. She had heard tales of Vestor's anger. "My Lord, there is more. If I may," she said, indicating that he should retake his seat. Vestor sat down slowly, his eyes never leaving her face.

"My Lord, I am a faithful servant and have only your best interests at heart," Nikka continued, before taking a deep breath. "It seemed to me that there was something amiss in the story they told. Dov was overly protective, not allowing me free conversation with the boy."

"Go on," Vestor said.

"I even tried a gentle dream probe on Steff, but Dov disrupted me."

"I'm surprised you were careless enough to get caught," he said with derision.

"Yes, well . . ." Nikka blushed. "We went our separate ways the next morning, but I was convinced something was not right."

"I trust your intuition, Nikka," Vestor said, starting to rise again.

"So you see, my Lord, I did what I thought you would have me do."

Vestor remained seated and asked, "Yes?"

"I hope you don't think I've taken liberties, but under the circumstances I thought it would be best—"

"Get to the point!"

"I went to the closest guard station and requested trackers be sent to follow them. I implied I was speaking on your behalf. I told them to take *extreme* action if Dov and Steff's activities appeared treasonous," she said in a rush. "I trust I acted correctly," she added, almost in a whisper.

Slowly, Vestor leaned back in his chair. He picked up his goblet and took a sip of wine, observing and enjoying her discomfort. He allowed a few moments to pass before speaking. "Nikka, my dear, you are as clever as you are beautiful. You have done exactly as I would have wished." A small but genuine smile touched his lips.

Nikka breathed an audible sigh of relief. She sank into her chair and tried her best to look calm. "I am grateful to hear that, my Lord. I requested reports be sent directly to you and came here to inform you as soon as I could."

"I am very pleased."

Her confidence restored, Nikka smiled coquettishly. "You will find I can be very pleasing, my Lord."

Vestor leaned toward her and smiled sardonically. "I have no doubt about that," he said. Vestor put his wine glass down, stood up, and offered his arm. "I believe I do have time for some dinner after all, my dear."

Nikka felt a rush of excitement as they walked out of the hall. She had heard tales of Vestor's gratitude.

❀ ❀ ❀

THE FIRST REPORT ARRIVED ON Vestor's desk eight days later. Dov and Steff did appear to be traveling toward Tinton as they had claimed. The second report was more worrisome.

> *Subjects arrived at Tinton. Avoiding detection, younger man left the city. Whereabouts unknown. Have sent scouts to pick up trail.*
> *We remain with the elder.*

"Dov, what are you up to?" Vestor growled as he paced the room.

The third report caused Vestor to hurl a paperweight through one of the windows.

> *Persuaded doctor to cooperate. Information revealed. Your nephew is traveling to Carroo. What are your orders?*

Vestor called down the stairs, "Send Fizor to me!"

Fizor raced up the stairs. "What can I do for you, sir?" he asked, out of breath.

"Your future brother-in-law is engaged in seditious activities. He's headed to Carroo and needs to be stopped. Now."

"Of course, my Lord. I will issue orders immediately," Fizor said. He retreated down the stairs, yelling commands to his men. By the end of the day, riders were on their way to scour the land for Steff.

At long last, another report arrived. After reading it, Vestor sank into his chair, his head dropping into his hands.

Teller dead. Felled by arrow at border with Dute.

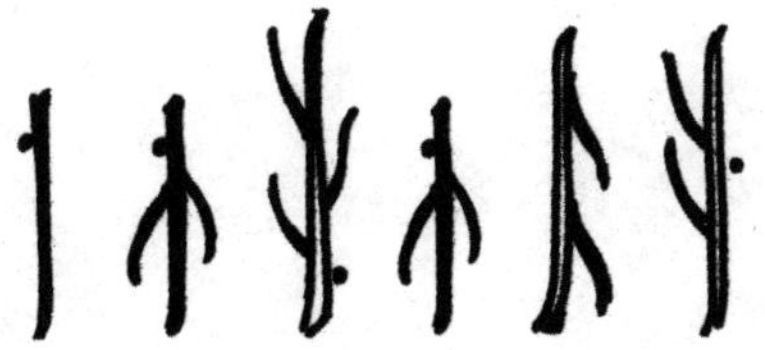

Chapter 14

The Green Mountains formed the border between Minca and Carroo, the tall, rugged slopes creating a natural barrier. The original pine forest, which gave the mountains their name, had been slashed and burned in the early years of the war. The forest was returning, but the darkness of charred wood would always underlie the green.

A lone hawk glided on the air currents high above the peaks. Below, a small figure perched in the branches of a tree, eyes closed, connected telepathically with the hawk.

"*They come,*" the hawk communicated.

"*How many are there?*"

"*Many.*"

The young guardian sounded out a series of low-pitched tones. After a few moments, another sequence of sounds carried through the trees. Then a second could be heard, then a third, and a fourth from farther away.

The hawk gave one lone call and flew away. The guardian looked toward the mountain pass. This was one of the old trails to Minca, one of the few passes that led into Carroo from the outside. No one had come through in years. Guardians, with the help of their nonhuman friends, were stationed along the border, watching, vigilant, ready to defend their tribe.

Now, with the hawk's warning, the five prepared for whatever was to come. It was a short wait before they saw movement in the mountain pass, and even at this distance, they could hear shouting. They waited quietly. One man came through the pass, running fast. He was stumbling and cursing, calling out to the Goddess for help. Others followed behind. There were ten of them, not in such a hurry. Occasionally, one would stop, take aim, and shoot an arrow or throw a rock at the man running before them. Jeers and laughter filled the air when the missiles missed their mark.

The Carroo felt a mental nudge from one of the other guardians. Focusing, they mind-linked to hear the communication.

"*This is peculiar, Réan,*" the guardian said.

"*It could be a trap. Hold strong. It won't be long. They are almost in place.*"

When the runners from Minca were in the correct location, the guardian gave a signal. Instantly and with precision, hidden nets on the ground scooped up the runners, hoisting them into the trees. The first runner was trapped alone. Realizing what had happened, he collapsed, giving up. The others were trapped in twos or threes. Their response was different as they struggled and yelled. Some pulled out knives and tried to cut the ropes holding them, but these were Carroo ropes. They had been spun with incantations as well as hands and would never cut unless the proper words were spoken.

The Carroos climbed down from their perches and made their way to the trail, quietly and swiftly, knives and cudgels at the ready. When they reached the first trap, they looked up at the man in the net. He looked back and said, "I have come to see Mother Carroo."

The five Carroos looked at one another and held a silent conversation.

"*This must be a trap.*"

"*I don't know. The others were trying to shoot him.*"

"*They missed every time. We can't trust him.*"

"*What if he's telling the truth?*"

The young Carroo, Réan, said out loud, "Go get the other Mincans. Bring them back here. Then we'll decide what to do."

The other four nodded and strode up the trail. Réan squatted on the ground, observing the man in the net. This Mincan looked to be tall, about a head taller than Réan. He was filthy, his clothes torn and clotted with dirt. Yet there was nothing threatening about him. He seemed to be relieved to be hanging in a tree. *Are all Mincans this strange?* Réan wondered.

"I've been traveling for so long," the Mincan said wistfully, staring into the tree branches. Turning his head, he looked at Réan and asked, "Do you have any water?"

Réan reached into a vest pocket and brought out a flask, handing it up through the net.

"Thanks," he said. "What's your name? I can't thank you properly without a name."

"No need for names. I doubt you'll have time to use it."

"I hope that's not true. I must get to Mother Carroo. My name's Steff," he said with a slight smile. He returned the flask, then turned back to look at the branches, shifting into a more comfortable position. They both waited in silence for the others to return.

The men from Minca were a scruffy bunch, thin and raw. They were tied wrist to wrist and led by one of the Carroos. They were invited to sit, and when they refused, they were forced onto the ground. Réan stood and walked around the group slowly.

"Who are you? Why do you come to Carroo?" Réan asked.

"Don't say nothing," the oldest one grumbled to the others, "and don't look at none of 'em."

"They were chasing me," said the man hanging in the tree.

The older Mincan man tried to rise. "No, we wasn't. We was trying to stop you from making a mistake. No one's allowed to cross into Carroo anymore. We was doing you a favor. Now look where that's got us!" he growled as he was restrained by the Carroos.

"They were sent by Regent Vestor to stop me from coming here, from seeking Mother Carroo," the trapped man said.

Réan looked from one to the other and asked, "Why were you shooting at him?"

"Shooting? Eh . . . well . . . it was just a bit of fun." The man shrugged. "Ain't that right, boys?" The other men nodded and muttered agreement.

Réan circled the men in a mesmerizing fashion. Suddenly, Réan squatted down next to one of the younger Mincans. The startled man jerked back, shocked. That was the opening Réan needed. "Who's telling the truth?" Réan whispered quickly. Before he could think, the man pointed to the trapped man. His companion tried to lunge for him but was again restrained by the Carroos.

Réan stood and looked at the man in the tree. Reverting to silent conversation with the other Carroos, he said, "*Take these men back over the mountains. Then return to your posts. I'll deal with this one.*" The men nodded in agreement and tugged the captured men to their feet.

There was a good bit of shoving and shouting as the men were led away. Réan waited until they were out of sight before waving a hand toward the tree. With a thump, the net and its contents flopped to the ground.

Steff crawled out of the rope net, massaging his aching limbs as he stood. "Thank you, again." Then he asked, "Was that some kind of truth inducement you used on that fellow?"

"No. Simple people often resort to the truth when they're caught off guard," Réan said, sitting down on the ground and gesturing for the Mincan to join him.

Steff sat and asked, "What will your friends do to them?"

"Nothing much. Once they cross back into Minca, they simply won't remember where they've been or what they've been doing for the last few days."

"Really? Krickers! That's amazing."

After a few moments, Steff said, "We weren't sure there were any Carroos left. I'm very glad I found you."

"Mincan, you didn't find us. We found you," Réan said defensively. "Why do you want to see Mother Carroo?"

"My information is for her alone."

"Well, you may as well tell me. I won't take you to see her unless I feel it's safe."

Steff considered this. All of the Carroos were short, he had noticed, but this one was the smallest of the group. Despite his stature, he exuded confidence. He was dressed in shades of green and brown. *Perfect camouflage in this forest,* Steff thought. A large vest, which was covered in stuffed pockets, hung loosely over his tunic. *He must carry everything he needs to survive in that vest.* A neckerchief was tied around his neck. Cloth leggings protected his legs, but he was barefoot. His raven hair was chopped short and poked out from under a cap decorated with buttons and feathers. Compared to his dark hair, the Carroo's skin was very pale, almost translucent. *Now I understand why they call them "blue,"* Steff thought. Beneath dark brows, piercing blue eyes stared at Steff. He seemed perfectly prepared to wait all day for Steff's response.

Steff decided to trust the young man and asked, "What's your name?"

"Réan," he said simply.

"Pleased to meet you, Réan," Steff said, extending his arm. With a slight hesitation, Réan reached out and clasped his wrist.

"I'm brother to Mother Minca. She sent me here with a message for Mother Carroo. She's also sent an emissary to Mother Dute." After a pause, he added, "She had a vision for peace between us."

"Peace? Ha. Mincans don't want peace," Réan said scornfully.

Steff regarded Réan closely. He looked to be in his late teens. He would never have known a life without war, which would explain this cynicism. Steff sighed. "My sister was a child when our uncle took control of Minca. The war has been hard on Minca as well as Carroo and Dute. Our land is dying, and our people are starving. She is hopeful that the power of the Goddess can be restored before it's too late. To this end, she has sent me to talk with Mother Carroo." Straightening, Steff asked Réan, "Will you deny me the opportunity to speak with her? Will you send me back across the mountain and muddle my mind as well?"

Réan said nothing but observed Steff closely. Finally, he came to a decision. "Well, let's get going then," he said, getting up.

Steff smiled. Réan set off at a quick pace through the woods, farther into the mountains. After a while, he waited for Steff to catch up and chided, "I thought you were in a hurry."

"I'm not as young as I was when I started this journey," Steff replied, catching his breath.

"Well, you probably weren't as dirty or smelly either. Would you like to bathe?" Réan asked, gesturing to a small pond nestled in the trees to his left.

"Wonderful!"

He stripped off his boots and clothes and walked naked toward the pond. Réan watched the strapping young man, admiring his physique.

The water was bitterly cold, but Steff submerged himself with a sigh of delight. Réan handed Steff a packet of powdered soap-root from one of his many pockets. As Steff lathered up, Réan picked up Steff's clothes and handed them to Steff to wash.

When he was done, Steff got out and, shaking his head to shed some water, walked to a spot of sunlight shining through the branches. He spread his wet clothes out on the ground before lying down, relaxing.

They remained in silence, lost in their own thoughts. When his clothes were dry enough to put on, he dressed. Réan nodded toward the trail. They started off again.

"How long have you been traveling?" Réan asked.

"We set off at the Summer Solstice."

"Tell me," Réan said.

Steff began at the beginning, leaving out only the details of Cora's vision. His tale of adventure and pursuit managed to entertain Réan and distract Steff from his own weariness. Steff was pleased to get an occasional laugh out of Réan. When Steff told him about finding the mutilated Dute, Réan stopped, his face tight with concern. With a sad shake of his head, he led Steff onward.

As the sun set over the mountains, Steff told of his capture and escape from the Mincan men. "All my skill with

Rime meant little. I was outnumbered." Steff flashed a smile at Réan. "They thought they had me knotted tightly, but I tricked them. I filled my lungs full of air as they tied me up. When they tossed me aside, I was able to release my breath and the ropes were loose."

"Quick thinking," Réan said with approval.

"Well, it's an old trick but a good one. Once they were asleep, I was able to crawl away and head for the mountain pass. They came after me the next morning. And that's when you trapped us."

"It's getting dark," Réan said. "We've covered a long distance. We should stop."

Steff was amazed that most of the day had passed without his realizing it. He collapsed to the ground, his aches and exhaustion returning.

Réan cleared a spot of grass and weeds, gathered up dried pine needles and kindling, and made a small pile. From one of his vest pockets, he produced a bag. With a prayer of gratitude to the Goddess, he added a pinch of dried leaves from the bag onto the pile. Extracting some flint from another pocket, Réan sparked the leaves into a flame.

"What was that?" Steff asked. "I've never seen a fire light so quickly."

"Do you know the fireweed plant?"

Steff nodded. "The leaves are bright red in the fall. But I didn't know it could do that."

"On its own it won't. We add some Carroo energy to it. Then it becomes what we call flashweed. It will ignite even the wettest wood." Searching through his vest pockets, Réan retrieved dried mushrooms and spices. From a deep pocket, he pulled out a small, hammered metal bowl to cook in. Steff watched intently as Réan covered the dried food with water and settled it on the fire. With a flourish, he withdrew a spoon out of an inside pocket and began to stir.

Steff's stomach growled. Réan glanced at him and asked, "How long has it been since you last ate?"

"Since they caught up with me. They took my food and water and weren't particularly interested in sharing. Fortunately, they didn't find my message for Mother Carroo. I'm sorry I have nothing to offer for the meal."

"Don't worry. I have enough for tonight. I hope you like soup," Réan said with a smile. "There's plenty of food to forage this time of year. We won't starve."

"How far do we have to go?"

"It's a twelve-day journey to Cappett on the coast. That's where our Mother is. You won't remember how you got there, Mincan. You say you're here for peace, but we *will* keep ourselves safe."

"I understand," Steff said. "So, you've heard a lot about me. Tell me about yourself."

"Not much to tell, really."

"There must be something. You didn't appear out of thin air, did you?"

Réan poked the fire with a stick before saying, "No. I was born twenty years ago in the usual way. We lived in the foothills of the Green Mountains not too far from the border with Minca. My parents and sisters were killed in a Mincan raid when I was six years old."

He stirred the soup, a far-off look on his face. It was clear there was more to this story, but Réan didn't elaborate.

After a minute, Steff said, "I'm sorry about your family."

Réan came out of his reverie and shrugged. "I'm second cousin to Mother Carroo. I was brought to Cappett, to her household. That's where I grew up and was educated. I've been a mountain guardian for five years or so. Not much to tell."

Réan reached into another pocket and pulled out a collapsible cup. He poured some soup into it and handed it to Steff. He offered Steff some crusty bread from yet another pocket. Steff ate at once, contemplating the strange wonders of Carroo pockets.

Réan removed his neckerchief and wrapped it around his hands, picking the cooking bowl out of the fire. He took a sip of the soup before speaking. "It was a long time ago. I'm afraid I don't really remember them, not without Sighting."

"What's Sighting?"

"It's a meditation we can do. It enhances memories so you can see people or events more clearly. Depending on what the focus is, it can be fun. Sometimes it's just too painful. I don't use it to see my family very often, anymore."

They ate the rest of their meal in silence. Steff helped to clean up and extinguish the fire. The night air was warm, even in the mountains. Steff piled up some pine needles, creating a makeshift bed while Réan watched with curiosity.

"What are you doing?" Réan asked.

"I'm making a soft spot to sleep on."

"You sleep on the ground?"

"Yeah," Steff said. "Don't you?"

"No. Never. We sleep in the trees."

"What? How do you do that without falling? Do you tie yourself onto a branch?"

Réan stood up and instructed Steff to watch. He turned toward a tall pine, closed his eyes, and extended his arms. "Sister Tree, I ask for your help. Please hold me in your arms and keep me safe while I sleep."

The tree swayed, even though there was no breeze. Slowly, the lower branches bent toward each other, entwining and creating a solid nest large enough to hold Réan. Réan opened his eyes and grinned at Steff.

Steff's eyes were wide with astonishment. "I'd heard Carroos had special abilities, but this is incredible! I've never seen anything like it!"

"Shall I ask for you?"

Steff gave a quick nod. Réan asked another tree to help Steff. It took a few moments for the tree to respond, as if it were seriously considering the request. Eventually, the tree moved its branches and created a nest large enough for Steff.

"Do you need help getting up there?" Réan asked.

"I *think* I can climb up by myself," Steff said, slightly affronted. "I'm not that feeble."

Réan laughed and scrambled up into his sleeping nest. Getting up the tree was harder for Steff, but he wasn't going to admit it. Rolling into the branch bed, Steff felt wonderful, comfortable, and secure, with the lovely scent of pine.

"Don't forget to thank your tree before you go to sleep," Réan said. "You don't want to be dumped out in the middle of the night. Sleep well."

Steff wasn't sure if Réan was joking or not, but he wasn't going to take any chances. Whispering softly, he said, "Thank you, Sister Tree. This is a beautiful bed. I am very grateful." He felt the branches tighten slightly, as if she were giving him a hug. Steff smiled at the thought, closed his eyes, and slept solidly until morning.

Chapter 15

Steff and Réan walked west over the mountains, gathering berries, nuts, and other edible plants for their meals. Each evening, Réan prepared their sleeping nests. He encouraged Steff to try talking to the trees himself. Nothing happened at first, but then, one evening after Steff asked for help, one of the pine trees started to quiver. Excitedly, Steff turned to Réan with delight. Réan was quivering himself, trying to contain his laughter.

"What's so funny? I asked politely, and look! The tree's moving!"

"She's not moving to make you a nest, Mincan. The tree is laughing at you!"

Steff whirled back around to face the tree. It *did* seem to be laughing. Exasperated, Steff fell to his knees. Throwing his hands into the air, he squawked, "Blessed Goddess. I give up!" and fell, quite dramatically, facedown onto the earth.

Réan was laughing out loud now. Steff rolled over and started laughing too. Réan blurted out, "You'll never pass for a Carroo."

"I know. I'm much too tall and much too pink."

That got them laughing even harder. The stand of pines started moving, as if they were joining in on the laughter. When their giggling subsided, Steff got up and executed a formal bow to the pines. "Please forgive my Mincan heritage. I mean no insult."

With that remark, the pine tree he had originally approached seemed to bow in return. It then bent its branches and formed a nest for Steff to sleep in. Réan nudged him with his elbow. "Good for you, Steff. You've won them over. They will spread the word that you've received approval," Réan said. "Whenever you need a sleeping nest, ask any evergreen and you will be accommodated."

With a sense of awe, Steff bowed again to the pine trees. "Thank you. I am blessed by your generosity," he said with sincerity, and he climbed the tree.

Climbing into his own nest, Réan called out, "Good night."

"Good night, Réan. Thank you . . . for everything."

❊   ❊   ❊

STEFF BEGAN TO COMPREHEND the deep connection Carroos had with nature. Réan acknowledged every creature they encountered. He silently expressed gratitude toward the earth, animals, and plants. It gave Steff a new perception of a world he had always taken for granted.

Réan was fascinated by the Mincan flair for crafting and inventing. One evening, Steff built a dam in a shallow creek to deepen the water enough to soak their feet. Another evening, he spent some time in quiet enjoyment, arranging stones and pebbles. When he was done, he presented Réan with a small geyser of water for a drinking fountain. Réan was amused by the construction. Sensitive to the Carroos' philosophy of nature, Steff replaced every stone as close to its original position as possible before they moved on.

Each day that they traveled, Steff observed a hawk in the sky. He considered the possibility of it being the same hawk each day. He asked Réan if he was correct.

Réan glanced up and saw Nesset soaring high above. "You've got good eyes, Mincan. That's Nesset. She and I are friends. Nesset was the one who told us you were coming the other day."

"Told you?"

"Yes. We can communicate through our thoughts with most nonhumans, in the same way we Carroos can communicate with each other. Birds are easy to mind-link with. Don't Mincans do that too?"

"Sometimes I know what my sister is thinking, but I don't think it's the same. And I don't know anyone who can do that with animals or birds, not even Dov."

"That's too bad. You can't imagine what you're missing," Réan said. After observing Nesset, Réan laughed. "I think Nesset is keeping a watch on you. If you try anything shifty, she'll fly down and pluck out your eyeballs."

"Thanks for the warning, friend," Steff said, not sure if Réan was teasing.

Walking to a small clearing, Réan reached into a deep pocket in his vest and pulled out a piece of heavy felt. He wrapped it around his forearm and tucked the edges in, securing it. Then he extended his arm straight out from his shoulder. Within a minute, Nesset swooped down out of the sky and landed on Réan's arm. Réan talked to Nesset soothingly and stroked her feathers. He motioned for Steff to come closer.

"Nesset, this is Steff. Steff, this is my sweet friend, Nesset."

Nesset cocked her head to see Steff better. He nodded slightly in acknowledgment. They appraised each other and seemed pleased with what they saw. Nesset turned to Réan, gave a little coo, and flew off.

"She approves of you, Mincan. And she's *very* particular."

"I'm honored," Steff said sincerely.

Réan punched him in the arm, laughing.

❖ ❖ ❖

STEFF AND RÉAN WALKED ALONG a ridge, the Green Mountains softening into rolling hills as they neared the sea. A trail descended to a wide green valley below. Wildflowers bordered the trail, a lovely fragrance wafting up to the travelers. Deciduous trees encircled the valley's mossy meadow, whose center was marked by a tall pine. Their journey had come to an end, but Steff couldn't see Cappett.

"Well, what do you think of Cappett?" Réan asked, waving his hand toward the valley.

"Very funny, Réan. Where is it?"

"Right in front of you, Mincan."

"I see trees and grass and the sea beyond. That's it."

Réan looked at the valley and then back at Steff. "Oh! I wasn't thinking. Come here and bend down."

Steff did as Réan requested. Very gently, Réan blew into Steff's face. It tickled in a pleasant way.

"Now look," Réan said with pride.

Steff turned back to the valley. A new vision appeared before him. In the center of the valley, a large circle was outlined in boulders and surrounded by flowers. At the apex, in front of the pine, was a very tall standing stone. Radiating out from the circle of boulders was a maze path defined by vegetable gardens of wondrous varieties. The trees surrounding the valley were festooned with multicolored ribbons that moved gently in the breeze. Over forty people were there. Carroos worked in the garden and walked through the forest while children played, laughed, and sang in the center circle. Wild animals and birds were there too, without fear. The sight and sounds were so peaceful and welcoming, Steff felt a tightening in his chest.

"It's beautiful."

"It's home."

They started down the trail. Their arrival created a swift reaction. The children and animals ran to the trees. The adults moved into a tight group at the base of the trail, barricading the entrance to the valley. Steff and Réan stopped a distance from the crowd. A silent conversation between Réan and the other Carroos ensued, and eventually they parted, allowing access to the valley.

"Come, Steff," Réan said, leading the way. The Carroos ushered them through the maze to the circle. Réan stopped in front of the tall stone and stood in silence, Steff at his side. Steff didn't understand what was happening. The Carroos moved around the circle, standing in front of the boulders facing the monolith. They, too, were silent.

A sudden swirl of air caused Steff to blink his eyes. When he opened them again, there, standing before the monolith, as if she had appeared out of the air, was a tiny old woman. Steff realized she had been there the whole time, invisible to his non-Carroo eyes, questioning Réan wordlessly.

Steff knelt down onto one knee and bowed his head, putting him almost at eye level with the small woman. "Mother

Carroo, I am Steff, brother to Cora, Mother Minca. I come in peace."

Mother Carroo stepped past Réan and took Steff's face into her hands. With her eyes closed, she held his face gently for a minute or two, and then nodded.

"Rise, Steff. You are welcome," she said in a high, gentle voice.

Steff stood up. Mother Carroo was barely taller than his waist. She tilted her head up to him, and Steff was shocked to see that her eyes were a milky white. Mother Carroo was blind! She had a winsome face, with laugh lines surrounding her mouth and eyes. Her long white hair was braided and wound around her head several times before falling over her shoulder. Feathers and flowers were tucked into the braid, creating the effect of an organic crown. Her vest was covered in flowers embroidered by a delicate hand. Her simple tunic was of the softest green material and well-worn over her dark-green leggings. She, too, was barefoot.

"Take Steff to our guesthouse, then come to me, Réan," she said. To Steff she said, "We have much to discuss. Refresh yourself from your journey. We shall have time to talk after supper."

Mother Carroo nodded, then addressed the community. "Make our new friend welcome," she said. Without words, she urged them to be cautious until he earned their trust.

Steff's heart pounded. Réan gave his arm a playful push. "You're smiling like a child with a treat," Réan said with a grin. "Mother Carroo affects us all that way. It's good to be home."

"How long has it been since you were here?"

"I returned to the mountains just after the Summer Solstice. Come. Let me show you where you'll be staying."

As they left the circle, the Carroos crowded around them. There were a couple Carroos almost as tall as Steff, but most were considerably shorter. The sea of faces was overwhelming, the many voices indistinguishable. Réan grabbed his arm and pulled him along, saying to the others, "Give him space. There will be time to talk later."

When they were alone, walking to the trees, Réan said, "I love Cappett, but sometimes it's just so . . . so . . . crowded."

Steff chuckled. "I know what you mean. I live with my sister and housekeeper. Even with just the three of us, sometimes our home is *very* crowded."

"I thought you'd understand," Réan said shyly.

They walked deep into the forest before Réan stopped near a tall oak tree. "Here's our guesthouse," he said, pointing up. Long colorful ribbons hung from the branches above his head, like so many of the other trees. Liquid rainbows. The ribbons were attached to branches that had woven themselves into a platform high above the forest floor, carrying a tent the color of a clear, blue sky and painted with the images of plants, animals, and birds. Beyond the tent, what looked like a regular tree grew, the branches and leaves providing privacy.

Steff turned and looked at the tops of the other trees. Every one that had filaments hanging down had a tent platform above, each decorated in differing shades of greens and blues. The painted designs displayed distinct creative styles. There were animals, plants, or birds on some, while others were repeated patterns of lines or shapes. Each tent was beautiful and unique. When he was able to speak, he said, "Incredible!"

Smiling, Réan said, "To enter your space, you need to say, 'Carroo Carree.' Try it."

Grinning, Steff said, "Carroo Carree." He watched, his eyes wide, as the ribbons lengthened and knotted themselves into a ladder.

"Krickers!"

"Climb on up."

It was a long climb up to the platform. Réan followed him. When they were both on the platform, the ribbons untied themselves and fluttered in the breeze. Looking down, Steff asked, "How do I get down again?"

"Say the same thing in reverse."

Steff opened the tent flap and walked in. The room was almost three of his arm's length in each direction, and just tall enough for his height. On one side there was a sleeping pad. It had been made for Carroos and was a little short for him, but it looked comfortable and inviting with its embroidered patchwork quilt and pillows. A small flap in the wall was rolled up to let in light and air. There were two low chairs made from branches lashed together with colored twine, and a flat round stone served as a table. Two ceramic cups next to a jug of water with mint leaves floating in it and a basket of fruit alongside a small oil lamp completed the picture of serenity.

"There's the privy," Réan said, pointing to a fabric wall dividing the space. "There's water and towels for washing in there also. Someone will be in each day to remove any waste and tidy up. We'll find some extra clothes for you and give yours a proper washing. Is there anything you need?"

Steff shook his head.

"Well, I should go to see Mother. There will be a chime for dinner. We'll be eating at the circle, so just come over."

Steff collapsed onto the sleeping pad. "Thanks."

Steff was asleep before Réan climbed down the ladder.

Réan walked slowly to the Mother's tree behind the monolith. When he got there, he found the Mother sitting on a boulder at the base of the pine. Hearing Réan approach, she motioned for him to sit on an adjacent boulder. They faced each other and clasped hands. After kissing each other on the cheeks, they closed their eyes and leaned forward until their foreheads were touching.

"*Welcome home, dearest cousin. I have missed you.*"

"*I've missed you too, Titia.*"

"*You've brought an interesting puzzle with you.*"

"*Indeed.*"

"*What do you make of this Mincan? He seems to think you're a boy.*"

Réan smiled.

"*I chose not to correct his impression of me. I believe he is sincere in his quest for peace between us, but he is a Mincan, after all. I hope you're comfortable with my decision to bring him here.*"

"*I trust your judgment, dear one, and will keep your identity safe. I will talk to him this evening. It's been so long since we've had peaceful contact with Minca.*"

❀ ❀ ❀

AFTER HIS NAP, STEFF STEPPED OUT onto the platform, where he found a pile of fresh clothes. After washing, he tried them on. The sleeves of the tunic and the leggings were a bit short, but the material was soft. He felt clean for the first time in many, many days. To honor the Carroo tradition, he went barefoot.

Dinner in Cappett was a community picnic. Lanterns placed between the boulders provided a warm light. Caldrons of vegetable stew and loaves of whole grain bread were served with fresh berries for dessert. The Carroos sat on the boulders and on blankets around the circle, eating and talking. Steff felt welcomed. Some of the Carroos actually had relatives in Minca, and they plied Steff with questions about them and other concerns regarding Minca. There was little Steff could tell them, but they didn't seem to mind. They were pleased just to have him there. After dinner and clean up, the children performed traditional songs and dances for their guest. They were only slightly different from the ones Steff had grown up with. He smiled and tapped his foot along with the music. A small child grabbed his hand and tried to pull him into the next dance.

Laughing, Steff said, "No, no dancing for me. Thanks. But," he turned to the tin pipe player, extending his hand, "if I could borrow your pipe?"

Steff played a lively tune. Titia remembered the song from her visits to Minca before the war. To everyone's pleasure, she sang along with him in her high, lilting voice.

Réan sat across the circle, grinning, surprised at how comfortable Steff was in this new situation and how easily he was fitting into the community.

As the moons rose over the trees, the community quieted down. In the moonlight, parents gathered up their children and took them home for bed. The other Carroos left the circle for the woods alone and in pairs. People called down their ribbon ladders. Titia picked up a lantern, took Steff's hand, and led him to the boulders beneath her pine tree. When they were seated, Titia gently squeezed his hand.

"Tell me about Minca, Steff," she said, "and your sister, Cora."

That one simple question, the kindness in her voice, broke through all of Steff's bravado. Tears came to his eyes, a tightness in his throat. Burying his face in his hands, he let out a sob and wept.

Titia sat silently, a hand touching his shoulder. When his ragged breathing subsided, she said, "You've had a long journey."

He gazed into her ancient face. "There were times I didn't believe I would get here, Mother Carroo."

"Tell me."

Steff began at the beginning. It was the middle of the night before he finished his tale.

Titia sighed. "You have given me much to think about. You say you have a message from your sister?"

Steff reached into his tunic and pulled out the worn talisman. By the light of the lantern, he picked apart the stitches and withdrew the letter from within. Titia took it from him and held it close to her heart for a moment before opening it. She spread it flat on her lap, her fingers dancing over the surface. Steff watched with interest. *She can read Spirit Writing without sight!*

When she was finished, she carefully folded the letter and put it into one of her pockets with a sigh. "I have been waiting, praying, such a long time for this," she said, with tears in her eyes. "I had lost hope that a message would come in my lifetime. The barrenness of Minca's land is spreading to Carroo. I feel its encroachment like the chill of death. We Carroos are few in number. Without the balance of the Goddess, we are dying out."

The sorrow in Mother Carroo's expression touched Steff's heart. They sat in silence for a moment.

With a small shake of her head, Titia smiled ruefully. Squeezing Steff's hand, she said, "Sleep well. I will meditate upon your sister's words. We will discuss her message after the Autumn Equinox ritual."

Steff rose. With a slight bow, he bid Mother Carroo good night, picked up the lantern, and walked into the woods.

Glancing back, Steff saw Titia standing in the circle with her back to the monolith. Her arms were held wide in supplication, her face lifted toward the moons. She was smiling. The tears on her cheeks sparkled like diamonds in the moonlight.

Since leaving home, Steff had felt many things—excitement, pain, fear, illness. For the first time, he felt hope.

Chapter 16

A gentle rocking roused Dov to consciousness. His body was immobile, slightly numb. His sightless eyes were closed, but he felt the heat from the sun. He felt at peace. This, then, was death. He lay there for a long time breathing in the sweet air.

To his delight, he sensed movement at his side. He could smell a dog. Dov sighed. "Be content, Lali. We did our best. We are headed for life everlasting with the Goddess." The dog licked his hand.

"No, you're not," a rough voice said.

Dov was so shocked at the sound of the voice, he tried to sit up. A searing pain shot through his head, and he fell back with a groan.

"Stay where you are, stranger. You're in no condition to move."

Dov lay motionless until the pain subsided. When he felt able, he asked, "If I'm not dead, where am I?"

"You're in my boat, Mincan, in Dute."

Dov pondered this. "Who are you? Why can't I see? Why can't I move? Is this my dog?"

"That's a lot of questions," the man said. "To start, my name is Coren. I found you at the bottom of Kameeth Falls. You were unconscious, an arrow in your back, half in and out of the water. I thought you were dead. I saw no sign of a dog. This here's my dog, Sumoi. Seeing as you're a Mincan, I would have let you rot, but it didn't make no sense," Coren said.

"What didn't make sense?" Dov asked.

"You being shot up like that. That was a Mincan arrow. Besides, I found a Dute talisman on you. So, I pulled you out and did my best to fix you up. Aside from the arrow, you had quite a conk on the head and both your legs were broken. I have bound you from head to heels with poultices and bandages. You've been unconscious for two days."

"But my legs don't feel broken," Dov said in wonder.

"Aye. I've taken care of that too."

"Thank you. I'm very grateful," Dov said with sincerity.

They floated down the river for a while. Eventually, Coren asked, "Who are you, then, and why were the Mincans trying to kill you?"

"My name is Dov. I'm Mother Minca's Teller."

"I didn't think there was a Mother Minca anymore, just Regent Vestor running things up there."

"Mother Minca has been in exile since she was a child, but she is very much alive. She asked me to come to Mother Dute."

"Well, that's good then. I'm taking you to her. She can decide what's to be done with you."

They traveled in silence for the rest of the day. Dov was aware of the changes in movement as the boat shifted through the currents. Occasionally, as they passed through rougher water, Dov was jostled, but he felt only mild discomfort. He realized the potency of Coren's medicine.

At long last, Coren steered the boat to shore, stepped into the water, and secured the boat. Wading to Dov's side, he checked Dov's legs and bandages. He unwrapped the cloth around Dov's head and removed the wrappings from around his arms. Dov's tunic had been cut from neck to hem and wrapped around his body on top of the bandages. Dov reached inside to clasp the amulet Cora had given him, reassuring himself the message for Mother Dute was safe. He breathed a deep sigh of relief.

"You'll not be trying anything, Mincan, or I'll wrap you up tight again," Coren said.

"I don't think I'm quite ready to take you on," Dov replied with sarcasm.

"True enough," Coren said. He grabbed a bundle and waded to shore. Sumoi jumped into the water with a splash and followed Coren to the beach.

Dov's vision was blurry at first but came into focus after a few moments. Coren was a big man, burly and strong, half a head taller than Dov. He was stone-faced, but his brown eyes were kind. His ruddy complexion had darkened to mahogany from the sun, while his hair and beard were bleached pale blond. There were small ceramic beads of many colors braided into his beard and shoulder-length hair. He looked to be about Dov's age. He nodded at Dov as he took another couple of bundles from the boat, setting them high on the shoreline. When he was done, he came back for Dov. With a grunt, Coren lifted him easily, proving his strength. It was awkward, as Dov's legs weren't flexible, but Coren gently carried him to shore, placing him on the warm sand.

Propping himself up as best he could, Dov looked around. Coren's boat was about the length of three tall men and half as wide across at the widest point. A shallow draft vessel, it was constructed of wood weathered to a dull gray. There were strings of dried fish tied on racks in the center of the boat, and several storage baskets were lashed to the sides. Dov had been lying on top of some padding in the bow. There was a seat by the rudder in the back from which Coren could steer.

The river ran through the bottom of a deep gorge. The walls of the canyon were shades of pink and ocher, touched by the last of the sunlight. There was little vegetation and no sign of life other than themselves. Sumoi investigated the beach, sniffing and running back and forth, while, in silence, Coren started a small campfire and prepared a meal. Dov felt oddly content.

Coren cooked a thick, savory porridge with dried fish added to the oats. Dark, unleavened bread and smoked cheese accompanied the gruel. They ate their simple meal in silence.

After eating, Coren brought a small leather pouch to Dov's side. He motioned for Dov to lean forward. Coren undid Dov's torn tunic and removed the bandage from his back. "The arrow didn't hit anything vital, Mincan. The wound is healing nicely. You can do without the bandage, I think." He walked over to one of the bundles, pulled out one of his own tunics, and gave it to Dov. It was the same shade of dull blue as the tunic and leggings Coren wore. It hung loosely on Dov's body, and the material felt soft and comfortable.

Next, in silence, Coren unwrapped Dov's legs. Coren had tied a blanket around Dov's limbs both for comfort and to secure them to a thin plank of wood that went from Dov's heels to his buttocks. Beneath the blanket, each leg was wrapped tightly in linen bandages. Coren removed them. Dov's groin was also wrapped, much like an infant's. Coren removed all of the soiled material and replaced it with clean, new wrappings.

Dov stared at his naked legs in amazement. They looked pale and bruised and somehow not quite right, but he felt no pain and could see no obvious twist or break. Coren flexed and stretched Dov's legs, increasing the range of motion with each movement. It felt good. Coren then massaged a salve onto each leg before adjusting and rewrapping the bandages and splint. Next, he sat quietly for a few moments with his eyes closed, his hands holding Dov's ankles gently. He then chanted a song—or perhaps it was a prayer—too softly for Dov to hear, but he experienced a warm tingling starting in his feet and moving up his legs. When he was finished, Coren gave Dov a nod and went back to the fire to brew some herbal tea.

"How badly are they broken? How long will they take to heal?" Dov asked.

"More questions," Coren grunted. "You had a simple break in both thighs and a crack in the shin in the right. I expect you'll be able to walk by the time we get to Dermouth."

"Really? How soon will that be?"

"Ten or eleven more days, depending on the river."

"You are more than a healer. You're a magician!" Dov exclaimed.

"No, I'm not. You'll probably walk with a limp, but I expect you will not be in pain. I'm just skilled in the basics. If one of our gifted healers were here, you'd be doing a jig in three days' time." He poured the tea. To one cup he added powder from a separate pouch. Handing it to Dov, he muttered, "Drink this."

As soon as he sipped it, a deep heaviness permeated his body, dulling his aches. He also felt a keen desire to sleep. And so he did.

When Dov woke up, it was late morning. They were in the boat again and it was moving swiftly, dipping and shuddering as it surged forward. Dov's legs were wrapped tightly in place, permitting only minimal movement. His body was covered in a tarp, leaving only his face uncovered. He struggled to sit up, but the wrapping prevented him. He started to panic.

"Hey, Coren!" he called, twisting his head.

Coren was in the back at the rudder. "No time to talk, Mincan. We're coming to the Truler Rapids. Keep as still as you can. It'll be easier on you."

Dov settled back down. Breathing deeply to quell his anxiety, he deduced it would be in his best interest to remain still and let Coren do his job. Sumoi inched his way to Dov's side. He licked Dov's face and settled down next to him. Dov closed his eyes and prayed to the Goddess as the bouncing and battering increased. Water sprayed over his face repeatedly, each drop a shock of cold. It seemed to take forever to navigate the rapids, but they were through very quickly.

"Ha! Wasn't that fun, Mincan?" Coren laughed as the boat settled into the calmer waters beyond the rapids.

"Krickers! I've never been so bounced around. I'm even more grateful for your Dute remedies."

"Oh, you Mincans always were a sorry lot. My great-uncle was Mincan, and he couldn't abide running the rapids."

"Perhaps it's an acquired taste."

"Maybe Sumoi and I can change your mind. There are plenty of rapids between here and Dermouth. We'll be going through the Big Truler Rapids this afternoon. And then there's the Tundra Waterfall."

"Waterfall! Surely you're not serious about going over a waterfall?"

Coren chuckled behind him.

"We'll be going under, not over," he said with a laugh. "And they're real pretty."

Late in the afternoon, Dov heard the rapids approaching ahead. As they got closer, it sounded more like booming thunder than flowing water. Dov's anxiety rose. Before they got too close, Coren steered them to the riverbank. Jumping into the water, he secured the boat. Deftly, Coren shifted some boxes, rearranged the padding, and helped Dov into a sitting position to free his arms. He tucked the tarp snuggly around Dov's torso and legs. From this vantage point, Dov saw the churning water sluicing between huge boulders—there didn't seem to be any safe way through. Dov's anxiety became panic. Coren climbed to the top of a large boulder and surveyed the rapids beyond. He spent some time judging the rapids and planning his run. When he returned to the boat, he was whistling a merry tune.

"I've only been in boats on calm, clear lakes in Minca," Dov said with a slight tremor in his voice.

"Oh, not to worry. I do this three or four times a year." Coren pulled a bottle out of a satchel tied to the side of the boat. "Here," he said, handing it to Dov. "This will keep you from feeling any pain as we run the rapids."

Dov took a sip and choked on the strong drink. "Is it medicine?"

"No, but it's medicinal. It's my homemade brandy. Let me have some too."

Dov handed the bottle to Coren, who took a long, deep swallow. Grinning wickedly at Dov, he said, "It never hurts to be a bit tipsy when you go through the Big Truler." He took another long swallow.

Dov pondered his companion's ability to maneuver the boat through the rapids while tipsy. "I think I could use some more of that myself." Grabbing the bottle, Dov took one big swig, then a second. The liquid burned his throat as it went down. Perspiration broke out on his forehead, but the panic receded, replaced by excitement. Dov handed the bottle to Coren and grabbed the sides of the boat. "I'm ready. And may the Goddess guide you well!"

With an excited whoop, Coren stowed the bottle, untied the rope, and jumped back into the boat. His landing propelled the boat back into the current, and they headed toward the rapids. Sumoi, barking vigorously, crouched next to Coren.

Time seemed suspended as they buffeted through the Big Truler. Dov saw each boulder they passed and felt the rise and fall of the boat as they moved through the water. The boat skimmed over rocks and boulders, slamming into the water beyond. Waves sloshed over the sides, drenching them. A rainbow mist encircled the boat, and the strings of dried fish danced on the racks in a frenzy. Although Dov knew he was screaming, his voice was drowned out by the sound of the water crashing around them. The river spit them out at the end of the rapids into a clear and calm stretch of water. Sumoi was barking and Coren was laughing. Dov didn't know if it was Coren's skill that got them through unscathed or pure luck. It didn't matter. They were alive!

Chapter 17

The mutual exhilaration of the Big Truler Rapids settled something between Dov and Coren, and they developed an easy camaraderie. Coren didn't talk much, but, over time, Dov learned the man was a widower who lived with his daughter, son-in-law, and three grandchildren in Dermouth. He traveled up to Kameeth Falls several times a year to fish and gather herbs that grew in the northern region. Dov told Coren about his life in Minca, about Cora and Steff and his beloved dog, Lali, who gave up her life at the top of the falls. He filled the silences with stories and songs from Minca, which Coren found amusing.

In the evenings after their meal, Coren massaged Dov's legs, chanting and praying to heal the broken bones. After two days, Coren removed the wood splint from beneath Dov's legs, leaving them covered only by the linen. He gave Dov a pair of his leggings, which were baggy enough to accommodate the wrappings. With the cuffs rolled up, they fit fairly well, and Dov was able to bend and stretch his legs on his own. Coren retrieved Dov's boots from one of the baskets, and with their shafts folded down, they fit well enough for comfort and protection.

On the sixth day, Coren beached the boat midafternoon and disembarked to secure it. When he returned, instead of carrying Dov to shore as usual, he yanked Dov's boots off, lifted him up, and deposited him in the water. With a yelp, Dov grabbed the side of the boat.

"Mincan, I'll not be carrying you into Dermouth. It's time to get yourself moving," Coren said. He grabbed a bag of supplies and, turning toward shore so Dov couldn't see the grin on his face, left Dov in the water.

Cursing under his breath, Dov gingerly lowered himself to the riverbed and allowed his weight to settle on his feet. The water came to just above his waist, but it wasn't too cold, and he felt little discomfort. Carefully, still holding onto the boat, he took a couple of hesitant steps before releasing his grip on the boat and walked. Sumoi, who had observed Dov from Coren's seat in the back, jumped into the water and swam after him, barking his encouragement.

"Coren! Look, I'm walking!"

"For sure, Mincan. You'll not be ready to walk on dry land without help for a couple more days, but this will remind your muscles how to work. Don't overdo it. Just a few turns around the boat. Let me know when you're ready to come ashore, and I'll lend a hand."

Over the next several evenings, as they sat by their campfire, Coren fashioned a walking staff for Dov out of a spare oar. Inverted, the usual handgrip became a sturdy base of support. Coren carved the blade into a functional handle. Digging deep into one of his bundles, Coren came up with some beads and twine, which he used embellish the staff in the Dute fashion. With a shy smile, he handed it to Dov.

"It's beautiful!"

"No need to flatter me, Mincan," Coren said, his face flushed with pleasure. "Try it out and see how it goes."

Dov used the staff to pull himself upright. Holding it with both hands, he took a tentative step, paused, then took another. "You saved my life and restored my health. I am grateful, friend."

Coren grunted and stood. He walked to Dov and reached out to grasp Dov's wrist. "It's been a most interesting trip, Dov. I am happy to call you 'friend.' Let's walk down to the end of the beach and back."

❋ ❋ ❋

As THE DAYS WENT BY AND THEY traveled down the river, Dov saw evidence of civilization—more vegetation, grasses, and even small trees. Branches of the river flowed east and west, and there was Dute activity along those riverbanks as well. Some of it appeared to be food cultivation. Occasionally, Dov saw another boat tied up on the shore. He spotted caves in the canyon walls obviously used as dwellings. One day they passed two men perched on boulders fishing. Sumoi barked at them. They stood to wave at Coren, but seeing Dov, they quietly slipped behind the rocks.

At midday on the tenth day, the wide river split in two. Coren took the branch to the right. The river narrowed and moved more swiftly. The river churned up ahead, and in the distance a mist formed above the river. Before they got close to the mist, Coren navigated his boat around some rocks toward the shoreline and a grove of willow trees. Their branches hung down to the water, a living screen to what lay beyond. The willows camouflaged a large backwater, which was well protected by high canyon walls. At the far end, three boats were moored to a dock, while another was upturned on the shore. Five or six people worked on the boats and repaired fishing nets. When they saw Coren's boat coming through the trees, they waved and shouted greetings. They froze in place when they saw Dov.

"What's the matter? Have you not seen a Mincan before?" Coren called. "Come on, Jez, give me a hand here!"

The man called Jez was a slightly smaller version of Coren. They could have been brothers, they looked so much alike. He came forward and Dov threw him the mooring rope. When Coren's boat was tied up alongside the others, Sumoi jumped to the dock and greeted every Dute there. They petted Sumoi while staring at Dov.

Coren got out at a more leisurely pace, stretching and yawning casually. Dov struggled to get out of the boat, propping himself up with his staff. After a brief hesitation, Jez came to help him step onto the dock.

"This here is Jez. He's been my friend since we were lads. Jez, this Mincan is Dov. He's come to see Mother Dute," Coren said by way of introduction.

With a nod, Jez accepted Dov and the peculiar situation. The others were not so easily convinced and stayed at a distance.

Coren got back into the boat and unloaded the dried fish and herbs from his boat onto the dock. Jez picked up some bundles and carried them to shoulder baskets lined up onshore. Dov grabbed the rest and, walking with the aid of his staff, followed Jez. Coren secured a tarp over the boat and joined them. They loaded the fish and herbs into three baskets and strapped them on.

With Sumoi in the lead, the three men walked around the backwater and through a rock fissure that Dov hadn't noticed before. It was slightly more than shoulder width and led to a stairway chiseled into the rock that descended to the bottom of the waterfall. Open to the sky above, the stairwell was just bright enough for them to see where they were going. The sound of the water reverberated through the stairwell, making conversation impossible.

There were, perhaps, three hundred steps to the bottom. Dov struggled with the loaded pack on his back, but by bracing himself against the solid walls and using his staff, he managed to descend without incident. Even still, Coren stopped several times for Dov to catch his breath.

At the bottom they stepped out onto a rock ledge. Enveloped in a cloud of mist, Dov heard the waterfall in front of them but couldn't see it. With the stairs behind, there was nowhere to go; it was a dead end. He looked at Coren quizzically. Coren smiled and stepped backward through the mist, disappearing from view. Jez nudged Dov from behind, and he, saying a silent prayer to the Goddess, stepped forward.

Grabbing his arm, Coren pulled him through the mist and under the falls. Jez and Sumoi followed. They were on a narrow rock ledge behind the water. Lanterns were lined up on the floor, and Jez lit one for each of them. Holding his lantern high, Dov saw the ledge was a narrow pathway behind the waterfall. The sound of the water was almost overwhelming as it roared to the bottom of the falls. Dov looked over the edge, and a wave of vertigo washed over him. He leaned against the rock wall and closed his eyes, taking deep breaths. Sumoi came forward and licked his hand.

"You'll be fine, Dov!" Coren yelled into his ear above the sound of the water. "Don't look over the edge. Follow me."

After uttering another silent prayer to the Goddess, Dov opened his eyes. He nodded to Coren. With a grin and a wink, Coren led the way.

At the end of the falls, Coren led them into a tight tunnel that veered off to the left. The stone walls muffled the sound of the water. Eventually, the path widened into a small alcove where the men removed their packs and sat. Jez passed around a bottle of water. Coren knelt beside Dov and gently massaged his legs.

"We're almost there," Coren said. "Do you think you can walk a ways?"

"I'm doing fine. Just give me a few moments and I'll be ready to go on."

Dov felt excitement vie with trepidation. He remained unsure of the reception he would receive.

A golden light flowed in from the exit to the tunnel. They blew out their lanterns, hung them from hooks in the wall, and stepped to the end of the tunnel. A majestic view greeted Dov. A verdant green valley spread out before his eyes. To the left, another waterfall's spray created a rainbow as it fell to the canyon floor. From there, the river flowed through the valley. Fields of crops and fruit trees were planted along its banks. Framed by canyon walls of warm gold- and rose-colored sandstone, the valley extended far into the distance. Stairways were carved into the canyon walls, leading to cave dwellings. Multicolored flags and banners hung before the entrances, each decorated with images from nature, and Spirit Writing providing personalized shade and privacy. Dov, overcome by the beauty and serenity, crumpled to the ground and began to cry.

Concerned for his friend, Coren rushed to his side. Dov waved him off.

"I'm fine. I have been living in the gray ruin of Minca for so long, I had forgotten how beautiful the world could be."

Coren squatted beside him. "Yes, it is beautiful. Mother Deana moved Dermouth and her people to this protected valley in the fifth year of the war. Dermouth in the north was not safe. We hoped, by moving south, that Vestor would leave us alone. We keep patrols along the border, but Vestor's armies continue to push closer."

"When we arrived, it was barren land. Mother Deana encouraged one branch of the river to come to this valley," Jez explained, pointing to the waterfall. "We began planting and building. We have made it home."

"But come," Coren said, standing up. "You must meet Deana's daughter, Tasha, our Mother Dute."

Chapter 18

Twilight turned to darkness as the men walked the path along the river. The valley was deserted, but soon lights appeared in the many cave dwellings, illuminating the walls of the canyon with a soft glow.

It was not a long walk. When they arrived at the steps to Mother Dute's cave, Coren and Jez removed their baskets. Dov shrugged off his basket and leaned heavily on his staff, swaying slightly.

"Just a few more steps, Dov."

Leaving their baskets behind, the three men maneuvered up the wide steps carved into the sandstone. Sumoi brought up the rear. Music, laughter, and conversation could be heard through the colorful embroidered banners hanging at the entrance. Parting the cloth, they walked inside. Twenty people turned to meet the newcomers. Seeing Dov, they stared in shocked silence. The music stopped.

Dov, still gripping his staff, tried to take in the light and color. The comforting fragrance of the evening's meal reminded him he was hungry.

A child pushed through the stunned adults, making her way toward Dov. Several of the adults tried to grab her, but she slipped past them. Stopping in front of Dov, she looked up into his face and exclaimed, "You came!"

Dov looked down into a beautiful face surrounded by russet curls. Her dark-brown almond-shaped eyes were wide with expectation. Dov smiled weakly. His knees buckled, and he collapsed on the floor.

❀ ❀ ❀

DOV WOKE UP IN A COMFORTABLE bed. Beneath the blanket, he yawned and stretched. The aches and pains were gone from his body. Daylight streamed in through windows chiseled high in the cave walls. He wore a soft yellow flannel nightshirt. As he looked around the room, he realized he was not alone. The young girl from the night before was curled up in a chair next to the bed dozing quietly with an embroidery hoop in her lap. Hearing him move, she snapped awake.

"How are you feeling? Can I get you anything? I'd better call my mother," she said. Before he could say anything, she jumped up and ran, the embroidery hoop rolling away unnoticed. With a swish, she slipped through the curtains covering the entrance to the sleeping chamber.

A few moments later, the girl came back. Her mother followed. She had the same russet curls pulled back into a long braid, beads woven throughout her thick hair. She was a big woman and her skin was the color of her hair, warm brown with a hint of glowing pink. Her eyes were a dark brown. Her tunic was soft and flowing, a deep shade of turquoise. Her strong legs were covered in loose leggings of a dark blue. She walked with confidence and grace, and her face, while somber, was not unfriendly. She looked Dov directly in the eyes as she faced the bed. The girl stood behind her mother, peering around her side.

They observed each other in silence for a few moments. Then Dov pushed himself into a seated position. Clearing his throat, he said, "You are Mother Dute? I'm Dov—"

"I know who you are," she said softly. "My aunt Marna, our Teller, remembers you. I am Tasha, Mother Dute, and this is my daughter, Bejla."

"Marna?" Dov was overwhelmed. "She's alive?"

"I knew you were coming," Bejla said excitedly.

Dov studied the child.

"She did. She has visions," Tasha said, stroking her daughter's hair.

Dov blinked, befuddled.

"Enough for now. When you are fully awake, please come join us in the main room. We have plenty of food and plenty of questions for you. The privy is through there," she said, waving toward another set of curtains. "Refresh yourself. You will find clean clothes. We will expect you shortly." With that, she moved back through the curtains, pulling Bejla behind her.

Dov moved slowly to the side of the bed, swinging his legs to the stone floor. His staff leaned against the wall within reach. Grabbing it, he stood and stretched. He felt remarkably well and hardly needed the support as he made his way to the privy.

Dressed in a clean teal tunic and soft blue leggings, Dov walked out through the curtains. Several Dutes stood by the entrance to his room, regarding him warily. He nodded at them and gave them a slight smile as he passed. They followed him down the corridor to the main room.

As he entered, Bejla appeared at his side. She had been waiting for him. The Dutes who had followed Dov walked into the room and mingled with others who were already there. Mother Dute was at the far end of the large space talking with two older women.

Bejla took his hand and led him to a cushioned platform near the entrance to Mother Dute's cave. The banners had been rolled up, and the valley floor spread out before his eyes. It was a beautiful, busy place. Dutes worked in the gardens and orchard, fished in the river, walked, and talked. Farther down the river, herds of goats and sheep were corralled along the riverbank. Smoke rose in the distance, indicating the location of the Dute forge. Life seemed so normal, as if the war didn't exist here.

Bejla said, "The Goddess watches over us here in Dermouth. There are two other Dute valleys like Dermouth, but outside the valleys, the living is harder and more dangerous. Only the bravest Dutes dare to live up north close to the border." She leaned back. "Coren said he would come by later this afternoon. He wants to introduce you to his family."

Dov smiled at her. "I would like that very much. He saved my life."

"His granddaughter and I spend a lot of time together studying and playing. Her older brothers tease us a lot."

"Is that so?" Dov was already growing fond of the gregarious child.

"Tell me about Mother Minca."

Dov smiled wistfully, thinking of Cora. "Cora. Her hair is curly brown. She can look very serious, but she has a quick sense of humor. She is smart and creative and has the kindest heart I know."

Bejla clapped her hands and said, "I *knew* that's what

she looked like! She's pregnant, isn't she? I saw that in my vision too."

Dov, shocked into silence, simply nodded his head.

At that moment Tasha arrived, accompanied by the two women she had been talking to. Dov recognized Marna from their younger days. She had aged well. Her sun-streaked auburn hair surrounded a friendly face, laugh lines bordering her generous mouth and green eyes. The second woman looked more foreboding. Her features were similar to Marna's, but her mouth was set in a grim line and there was no humor in her green eyes. A faded scar on the right side of her face, sliced from forehead to chin, marred the deep earth color of her skin. A streak of white traced the line of the scar through her auburn hair.

Marna was the first to move. To Dov's surprise and delight, she enveloped him in a hug. "Welcome, Dov. I never dared hope to see you again."

Dov smiled and hugged her back. "Nor I you."

They might have remained embracing but for Bejla's tugging at their tunics. "Auntie Marna, we have to talk. There isn't much time. The Equinox is in three days, and we have to make plans."

The group seated themselves and Tasha spoke.

"I guess we should complete our introductions. Dov, you clearly remember my aunt Marna. This," she said, indicating the other woman, "is my aunt Mina."

Mina gave Dov a curt nod but didn't speak. Dov nodded in return.

Turning to her daughter, Tasha said, "Bejla, dearest, please ask Demi to bring some food and beverages. We need to nourish our guest if we are to ply him with questions."

When Bejla returned, Tasha continued. "Coren told us last night about the nature of your arrival. He showed us the Dute talisman he found in your pocket. I had given it to a friend, Pico, along with a message for Mother Minca. Can you tell us what happened?"

"I'm sorry, I cannot. Steff, Mother Minca's brother, and I were traveling together when we came across his body—Pico's body. I found the talisman. We buried him in the traditional Mincan way," he said solemnly.

"Bejla had a vision of our tribes reconnecting. That is why I sent him."

Dov paused before speaking again. "Cora, Mother Minca, also had a vision of the tribes coming together. She sent me south to you and her brother west to the Carroos."

"There are no Carroos left," Mina said, turning away.

"I think there might well be. I—we—believe they are using their gifts to keep hidden and safe."

"Let us hope you are correct," Marna said with a sigh.

Tasha said, "So, Dov, you have a message from Mother Minca?"

"I do." He pulled his talisman from beneath his tunic and carefully plucked at the stitches enclosing the letter. Presenting it to Tasha, he sat back as the others gathered close. They, of course, had no trouble deciphering the Spirit Writing. They appeared to read it through several times, occasionally glancing at Dov.

The food arrived and was placed before Dov. Tasha and her aunts stood. "Please excuse us. We will take some time with our elders to discuss this message. Enjoy your food. Bejla will stay with you. Perhaps we can talk later this evening." With a slight bow she turned and left with Marna and Mina following in her wake.

Bejla poured Dov a mug of tea and handed it to him. Dov inhaled the fragrance of cinnamon and cloves. It was delicious. Bejla poured herself a mug before curling up on the cushion close to Dov. They each took an oatcake and ate in companionable silence.

Dusting the crumbs off his lap, Dov said, "May I ask about your visions?"

"What would you like to know?"

"When did they start? What have you seen?" Dov asked.

"I had my first vision when I was little. I was outside playing. I felt funny and sat down. Far away I could see my grandmother, Deana. That was strange because she was traveling to the other valleys and wasn't supposed to be here. She seemed to be calling to me, but I couldn't hear her voice. Then she disappeared. She was just gone.

"I was really scared when she disappeared. I ran home to tell my mother. She thought it was nothing, but two days later we got word that my grandmother had been killed by a patrol of Vestor's soldiers. To prevent her healing, the Mincans had cut her heart out," Bejla said, her eyes welling up with tears.

Dov placed a hand on her shoulder in sympathy. "Ah, child, it cannot be easy being a Seer, to know so much for one so young. It must seem a burden."

She smiled in gratitude, then took a deep breath and continued her story.

"Deana's body was returned to Dermouth. The elders gathered to mourn my grandmother and celebrate my mother becoming the new Mother Dute. They also did a Seer's ritual for me. Seers are rare in Dute. The last one was four generations ago. It's not always a female, I've been told, but always in the Mother's bloodline."

"They are rare in Minca and Carroo as well," Dov said with reverence.

Bejla nodded. "The elders taught me what they could about receiving and understanding visions from stories passed down. I often see Mincan troops before they cross the border. That's been very helpful. I saw Mother Minca just the once. She looked so sad. And I knew she was going to have a baby. I also had a vision of the three tribes meeting again at the Heart Stone. That one wasn't very clear," she explained with a sigh. "I couldn't see who was there or when, I just knew it had to happen for peace to return."

She gave Dov a wide smile. "And you. I saw your face very clearly in a dream. I knew you were coming and that you were an honorable Mincan, traveling with good intentions."

"Thank you, Bejla."

"You're welcome," she said seriously. "Would you like to go out and see Dermouth?"

"I would," Dov said. "I feel totally recovered."

"Auntie Mina did some work on you last night."

"Mina?" Dov asked, surprised.

"Yes. She's one of our best healers. She strengthened the work that Coren had done before. She says you'll be fine. You just have to be active to get your strength back."

"She doesn't seem to like me very much."

"No. She doesn't trust you. You're a Mincan."

Dov didn't know Mina's story, but he understood the many reasons she wouldn't trust a Mincan. He stood up. "Where will you take me?"

Bejla grabbed his hand and pulled him toward the steps. "First, I'll show you our gardens. Then I'll take you to the waterfall. We can go swimming, if you like."

Dov followed with a smile, leaving his staff behind, unnoticed on the floor.

❖ ❖ ❖

DOV AND BEJLA MEANDERED through the gardens and orchards as the canyon absorbed the heat of the day. They sampled fruits and vegetables and greeted everyone they met. With Bejla at his side, Dov was accepted without question.

As they walked toward the waterfall, they heard the sound of laughter over the roar of the water. When they arrived, Dov was delighted by the sight. The falls pounded on rocks, creating a mist of water filled with rainbows from the sun. The water formed a large swimming hole. A number of people splashed, played, and swam in the water.

"Want to go in?" Bejla asked.

"Absolutely!"

Stripping down to their underclothes, they walked into the cool, refreshing water. After a swim, they dried off in the warm sun before dressing and heading back to Mother Dute's cave.

As they walked back, Sumoi came bounding out of an orchard to greet Dov. Kneeling to pet the dog, Dov spotted Coren and his family walking through the trees. Dov and Coren embraced, pounding each other on the back. When they parted, Coren introduced Dov to his family.

"This is my daughter, Eske, and her husband, Drer, their two boys, Rom and Dak, and Glissa, my little darlin'."

Eske and Drer clasped Dov's wrist warmly. The children gaped at Dov with curiosity. Once the boys realized he wasn't going to be any more interesting than any other adult, they ran ahead with Sumoi barking at their heels. Glissa took Bejla's hand, and they walked to Mother Dute's. Eske and Drer followed Dov and Coren down the path.

"I see you no longer need your staff. That's good," Coren said.

"I left it at Mother Dute's. I didn't even realize I'd forgotten it. Dute healing is quite amazing."

Tasha was waiting at the top of the stairs to greet them when they arrived. She invited them in for tea, fruit, and biscuits.

"Tell us about finding Dov," Bejla requested from Coren.

"Oh, he was a right mess, Bejla, lying facedown in the water, arrow in his back, conked out. But he's got the constitution of a horse, and I fixed him up all right. Once he came around, it was another story," he said, laughing, and gave Dov a shove. "This Mincan asked question after question. And when he wasn't asking questions, he was singing and telling stories. It was the noisiest trip downriver I've ever had!"

Everyone laughed, including Dov.

"Maybe you could tell the rest of us one of your stories," Tasha said encouragingly.

With the children clamoring for a story, Dov agreed. He told them the abbreviated version of "Tura and the Evil Troll." Sitting at Dov's knee, Bejla smiled sweetly, understanding the story and Dov's true meaning.

As evening fell and lamps were lit, Coren and his family prepared to go home, but they promised to see Dov at the Autumn Equinox ritual.

After their departure, Tasha sent Dov and Bejla to wash up before the evening meal. "Bejla, bring Dov to the study. We'll be dining there with the elders tonight."

Chapter 19

Réan did not return to the mountains but stayed in Cappett, often in private discussion with Mother Carroo. Left alone, Steff found ways to occupy his time rather than dwell on his concerns about Cora and Dov. Occasionally, he worked in the gardens with the adults, but he preferred to spend time with the children. In the mornings he joined them in their studies, and in the afternoons he helped with their chores.

They spent one afternoon making paper out of grasses, leaves, and flowers. They said it was for the Autumn Equinox ritual but wouldn't explain how it was going to be used. Steff was fascinated. In Minca, paper was made by special artisans. He had no idea how it was done.

The children gathered baskets full of plants. Next, they tore them into small pieces and placed handfuls into a large caldron and added water. As it heated over a fire, they added an assortment of powders to make the magic paper. When the cooking was done and the pot cool enough, the fun part began.

Rolling up her leggings, a small girl climbed into the big pot and stomped the plants and water into a pulp. The other children clapped and sang, the rhythm building in intensity, encouraging her to stomp harder and faster. When she got tired, she climbed out and another child took a turn. Then another and another. When the pulp was the perfect consistency, they scooped the slurry onto loosely woven fabric stretched over square wooden frames. Using wooden paddles, the older children spread the pulp thinly over the fabric. The frames were then placed in the sun. After a short time, the paper was peeled off the fabric and hung in the branches of the trees to finish drying. The paper was mottled in tone with flower petals embellishing each sheet.

When their chores were done, the youngsters played games. If it was warm enough, they walked down the steep cliff trail to the beach cove below for a swim.

Steff entertained the children with his Mincan innovations. He devised a pulley system to maneuver a large woven basket up and down the cliff face. It made transporting food and supplies to the beach an easy task. Steff convinced Mother Carroo it was a safe way for her to get to the beach, as navigating the path was slow for her. She laughed the entire trip down and gave him a big kiss when he pulled her back up to the top.

In the evenings, the community gathered for their communal dinner at the circle of stones. If the weather was rainy, they met in a grove in the woods. The trees entwined their branches to create a dry shelter for the meal.

At the end of the day, the close-knit Carroos entertained each other with stories, songs, and dance. They encouraged Steff to participate, and he told them stories he learned from Dov, as well as ones he made up on the spot. Life in Carroo seemed carefree. Only in the quiet of his sleeping tent did thoughts of Minca and Evil V come to haunt him.

Time went by quickly. On the afternoon of the Autumn Equinox, the community gathered in the circle of stones. Adults carried baskets of food and drink for the ritual while the children carried their sheets of handmade papers. Once they arrived, they all stood in the circle expectantly.

Réan had explained to Steff that there was only one Carroo Teller still alive. She was traveling, with her apprentice, to other Carroo villages along the coast. For that reason, Titia, Mother Carroo, would be reciting the creation story. And so she did.

"As it was, in the time before time, the Goddess danced the dance of creation among the stars . . ."

After the telling, the community gathered up their baskets and walked the cliff path to the beach. Titia was lowered in Steff's basket, singing out a harvest chant during her descent. The others joined in.

We till the earth and then we sow,
With Goddess blessings, our plants will grow.

Beloved Goddess, Mother Carroo,
We harvest the blessings that come from you.

Through rain and sun and winds that blow,
We plant our seeds and help them grow.

Beloved Goddess, Mother Carroo,
We harvest the blessings that come from you.

They created a fire circle on the beach and built a fire to cook a harvest stew of grains with wild greens and to roast vegetables. When the meal was served, the Carroos sat in the sand around the fire. Mother Carroo said a blessing, and the meal was consumed with gusto.

As the sun set, lanterns were lit, and the children passed out their sheets of paper.

Réan snatched a piece of charcoal from the edge of the fire and broke it in half, handing a piece to Steff. "Here. Write down your most important wishes on the paper."

After taking a minute to compose his thoughts, Steff set to writing. Réan finished writing and tucked and folded the closely written paper, presenting it to Steff with a flourish. Réan had turned it into a little boat.

Steff smiled. "Show me."

All the Carroos were writing and folding. The youngest ones were assisted by their elders or drew pictures instead of words. As the sun fell past the horizon and the full moons rose in the sky, they finished their paper folding. In silence, they walked to the shore.

Titia held a burning stick and called out, "Beloved Goddess, beloved Kameeth, beloved Mother Carroo, we celebrate the Autumn Equinox, the harvest, the element of fire. We send to you our deepest wishes with love and appreciation for the many gifts you have already bestowed." She then lit the tip of her paper boat and placed it in the water. She passed the stick to the person on her right. He lit his boat and placed it in the water before passing the stick to the person on his right, and so on down the beach.

The waves, and a bit of Carroo energy, carried the burning boats out to sea. Looking up and down the coastline, Steff could just make out tiny glimmers of light from the other Carroo villages far away.

The Carroos watched until the last boat sailed out into the ocean and was consumed by fire.

The next morning, Steff again sat on the boulders with Mother Carroo. She told him her decision. At first, Steff was concerned Titia had selected Réan to go to the Heart Stone meeting. Cora had requested a female be sent, not a young man. He thought he should say something, but the beatific delight on Titia's face when she made her pronouncement put a stop to his words.

I have to trust the Goddess is guiding Titia, he thought. Besides, Steff enjoyed Réan's company, so he set his concerns aside.

The three discussed the safest way to journey to the Heart Stone. A straight, bold path through Minca would be unexpected and, thus, safest. Carroo gifts were essential for the trip. Titia announced they would travel as brother and sister. Steff was skeptical, but again he kept those thoughts to himself.

Réan used Carroo gifts to look like a Mincan woman, with longer hair and rosier skin. Steff realized Réan could easily pass as a young woman. "She" was quite pretty.

Late one evening, Titia approached Steff. She carried a small pot containing a green cream. With a grin, she dipped her finger in and swiped it across Steff's upper lip. Overnight, the downy hairs on Steff's lip darkened and coarsened. Two days later, he had a full mustache. He was shocked and secretly delighted.

Several of the Carroos made tunics and leggings of Mincan color and style for both Steff and Réan. Because they didn't utilize leather out of reverence for their animal friends, the shoemakers used their Carroo gifts to create fiber boots for Réan with the look and strength of leather. The many-pocketed vests Carroos wore would be inappropriate, so the Carroos stitched shoulder packs to carry supplies. Steff complimented them on their skills and assured everyone that the apparel would pass for Mincan-made.

Titia had some old Mincan coins to pay for food and lodging, if needed. Steff and Réan intended to forage for food and camp, when possible, but were grateful for the money.

Not long after the Autumn Equinox, the Carroos gathered in the stone circle at dawn. Mother Caroo blessed Steff and Réan and presented them with talismans for their journey. She also gave Steff a large knife and scabbard. The blade was inscribed with Spirit Writing, the grip carved from oak. It was beautiful.

"This was my father's blade. I want you to have it."

Steff was deeply touched.

The entire community walked them to the path leading out of their valley. And so they departed, a tall mustachioed Mincan with his diminutive sister. As Steff and Réan walked up the trail, they heard the Carroos singing their farewell.

Between the mountains and the clear blue sea,
there is a land that calls to me.

If I should leave and dare to roam,
this is the place I will call home.
'Tis where I was born and wish to die,
the land between the sea and sky.

Between the mountains and the clear blue sea,
there is a land that calls to me.

All the Goddess's creatures within this dell
are friends of Carroos. All is well.
May we live here forever in harmony,
with our brothers and sisters of the earth and sea.

Between the mountains and the clear blue sea,
there is a land that calls to me.

We give thanks to Kameeth and her daughter Carroo.
To the Goddess above, we send love to you.
'Tis where I was born and wish to die,
the land between the sea and sky.

Between the mountains and the clear blue sea,
there is a land that calls to me.

Steff turned and waved at the Carroos. Glancing at his companion, he saw tears on Réan's cheeks. Réan kept walking and did not look back.

Chapter 20

Bejla led Dov to the study, a small private chamber at the back of the cavern. Lit with oil lamps, it was warm and intimate. The walls were covered with tapestries depicting the flora and fauna of Dute. In the center of the room, a round table was set with plates and flatware forged from the bronze for which Dute was famous. In addition to Tasha and her aunts, four elderly Dutes awaited their arrival. To Dov's eyes, they seemed as ancient as the sandstone that formed the valley. The elders were introduced as Sløg, Maev, Tria, and Bérga. He was greeted warmly.

Over dinner, the elders engaged Dov in conversation about the situation in Minca, Mincan friends from long ago, and Vestor. They finished their repast with fresh fruit. There was apple brandy for the adults; Bejla was given warm cider.

"Dov," Tasha said, "we have talked about the message you brought from Mother Minca. We also have the vision from my daughter that predicted this gathering. We trust the Goddess is leading us toward reconciliation and peace. It is essential for our survival."

The four ancient ones nodded their heads in agreement. Then Bérga spoke. Her voice was so soft, Dov had to strain to hear her words.

"Every incursion by Vestor's troops has forced us farther south into hiding. Our resources and fighters have been pushed to their limits by this eternal war. If we do not restore the Goddess, restore the balance, all will be lost."

Tasha gave Bérga's hand a gentle squeeze and said, "We will send Mina as our representative."

Dov glanced at Mina, whose stern face registered resignation. "Are you willing to come with me?" Dov asked.

"I go where the Goddess sends me."

And so, it was settled.

❋ ❋ ❋

THE NEXT THREE DAYS WERE VERY busy, both with preparations for the journey to the Heart Stone and for the Autumn Equinox ritual. Dov and Mina sequestered themselves in the study, poring over maps, seeking the best route to the Heart Stone.

"I think we should retrace my journey upstream to Kameeth Falls. From there, it's a more direct route to the Heart Stone."

"That is true, but I expect your Mincans will be watching the falls. We should go downstream from Dermouth," Mina said forcefully. "Look," she said, pointing at the map. "There are older routes that haven't been used in years. They may be forgotten and unguarded."

"But time is of the essence. If we went back to the falls—"

"We could both be killed. We'd never get to the Heart Stone."

Before their debate devolved to snarling, they conferred with Tasha.

They found Tasha and Bejla on the platform overlooking the Dermouth valley. They sat amid paper and glue pots constructing paper balloons. Before Mina could spread out their map, Dov picked one up and asked, "What, in the Goddess's name, is this?"

"It's a fire balloon for the Autumn Equinox," Bejla said. "We make the balloons and write our wishes on them. Then we light them and send them to the Goddess."

"Don't they just burn up?"

"We attach a small bronze cup with wire," Tasha explained. "We put a bit of oil in the cup, add a wick, and it's ready to go. The oil candle heats the air and lifts the balloon. Our messages are 'delivered' before the balloons are consumed by fire. It's been a Dute tradition forever. Would you like to help?"

With a glance at Mina, Dov said, "I'd love to, but we've been looking at maps and strategizing a route. We wanted to ask your opinion."

"Why don't you both join us," Tasha suggested. "You can help glue while we talk."

Mina rolled her eyes and sat down. Dov smiled and sat next to Bejla. She showed him how to glue the paper together.

The four worked together in silence. Dov noticed that Mina's expression softened with her concentration on the gluing. She appeared content, as if this were a pleasant interlude in contrast to her conversation with Dov.

"So," Tasha said, "what are you thinking?"

Mina spoke up. "Dov wants us to retrace his journey back to Kameeth Falls. It's the easiest path between Minca and Dute, and the shortest to the Heart Stone. I'm concerned that the Mincan troops might be watching the falls. I think we should head farther east and take a more obscure trail. It would take longer, but I think it would be safer."

"I'm worried about the time and Vestor's army," Dov said. "If we need to be at the Heart Stone by the Winter Solstice, taking a longer route might be a problem."

"I appreciate both of your concerns. Let's turn it over to the Goddess while we work on the balloons and see if she has an answer," Tasha said.

They continued gluing until there were enough paper balloons for the Mother's extended household. Tasha then demonstrated the wirework to Dov. They commenced the finishing process of adding the rims and cups. At one point, Bejla stopped working and seemed to doze off. Tasha glanced at her daughter and smiled. "The Goddess is speaking to her," she whispered to Dov.

Mina attached a cup to the final balloon. With a whispered suggestion from Tasha, the three closed their eyes and meditated in silence, surrounded by paper balloons.

They were aroused from their meditation by Bejla, who came to each person and kissed them on the forehead. As they opened their eyes, they knew from her expression that the Goddess had given her a message.

"Dov, Vestor believes you were killed at the falls, but I did see troops stationed there. I saw Coren taking you both on a boat down the river, far past the foundry, to a place with a small landing surrounded by tall boulders. There is a path that leads to Minca through a gorge, to the headwaters of the Rone River in the Eastern Mountains."

Mina pulled out the map and spread it out for all to see. The starting point that Bejla referred to seemed obvious.

"The Rone River flows west until it reaches a confluence with the Minca River," Mina observed. "That will bring us close to the Heart Stone. Traveling by water would make up for lost time."

Dov nodded his head in resignation. "We will go where the Goddess tells us."

Folding up the map, Mina said, "I will talk with Coren tomorrow." She started gathering up the balloons.

They all helped to string the balloons onto a cord, which was then attached to a pole and set in a corner.

"It looks like a string of very odd fish," Dov said.

"You're right," Tasha agreed with a grin. "That's why the children call them 'fishes wishes.' Stringing them makes it much easier to get them to the ritual site."

Bejla asked Dov, "If you don't make fire balloons for the Autumn Equinox, what do you do?"

Dov smiled. "Do you have some more paper?" he asked.

Bejla ran off to find some. Tasha and Mina sat back down on the platform. When Bejla returned, Dov took a piece of paper and trimmed it into a square. Holding it up, he said, "First, we write our wishes on the paper, but then . . ." While the others watched, he folded, turned, tucked, and folded the paper some more. When he was finished, he held out his hand. Dov had folded the paper into a perfect miniature paper dragon. "It's a fire dragon. We release them into a bonfire to deliver our wishes to the Goddess."

Tasha, Bejla, and even Mina grinned with delight. They all wanted to learn how to fold the paper dragon. With pleasure, Dov taught them the intricate process. They made many dragons and were still folding paper when they were called for supper.

❈ ❈ ❈

MIST HUNG OVER THE RIVER ON the dawn of the Autumn Equinox. It burned off as the sun rose over the canyon walls, promising a warm, beautiful day. After breakfast, Mother Tasha's household packed all the items needed for the Autumn Equinox celebration—food, bowls, and flatware along with bedding and games. Dov was given the honor of carrying the "fishes wishes" pole. When everyone had their bundle, they moved out of the dwelling and along the ledge to a steep set of stairs chiseled into the rock face, leading to the top of the cliff.

❀ ❀ ❀

DOV WAS OUT OF BREATH WHEN he reached the summit. Far below, the valley stretched from the tunnel where he had entered Dermouth, past the waterfall, and on for several leagues. Then the canyon turned, and the valley disappeared out of sight. Dermouth dwellings lined the walls on both sides of the river. People were carrying bundles to the top of the mesas on each side of the river. Those who had already arrived erected canopies on the wide, flat expanse. The brightly embroidered fabrics shimmered in the sunshine. Dov helped Tasha's family set up their canopy and admired the craftsmanship of the holes cut into the stone mesa, which accommodated the rigging poles and made the temporary campsite possible. The "fishes wishes" pole was attached to the rest of the rigging, allowing the fire balloons to sway in the breeze.

The Autumn Equinox was a festive time. The smaller children played games in and around the canopies. The older children competed in relay races. Kites flew in the air. Friends mingled and talked. There was music and dancing. Food was proffered at every interaction. Naps were taken in the shade of the fabric canopies. Friends and neighbors called and waved back and forth across the valley from one mesa to the other.

Coren and his family arrived at Mother Tasha's campsite at midafternoon. They brought their own bundle of blankets, fire balloons, and a puzzle Coren had crafted for the children to put together.

In the late afternoon, cooking fires were started, and dinner was prepared. As the many families settled their cooking pots into the hot coals to cook, a silence settled over the canyon and the balloons were meted out. The Dutes took time to think about and write their wishes on the paper. As if there were a silent signal, people on both sides put down the balloons and walked toward the edge of their mesa.

Marna, in her role as Mother Dute's Teller, stepped forward and onto a cantilevered rock overhanging the canyon floor below. She seemed to be standing in midair. Her brilliant rose-colored tunic and dark-blue leggings were embroidered with Spirit Writing. She wore a cape of a deep-red fabric lined with turquoise, which blew in the wind like the wings of a firebird in the last rays of the sun. She raised her arms to the Goddess, and in a deep, resonant voice, she began the creation story.

"As it was, in the time before time, the Goddess danced the dance of creation among the stars . . ."

Marna projected her voice into the valley below, which acted as an amplifier. Every person in Dermouth could hear her.

When the story was complete, Marna nodded and stepped back onto the solid surface of the mesa. The Dutes erupted into cheers. They then began their harvest chant. It was a call and response across the divide.

Hello, my friends!
Hello to you!

What brings you here?
The Summer's through.
It's the Equinox and time to play!
And be grateful for this lovely day!
We thank the Goddess.
We thank Kameeth.
We thank Mother Dute.
For the food we will eat!
May you be safe and happy.
May your wishes come true!

People laughed and cheered. Oil lamps along the cliff's edge were lit at intervals as the sun slipped below the horizon. Waving to friends and family, the Dutes returned to their cooking fires and served their harvest feast.

Dov enjoyed the Autumn Equinox fare. There was a fish casserole consisting of layers of fish, rice, vegetables, and cheese cooked in a wild mushroom broth. Minted water was the traditional drink. With a smile, Coren explained it was to prevent an overconsumption of wine and the possibility of people falling off the cliff. For dessert, Dov was presented with a traditional Autumn Equinox puffed bread ball, which resembled the round and hollow fire balloons and was about the size of his fist. Bejla demonstrated how to take a small bite out of the doughy shell so Dov could pour honey inside to represent the fire. It was the perfect sweet.

Dov was unused to such rich food. There was poignancy in this moment. Like Tura's land in the children's story, Minca's lifeblood was draining away. Dov's enjoyment of Dute's Autumn Equinox was tinged with a deep sorrow for his homeland.

Bejla, sensing Dov's sadness, knelt beside him. She took his hand and whispered, "It will all be put to right, Dov. The Goddess is guiding us to peace."

Dov smiled and squeezed her hand.

By the time dinner was cleaned up, the sun had set, the full moons had risen, and the stars sparkled. The moons and oil lamps provided enough light to guide the group to the edge of the mesa. There they took turns lighting the wicks and watching as the hot air lifted the balloons. All along the mesas on both sides of the valley, balloons came to life and rose into the night sky. The balloons lifted higher and higher, looking like new stars amongst the old, until, one by one, they burned out.

❊ ❊ ❊

MORNING ROSE OVER THE MESA. The group broke their fast with tea, bread, and fruit before packing up their belongings. Coren hugged his family goodbye and returned with Mother Dute's household to their dwelling below. There he helped Dov and Mina gather up their travel gear before they all walked down to the river. Bejla, Tasha, and Marna accompanied them. A punt was tied up along the shore. After many hugs and kisses and words of advice, Mina, Dov, and Coren arranged themselves and their packs on the punt. Coren, standing in the back, picked up a long pole, shoved them away from the shore, and maneuvered them downstream. Dov and Mina were on their way.

For as long as she could keep up with the punt, Bejla ran along the path beside the river. "The Goddess goes with you. Dov, give my love to Mother Minca! We shall meet again!"

Dov, filled with affection for this little girl, smiled and waved. "May the Goddess hold you gently in her heart," he called back as they floated away.

Chapter 21

The mountain air turned cooler as the Autumn Equinox approached. The days were often overcast, foreshadowing the winter to come. On one crisp, sunny day, Rilda and Cora took advantage of the weather to hang their wash on the line in the garden. The women were talking when they heard the ringing of chimes.

"It's Shree!" Cora said, dropping wet clothes back into the basket. She ran toward the house, and Rilda scurried along behind her.

Shree had pulled up outside the courtyard wall. "Hello, my darlings!" she called out as she jumped down from the wagon.

At a distance, she looked remarkably like Rilda. They were the same height and equally plump. But Shree's face was weathered from her years on the road, and her nose was a sharper version of Rilda's. She wore her graying hair in a long braid down her back. Her eyes were a deep hazel, rather than blue, surrounded by laugh lines. Her manner was gruff, but her softer side was close to the surface.

The three women embraced each other in a heartfelt hug. When they broke apart, Shree placed her hand on Cora's slightly rounded belly. "Cora, darling, you are a beautiful mother-to-be. How are you feeling?"

"I feel very good—even better now that you're here."

"Let's get Pec stabled," Rilda said pragmatically. "We should finish hanging up the wash before we settle in for a cup of tea."

Shree unhitched Pec, a large draft horse, and led him into the stable, leaving the wagon behind. Once Pec was settled in the barn, contentedly eating a well-deserved meal, the three women returned to the garden. As they hung the rest of the wash, Shree gave them the news from her travels.

"There is good news. The Resistance managed to capture the Western Fort. They are using it as a base. The army had it well fortified with provisions for the winter, and our friends are distributing the food and supplies to the western communities. It is fair to say that the area is safe from Vestor's army at least through the winter.

"However," she said, her tone changing, "there are reports that troops are gathering at Kameeth Falls. I fear Vestor is planning another incursion into Dute."

Cora gripped Rilda's hand.

"I have some other disturbing news," Shree continued. "Adja, Tinton's herbalist and friend to the Goddess, was tortured and murdered. I understand Dov and a friend had been in Tinton around the same time."

"Dear Goddess," Rilda said with a gasp.

Cora turned pale and sank to her knees.

Shree looked at the two women. "Perhaps it is time to tell me what is going on and why you sent for me."

"You're right," Cora agreed as Rilda helped her stand back up. "The wash is hung. Let's go inside."

Picking up the empty wash basket, Cora walked to the

house. Shree and Rilda followed. When they were seated at the table, mugs of tea in front of them, Cora began the story. Rilda chimed in with details. Shree snorted derisively when she heard about the wedding patterns sent from Merton. "You wouldn't believe what's happened to women in Merton," she said. "The last time I was there, I didn't see one woman walking alone on the streets. Some young men yelled at me and threw clumps of mud at my wagon because I was traveling without a male escort. I got out of there in a hurry and vowed never to return until the world was set right."

The women sat in silence, sipping their tea, lost in their own thoughts.

"So," Shree said, smacking her hand on the table. "What can I do to help? Cora, are you able to travel? You're well along in your pregnancy. It's a long, hard road to the Heart Stone in the best of times."

"I had originally thought to get there with my pony hitched to our cart. Rilda has suggested I *might* reconsider that," Cora replied, nudging Rilda. "We were wondering if you might take me there."

"Of course," Shree agreed without a moment's hesitation. She reached out and squeezed both Rilda and Cora's hands. "I'm still free to travel in Minca and have trusted friends we can rely on. When do you want to leave?"

"I'd like to leave soon after the Autumn Equinox. I need to be there by the Winter Solstice."

"That gives us a couple days to prepare. Are you hosting the Equinox here?" Shree asked.

"Not this year," Rilda said. "We're going across the valley. Maji and Ayfer had a barn raising last summer. They've asked Mother Minca to do a blessing at the Equinox," she said, smiling at Cora, "and have invited the neighbors for the festivities."

"That should be fun," Shree said. "Now, Cora, would you like to see your future home?"

The three went out to Shree's caravan. It resembled a small cottage atop four big wheels. It was an arm's breadth wide and just a bit longer in height and length. It was painted in muted colors with Spirit Writing along the skirting board. There were small windows tucked under the eaves. Under each window was a flower box with medicinal herbs and flowers. A ladder was strapped to one side under the windows. Boxes and trunks full of the necessities and fripperies that Shree brought to trade were secured on the flat roof. Wind chimes dangled from the roof above the door in the back, adding their dulcet tones to her journey and announcing her arrival.

Opening the door, Cora looked inside. It was a compact space for living with hardly enough room to stand. Cupboards were built on one side to carry Shree's food and personal items. A small wood stove in the corner provided heat and a cooking surface. A low, narrow bed ran the length of the other wall, with more storage underneath. Baskets hung from the rafters, packed with dried medicinal herbs and flowers. A woven carpet on the floor added color.

Cora had seen Shree's caravan many times over the years but had never really inspected it. It was charming, neat, and very cramped. Her heart sank. Cora didn't know how more than one person could live in the space. She looked at Shree, tears in her eyes. Shree just grinned. Reaching out, she pushed a small piece of wood that was part of the door-frame. The caravan floor, rug and all, slid beneath the narrow bed, revealing a deep recess underneath. The outside skirting board and the Spirit Writing distracted the eye from recognizing the depth of the cart.

"I've transported many things in here—food, weapons, people. I got Kip through Merton a while back. With a few blankets and pillows, it's not uncomfortable. In case of an emergency, you should fit nicely, even in your delicate condition," Shree said, motioning to Cora's belly. She moved the piece of wood back into the doorframe, and the floor slid back into place.

❈ ❈ ❈

THE WOMEN RODE ACROSS the valley, arriving just before noon on the Autumn Equinox. Rilda and Shree chatted about old times along the way while Cora sat in comfortable silence in the back of the cart. She was wearing her best brown tunic and leggings. Her mother's brooch served as the clasp for a deep-blue cape lined with yellow silk, the traditional ceremonial garb. It was slightly worn, but it carried the energy of generations of Mother Mincas. Cora hoped her clothing could still hide her pregnancy. It was safer for all if this information remained private. Using the skills from her Carroo bloodline, Shree added a slight "cloaking" to aid the illusion.

Pec pulled the farm cart loaded with the three friends, food to share, and a stack of wood for the bonfire. The other families had already arrived at the farmstead and were busy with preparations for the celebration. The cattle had been relegated to the field to clear the barn for the blessing. Garlands of autumn leaves, pine boughs, and fall flowers decorated the barn door. A circle of plank tables was set up in the farmyard, and in the center was a pile of wood for the Autumn Equinox ritual, far enough away from the barn and house to be completely safe.

There were ten extended families in the valley. The earth holidays were important social times for their scattered community. The arrival of Mother Minca's group drew everyone around, marking the official start of the celebration.

"They're here!" the children cried out.

Ayfer, smiling broadly, helped Shree and Rilda down. The young children surrounded Cora, giving her hugs and kisses and pulling her to the small crowd of neighbors, where she was greeted warmly.

While the sun was still high in the sky, the families and friends talked, laughed, played games, and prepared the meal to share. In the late afternoon, Cora called them together. They formed a line along the eastern side of the barn. With Cora in the center, they placed their palms upon the wall. Cora called out, "We call upon the Guardians of the East, of new beginnings, and early morning sun. Bless this barn and keep her safe. May these walls protect all within."

Then the group silently moved to the southern, western, and northern sides of the barn. Cora called in the Guardian of each direction and repeated her appeal. Still in silence, they entered the barn and stood in a tight circle in the center, holding hands. After a moment of quiet, Cora began a blessing song in her clear, strong voice. Everyone joined in.

We sing our gratitude to the Goddess
for giving us this world.
We sing our gratitude to Kameeth
for giving us life.
We sing our gratitude to Mother Minca
for giving us love.

Goddess blessings. Goddess blessings. Goddess blessings.

We gather strength from the divine Goddess
to build our lives upon this land.
We gather strength from the divine Kameeth
to build with love and joy.
We gather strength from the divine Mother Minca
to build for the future.

Goddess blessings. Goddess blessings. Goddess blessings.

We sing our gratitude to the Goddess
for giving us this world.
We sing our gratitude to Kameeth
for giving us life.
We sing our gratitude to Mother Minca
for giving us love.

Goddess blessings. Goddess blessings. Goddess blessings.

Following the benediction, the group returned to their chores and preparations for the evening meal. Maji and Ayfer herded the cows back into the barn for milking while Rilda and Shree helped put the food out on one of the tables. Torches were set up to encircle the farm buildings with light. The children and several of the adults sat with Cora. She told them stories, and they all sang songs. As the moons rose, Cora stood up. "Let's light the torches," she called to the crowd.

Once the torches were lit, the children led the way to the table where the food was laid out. Rilda's bread, shaped like a fire dragon for the Equinox, was placed in the center of the table. Surrounding it were casseroles, soups, cheeses, fruit pies, and crumbles. The neighbors had prepared a sumptuous feast. The richness of the food and careful preparations marked the special earth holidays. Those in attendance gathered around Cora as she gave the Equinox blessing.

We give thanks for the love and friendship that brings
us together.
We give thanks for the food and the nourishment it provides.
We give thanks to Kameeth, Mother of us all.
May peace be with us on this Autumn Equinox.
Earth, air, fire, and water.
Blessed be.

With their attention focused on the blessing, few heard the sound of approaching horses. In the silence following the blessing, a voice called out, "Greetings! I understand you're in need of a Teller tonight."

Before the crowd was a beautiful woman astride a dark horse, a packhorse following not far behind. Her elegant clothes and extraordinary auburn hair were in sharp contrast to the simple attire of the valley residents.

Cora, gracious in her role as Mother Minca, stepped forward. "Welcome to our Equinox celebration."

As she moved to greet the newcomer, she heard Shree's voice inside her head clearly. One loud word.

Beware!

Chapter 22

Cora's step faltered a bit upon hearing Shree's voice. Panic gripped her, but she did her best to hide it. Intuitively, she shifted into a modified version of her Vestor persona, but not too extreme to cause concern amongst her neighbors.

"I'm so glad you lit the torches. I was afraid I would miss the celebration."

"Oh," Cora said, "that would have been terrible! You could have wandered the valley alone until daylight!"

"I'm Nikka," the Teller said as she dismounted, extending her arm.

"I'm Cora, Mother Minca." Cora took her wrist and executed a slight curtsy. Cora was struck by the opulence of this woman, a vision in warm hues and softness. *Who is she? Why is she here?*

Ayfer stepped forward at that moment. "Welcome to our farm," he said. "May I stable your horses?" Nikka handed him the reins to her mount and packhorse. With a dismissive nod to Ayfer, she took Cora's arm and walked toward the circle of tables.

"Cora, my dear, I am so pleased to meet you. I ran into Dov and your brother at the Teller's cave this summer. What a delightful young man he is."

"How lovely," Cora said with an innocent smile.

"Steff told me about your forthcoming nuptials. How very exciting."

"Yes. I cannot wait until the Winter Solstice. The general seems to be a kind and gentle man. I'm sure I will enjoy being his beloved. And the wedding will be so, so beautiful!" Cora responded with girlish enthusiasm.

"Dov said he was traveling this fall, so I thought I would take the opportunity to offer my services. I, too, am a Teller. I felt I had to come and meet you for myself."

"How kind of you. Please, come share our meal, Madame Teller."

"Please call me Nikka. I feel as if I know you already."

Cora led Nikka to the valley residents, introducing her to each one. Nikka smiled warmly at every individual. They, in turn, nodded or curtsied and stared in awe. Cora insisted that Nikka, as the honored guest, be served first. Recognizing Shree, who was helping Rilda serve the food, Nikka gave her a curt nod. Shree responded with a demure smile and low curtsy. Cora realized Shree, too, had an obsequious persona when needed.

Cora waited for everyone else to be served. Glancing at Nikka to be sure she was occupied, Cora held out her plate and whispered to Shree, "Who is she?"

"She's a famous Teller from the west of Minca. She is also an informer for your uncle. I'm concerned that she's here."

"She said she had seen Dov and Steff."

"That would explain why she came," Rilda said.

After the meal, Nikka entered the circle. Moving around

the unlit bonfire, she intoned the creation story. She moved like a dancer, her auburn tresses falling loose around her shoulders, the movement of her hands, the flow of her body, and the bejeweled tunic mesmerizing her audience. The familiar words took on a whole new depth of meaning.

"The Goddess was pleased. Her dance was complete. Under her loving eye, our dance began."

With these final words, Nikka swirled around the stacked wood and, with a sweep of her hands, ignited the wood as if by magic. There was an audible gasp from the onlookers. Nikka stood before the fire with her arms outstretched. The flames lit her beautiful face with a warm glow and cast a long, dark shadow behind her. The valley folk sat in silence for a long moment before they erupted in cheers. Smiling, Nikka walked around the fire, nodding and accepting the appreciation for her performance. Cora looked across the circle at Rilda, who sat next to Shree. They had frozen smiles on their faces.

The rest of the evening was a blur to Cora. Even with Shree and Rilda close by, she was extremely anxious; smiling and acting calm was a challenge. The children passed out paper and charcoal sticks. Wishes were written, paper dragons folded. Men, women, and children approached the fire one by one in silence. With a quiet prayer, they sent their dragon to the flames.

After the ritual, the community took turns telling stories and singing songs long into the night. By the time the fire became embers, the moons were high in the sky. Some neighbors were camping overnight at the farm, while others packed up their belongings and headed home in the moonlight. Ayfer and Maji insisted Nikka stay the night at the farm. She accepted gracefully. As Cora, Rilda, and Shree were packing up their wagon, Nikka approached.

"May I come visit tomorrow?" she asked, clasping Cora's hand.

Smiling demurely, Cora nodded. "Of course. Please do. Why not join us for lunch? Ayfer can give you directions."

As she held Nikka's hand, a tingling sensation flowed through Cora's palm. The hairs at the back of her neck stood up. She pulled her hand away, muttered a quick good-bye, and climbed into the cart. Shree encouraged Pec on his way. Cora kept her eyes on the Teller until they could no longer see her.

"Something happened when we were leaving. When she touched my hand, it felt strange and prickly."

Shree thought for a moment before responding. "Nikka has more Carroo blood than I do. Skin on skin. I imagine she was attempting to connect with you energetically, to garner information without having to ask. The prickling would have occurred when she encountered the cloaking with which I surrounded you. That's too bad. I'm sure it will make her suspicious. We will need to be on our guard when she comes to visit. Avoid physical contact, Cora, and don't look her in the eye either. I know you can come across as shy and hesitant. Use that to your advantage."

"Do you think she could tell I am pregnant?"

"I *think* my work would have prevented that," Shree said in a slightly concerned tone.

"Let us pray to the Goddess that you are right, cousin," Rilda said softly.

❊ ❊ ❊

THERE WAS A FLURRY OF ACTIVITY in Cora's home the following morning in preparation for Nikka's arrival.

In the evenings, Rilda and Cora had spent their time

sewing wedding clothes, just in case Vestor or Fizor arrived unexpectedly. They had also been using scraps of material to make baby clothes. Rilda tidied the tiny paraphernalia away and laid out the trousseau for inspection by the Teller.

Cora had been working in the toolshed on the boots and slippers from the leather Vestor had sent. The boots would be practical for her travels. The slippers were just for display. She added some finishing touches to her work before taking care of the horses and gathering vegetables from the garden.

Shree walked the boundaries of Cora's mountain home reciting incantations and hanging herbs and dried flowers over the entrance for protection. Shree was certain Nikka would know there was protection in place but not what secrets were being shrouded.

The preparations complete, the women worked together making lunch. Rilda scurried around the kitchen. She stirred soup, sliced bread, and issued instructions to the others. Glancing up, she realized Cora was pale. She stopped what she was doing and hugged Cora tightly. "We will get through this, sweetest. The Goddess is watching over us," she assured her.

"You sound so sure," Cora said feebly.

Shree looked up from setting the table. "Well, I agree with Rilda," she said jovially. "We'll find out. She will be here soon."

Pulling away from Rilda, Cora smiled at the two wise women. "Between the two of you, I cannot give into my doubts. Thank you. I . . ." She stopped at the sound of horses. With a nod from Rilda, Shree left the house to help Nikka with her horses.

Lunch was a slightly strained affair, conversation somewhat stilted with long silences. Cora kept her eyes downcast.

Rilda chattered. Nikka's inquiries about Cora's life in the mountain valley were unenthusiastic and met with the same sentiment. Shree barely said a word. At the end of the meal, Nikka asked about the wedding.

Cora perked up immediately. "I have waited so long to be wed," she said with a smile. "Do you know General Fizor?"

"He's a very distinguished soldier," Nikka replied. "I have never met him but have heard tales of his bravery. He is Regent Vestor's right-hand man. You are a lucky woman."

Cora chatted about the anticipated trip to Merton, her groom-to-be, and all her preparations to become the most ideal wife.

"Please, come look at my wedding tunic. I simply must know if it is suitable for Merton. Rilda is such a fuddy-duddy! She wouldn't let me follow the pattern specifications. I'm sure it's not nearly as elegant and, might I say, revealing, as it should be to suit a man of the general's stature. I would so, *so* appreciate your thoughts on this, Nikka. You are quite beautiful and stylish!" she said in a rush.

Nikka followed Cora out of the room.

Rilda and Shree smiled at each other and began clearing the dishes.

"Do you think she's going to want to stay here?" Rilda asked in a hushed tone.

"We can't let that happen."

"I don't know how long Cora can maintain this facade."

"I don't know how long my protections can withstand Nikka's attempts at penetration either," Shree said. "I can feel her trying."

"Shh. They're coming back."

The two women continued their work as Nikka and Cora returned.

"I told you so, Rilda!" Cora said with annoyance. "The wedding tunic is much too demure for a bride these days, Nikka says."

"That's not exactly what I said," Nikka responded. "I just thought you would look stunning with a deeper plunge in the back."

"That's exactly right," Cora said with feigned indignation.

"Come. Show me what you would like to change," Rilda said as she led Cora back out of the kitchen.

Nikka leaned against the wall nonchalantly, her arms folded across her chest. She eyed Shree carefully. Although she had her suspicions, she wasn't sure where Shree's loyalty lay. Shree put the dried dishes back into the cupboard without glancing in Nikka's direction.

"I haven't seen you on the road in a long time. Where have you been traveling over the past couple of years?" Nikka asked, retaking her seat.

"I've been traveling in the Eastern Mountains for the most part. And you?"

"Oh, here and there. Will you be staying here long?"

"Rilda is my cousin and it's been a nice visit, but I'm anxious to get back on the road. What are your plans?"

"I will meander a bit before returning to Merton. I'll certainly be there for the Winter Solstice. I wouldn't miss this wedding celebration for the world."

"Me either. It will be such a wonderful event. I believe Vestor made a good choice for Cora, don't you? I'm planning to leave this afternoon. Would you like to join me for part of the journey?"

After a moment's hesitation, Nikka nodded. "Why, that would be lovely!" And it was settled.

When Cora and Rilda returned, Shree announced she and Nikka would be leaving. She excused herself to go to the barn to hitch up her caravan. "I'll help you, Shree," Cora said, following her out of the house.

Once in the privacy of the barn, Cora whispered plaintively, "You're leaving?"

Shree heard the fear in Cora's voice. She gave her a small smile. "Not to worry, Cora. I will explain," she said, handing Cora a brush. "Would you give Pec a brushing?"

While Shree busied herself rearranging goods stored in the caravan, Cora took the brush and walked up to the horse. Patting her flank, she started brushing. Her anxiety caused her to use short, rough brush strokes at first, but the familiar scent of a horse combined with the sweet smell of feed and the earthy barn soothed her. As her strokes became rhythmic, her panic receded.

"Your ploy worked, Shree," she said over her shoulder with a rueful laugh. "I'm much calmer now. So, can you tell me what's going on?"

Shree stopped arranging the goods in her caravan and came to Cora. Speaking in a low voice, she explained, "I want to allay Nikka's suspicions and keep an eye on her. I will return for you once I know Nikka is well away. We have some time to get to the Heart Stone."

Cora considered Shree's words and answered, "I understand. It's a precaution we need to take. Thank you for all your help."

By midafternoon Nikka and Shree were on their way. Rilda set about making some fruit preserves from the late fall berries that grew in the garden. Cora, exhausted from the visit, went to the ritual space to sit in meditation and connect with the Goddess.

"Dear Goddess, Kameeth, and Minca, Mother of us all, I ask for protection, care, and guidance on my path. Speak to me clearly that I may understand. Keep my loved ones safe. Help us undo the harm that has been done to this land."

Sighing deeply, she closed her eyes.

Chapter 23

Vestor received a message from the west. Steff had been captured close to the border with Carroo. He waited impatiently for the patrol to arrive with his errant nephew, but it never did. Instead, a second message arrived.

> *Prisoner missing; patrol mind-washed by Carroos.*
> *Instructions?*

Vestor paced the perimeter of his tower room. He thought, *Steff is in the west. Dov killed in the south. What is this plot?*

Nikka confirmed his fears when she returned after the Autumn Equinox.

"My Lord, I come to you with grave concerns," Nikka said, moving close to the rigid man. She stretched out her hand and touched the tightening muscles of Vestor's arm.

"Tell me," he said, his voice icy.

"I traveled to the east as you requested. I timed my arrival for the Autumn Equinox. Everything seemed perfectly normal. The gathering was at a neighboring farm. Everyone was most welcoming and friendly."

"And?"

"I could feel protective energy around Cora. It was beautifully placed, too subtle for the local folks to sense. When I saw Shree there, I knew I wasn't mistaken."

"I should have had her killed years ago," Vestor said.

"Yes, well, I did my best and played my part as a traveling Teller. The following day, I paid a call on Cora. That was when I knew something was seriously amiss. The entire property was protected with old spells, and Cora was awash in protective energy. That other woman, Rilda? She hovered like a mother bird.

"I assume Shree had suspicions about me and my motives. I hadn't been sure about her loyalties before this, but I have enough Carroo in me to recognize someone else with strong Carroo skills. I realized there was little I could do there with those protections in place, and I had no excuse to stay uninvited. When I learned Shree was leaving that afternoon, I went with her. We traveled together for a while. I hoped to deduce *something*, but her energy was impossible to read. As soon as I could, I sent word to the soldier's base across the valley from Cora's home. I suggested they needed to keep a closer eye on the activities at Cora's. I trust you will receive information from them directly."

"You have no clear sense of what was going on?"

"No, but putting together my encounter with Dov and Steff, I can deduce they are clearly moving against your interests."

"I am sure you are correct, but tonight you need not worry about it. Let my people get you settled. We shall meet in my private chambers for a quiet dinner," he said. Taking her hand, he turned it over and kissed her wrist. "You have served me well, Nikka. Let me show you my sincere gratitude."

Nikka smiled and, after dropping a small curtsy, she descended the staircase.

Scowling, Vestor sat down at his desk and wrote his orders. Whatever his niece was plotting had to be stopped.

Bring my niece to Merton immediately. Use force if necessary.

"Fizor!" Vestor bellowed.

The general ran up the stairs quickly and stood at attention.

Vestor handed him the orders. "Your bride is conspiring against me. Send a rider with these orders to the base in Cora's valley as swiftly as possible. When he has gone, report to me."

Fizor hurried to do Vestor's bidding. When he returned, he found Vestor studying his map. Vestor related Nikka's report in detail.

Fizor's expression hardened into a deep scowl. "What can I do to stop them?"

"Send two platoons to the Green Mountains," Vestor commanded. "We must guard the border. And two more here," he said, tapping the map by Kameeth Falls.

"It shall be done, my Lord," Fizor said.

"Prepare my royal guards for travel. I believe we will be departing soon."

With the necessary steps put into action, Vestor relaxed. The waiting was over. He was prepared, militarily, for whatever was to come. His senses were heightened. Smoothing his dark hair back from his forehead, he smiled to himself. Tonight, he thought with anticipation, he would take advantage of the pleasant, sensual distraction Nikka could provide.

Chapter 24

Coren and Dov fell back into their familiar travel patterns as they moved down the river. Dov told stories and Coren grunted his approval. They laughed together and were comfortable in their silences. Mina sat alone at the bow of the boat, a silent reminder of their journey's purpose. Occasionally, she took over for Coren guiding the boat and participated in making and breaking camp. Her cooking skills were better than either Coren or Dov's, and they welcomed her assuming the role of chef. But she didn't speak often and assiduously avoided Dov. Both men respected her reticence.

Six days into the journey, they camped by a small, clear creek that flowed into the river. After dinner, Mina announced that she was going to walk up the creek to bathe and meditate in private. After she had gone, Coren stirred the embers of the campfire, and the two men sat in silence for a while.

Then Coren began a story of his own. "I grew up in the north, in the original Dermouth. Deana was our beloved Mother, full of life. Her older brother, Lutfan, was our Teller.

He was married to Jennis. Marna and Mina were their two children. They were as close as two sisters could be. We grew up together, fast friends. It was a happy time.

"Marna was clearly destined to become a Teller as well. She apprenticed early and traveled throughout Dute with Lutfan, her father and mentor. Mina was gifted in healing. She worked closely with Mother Deana, learning the old remedies and ways of healing. She married and started a family of her own. Her husband, Nesrin, was a particular friend of mine. We worked together with Jez in the foundry and fished together in our spare time."

Coren stopped talking. Dov waited in silence. This was the most Dov had ever heard Coren speak before, but he wasn't finished. After a minute, he resumed.

"We heard of the Mother Minca's death but did not understand the Dutes and Carroos were blamed."

Coren stirred the embers again. "Were you ever in Dermouth?" he asked. "It was a beautiful town up north in the Valley of Trees along the banks of a small tributary to the Rone River. There were two or three hundred of us there. We had no protection from invaders. There was no need.

"The first attack caught us off guard. They came from Minca at night and in silence. All of the homes on the northern bank were destroyed, burned," Coren said, staring deep into the embers. "Most of the Dutes were killed. Friends. Family."

His voice cracked with emotion. "The Mincans started to cross the river to the south bank to complete their devastation. The commotion had alerted the rest of us. We were able to push them back into the river, where we fought for our lives. By morning, the river ran red with blood. We had defeated them, but no one truly understood what had happened or why. There had never been fighting—killing—like this in all of history."

Dov nodded solemnly.

"We went from burned home to home, looking for survivors. The Mincans decapitated many of their victims to prevent us from healing our brethren. We found Mina unconscious outside her home. She had a deep gash across her face; burns covered most of her body. Her dead son was in her arms; her husband was inside, headless and burned beyond recognition.

"We carried the wounded across the river, and Mother Deana organized the healing space. All efforts were put into restoring our kin to health. Mina allowed the healers to treat her burns but refused the healing of her head wound. She has carried that scar for thirty years, in sorrow and in memory."

"There are other, deeper scars as well, Coren. No wonder she carries such anger and mistrust. Thank you for telling me this. I respect her too much to intentionally wound her further," Dov said.

There was another long pause before Coren continued. "After we buried the dead, Mother Deana sent runners out across Dute. We learned other communities had been attacked. Within a year, we started the move south, ceding land to the Mincan army. We had few weapons, just our hunting bows, but we did our best to resist. We used our skills to heal our wounded and turned our skills against the invaders. After many years of war, we were able to settle in areas of Dute that were naturally defensible. There have been fewer incursions from the north, but we will not let down our guard. We know that Vestor's plan is to rule us all."

"Indeed. And where he rules, the land is dying," Dov said. "We must return the land to the Goddess."

Mina heard Dov's words as she returned to camp. "Your words are true, Dov," she said, surprising both men. "The Goddess is calling."

With a nod to the men, Mina unrolled her bedding and settled herself for sleep.

❊ ❊ ❊

AT LAST, THEY ARRIVED AT THE gorge. The old maps indicated a wide creek flowing through the crevasse from the mountaintop. What they found instead was a wide creek bed with just a trickle of water flowing through it. They checked the map to be sure they were in the right place. They were.

The three unloaded the punt and set up camp for their last night together. Coren caught fish for their supper, and Mina prepared a dish of grains, herbs, and vegetables. Dov organized their packs for the journey up the mountain. They would carry tools to help them construct a makeshift raft, and each would have Dute bows with bronze-tipped arrows. With their spare clothing, camping gear, and food, the packs would weigh a considerable amount, but Dov and Mina were physically and emotionally prepared.

As the waning moons rose over the river, they sat down to eat. It was a delicious meal, well cooked and nutritious. Sitting in the glow of the campfire, Dov spoke.

"When we envisioned this journey at the Summer Solstice, I wondered if I would ever make it to Dute. If it hadn't been for you, Coren, I wouldn't have. I am very grateful, both for your healing and your friendship.

"Mina, I am grateful that your trust in the Goddess is stronger than your mistrust of me. I believe we are on a sacred journey together for reasons the Goddess alone understands."

Coren responded with a grunt.

Mina looked directly into his eyes and said, "Dov, I go willingly."

In the morning, Mina and Dov bade Coren farewell. They watched him head upstream before shouldering their packs. Mina took the lead. The first quarter league was an easy walk. Then the creek bed began a steady rise in elevation, and it was sometimes necessary to assist each other climbing over large boulders. Taking few breaks and walking in almost total silence, Dov and Mina communicated with hand signals and nods of their heads. It was functional, if not friendly. They walked until dusk, and by the light of small oil lamps they set up camp and ate a quiet supper of smoked fish and dried fruit. They made themselves as comfortable as possible among the rocks and tree roots before extinguishing the oil lamp.

"Rest well, Mina."

In the darkness, Mina said softly, "Good night, Dov."

Dov smiled to himself. Mina sounded *almost* amiable.

❈ ❈ ❈

EACH DAY THE CLIMB BECAME more difficult. The rocks and boulders became more treacherous, and soon they were scrambling over the terrain of what used to be waterfalls using rope and tackle to gain the higher ground. Whatever path had existed before had been totally obliterated. Ahead and high above, they saw the tops of the Eastern Mountains draped in their year-round blanket of snow. Fortunately, they would not be going that far. The headwaters of the Rone River originated in the temperate zone. At this time of year, it would be cold but manageable. They had packed quilted tunics, woolen leggings, and gloves to keep warm.

Late one afternoon, over a supper of fish soup, Mina gazed into the distance, lost in contemplation. At last, she said, "On the map, this gorge was marked as a pathway from Dute to Minca. Granted that map is many years old and no longer entirely accurate, but I don't think the Goddess created the obstacles we are dealing with. I think Vestor has tried to close off this border crossing."

"You don't think these are natural rock falls?"

"No. They look human-made to me."

"You may be correct." Dov thought for a moment. "That could be in our favor. If Vestor believes this crossing is inaccessible, it may not be watched."

"Perhaps, but we shouldn't let our guard down. I think we have just a couple more days of climbing to the top. What do you think?"

"I agree. I'm ready to be done with climbing. A river journey sounds delightful after our climb today."

Mina laughed softly. "I suspect we'll be going through enough rapids and rough water to change your mind within the first few days, Mincan."

"Good Goddess, I hadn't thought of that. I'm sorry Coren didn't leave us some of his brandy," Dov said with a chuckle.

That evoked a genuine laugh from Mina. "Not to worry. I've been running the rapids as long as Coren has. And I've been doing it without the aid of alcohol. It's up to you, with your Mincan skills, to build us a rapids-worthy raft."

"I will sincerely do my best," he said with a smile.

Dov took Mina's bowl and scrambled over to the trickle of water coming through the rocks. As he washed their bowls and cooking pot, Mina observed him closely.

Dov was unlike any Mincan she could remember, and that was a good thing.

❀ ❀ ❀

IN SILENCE, THEY REACHED THE end of the gorge, its walls rising high on either side. It was a challenge climbing the rocks and boulders that blocked the narrow fissure. Dov shinnied over the top first. Mina had been correct. The border crossing had been intentionally blocked. Taking off his pack, he extended his hand to Mina. Gratefully, she accepted it, climbed out, and took off her pack. They stood for a moment to catch their breath.

Without warning, a large stone flew through the air and struck Mina on the side of the head. She fell over in a heap behind a large boulder. Dov saw another stone coming toward him and threw himself out of its trajectory and behind another boulder. Mina's pack was within reach. He grabbed it as another stone hit the boulder. Without a second thought, Dov snatched Mina's bow and arrows, stood up, and let one fly in the direction the stone came from. It missed its mark. Ducking behind the boulder again, Dov waited as more stones flew at him. He sensed a pattern. One, two, stone flies. Pause for a count of seven, another stone. One, two, stone flies. *So, there are two of them, off to my left.*

Calculating when the next stone was due, Dov inched his way to the far edge of the boulder. Two figures moved amongst the shrubs on the opposite side of the Rone River. It was a difficult shot. One of the figures stood up, sling in hand. Simultaneously, Dov stood and let loose an arrow. It pierced the shooter through the shoulder. The other cried out and stood to retaliate, but Dov was faster with his arrow. This arrow caught the shooter in the chest, killing the second person immediately.

Dov, arrow at the ready in case the first person was armed, ran through the swiftly running water. Reaching halfway up his calves, it was bitterly cold with a very strong current. He found the wounded person, a woman, clutching the dead body of a man. She wept silently, uttering over and over, "We have failed. We have failed. All is lost."

Without hesitation, Dov removed the arrow from her shoulder. He pulled some rope from his pocket and secured the hands of the wounded woman behind her back. She glanced back at Dov before turning back to the dead man. "We have failed. We have failed," she sobbed.

"I will be back to tend to your wound," Dov told her. He crossed the river again to aid Mina. He found her struggling to sit up. As he went to her, she waved him away. Leaning over, she vomited onto the ground. Dov helped her move to a clean, flat area of grass. He brought some water from the river and gently washed her face and wound.

"I think you will be fine. You probably have a concussion. The best thing is for you to rest."

"I will, but first bring me my pack."

He did as he was told. Mina rummaged around in it and pulled out a dark-brown leather pouch, which she handed to Dov. "Inside you will find a flask with a red stopper. Pour six drops into a cup and add water. Drinking these herbs will help me sleep and heal the concussion. Will you be safe? How many are there?" she asked as he followed her instructions.

"There were only two, as far as I could tell. I killed one and wounded the other," he said, lifting the cup to her lips. "I will attend to her wound as soon as you are comfortable."

Mina put her hand out, clutching Dov's forearm. "Thank you," she said, attempting a smile, which turned into a slight grimace. Her eyes closed, and Dov laid her back onto the grass. She slept.

Once again, Dov crossed the river. When he approached the attackers, he saw the woman had collapsed on the dead man and rested her head on his chest. She wasn't breathing. He felt for a pulse in her neck, but there was none. *She was wounded in the shoulder and hasn't bled that much. She shouldn't be dead!* He rolled her over. Her head fell back with a thud. Her lifeless eyes stared into nothingness. Her mouth sagged open, her tongue engorged and black. *Poison!*

Chapter 25

Steff and Réan retraced their journey to the mountain pass in the east. Réan was troubled by Steff's behavior. Since Réan's transformation into a Mincan woman, Steff was acting oddly solicitous. As Steff once again offered Réan a hand crossing a stream, Réan yelled, "What is wrong with you?" She kicked water at Steff. "You've been treating me as if I were a delicate fruit that might bruise. This is ridiculous!"

Steff was taken aback. A blush creeped up his neck. "I'm sorry. You just look so different."

"I'm *supposed* to look different, idiot! Do you treat your sister this way?"

"No, but . . . but . . ."

"Then just stop! It's me, Réan. I'm the same person you met when you got to Carroo. I'm quite capable of walking without assistance."

Steff was embarrassed. Réan, in this female guise, was very attractive. It brought up sexual feelings he wasn't prepared for. He mumbled an apology before walking up the trail.

Réan ran up from behind and clapped Steff on the shoulder. "All right, then. Help me take off these boots. They are hurting my feet, and I refuse to wear them until I must."

Steff smiled and the tension lifted, their camaraderie restored.

Nesset had no difficulty recognizing Réan in this Mincan incarnation. She flew high above the pair of friends. According to Réan, Nesset intended to make the journey with them.

As they neared the border with Minca, Réan communicated telepathically with the patrol in the mountains. She asked them to join them for an evening meal. Réan also let them know she was keeping her gender a secret from Steff. When they arrived at the meeting place, they howled with laughter at Réan's disguise. They stopped laughing, however, when they heard about Réan and Steff's mission. Over their simple meal, Réan's friends asked about their families back home and the Equinox celebration. They plied Steff with questions about his sister and life on the other side of the mountains. Several offered to go with them. Steff detected signs of relief from the patrol when Réan assured them it wouldn't be necessary.

"Thank you," Steff said with sincerity. "Your offer to come with us means a great deal."

The young men stood, and with brief hugs for Réan, they returned to their posts.

After a night sleeping in the trees, Steff and Réan crossed the mountain path and into Minca, traveling south and east to the Heart Stone. With Nesset as scout, they were able to avoid the inhabitants of the western territories as they traveled, sticking to the forest to avoid farms and villages. Things went well for the first eight days. Then, late one afternoon, Réan grabbed Steff's arm, stopping him in his tracks.

"Steff, Nesset's sent a warning," Réan said in a harsh whisper. "There are army troops coming this way from the north. Quickly, to the pines!"

The two ran to the nearest trees, asking for protection on the way. The pines welcomed them into their boughs and kept them hidden until the men were long gone.

As the days passed, Nesset warned of other patrols. Clearly, Vestor's soldiers were on the lookout for something, someone. Fortunately, Nesset was able to give them adequate warning.

They reached the Roaz River but stayed in the woods on the ridge high above. Below they could see the Great Road that ran alongside the rushing water. Checking the map for the best crossing point, they marked a fording area several days' journey farther south at the town of Zai and set off in that direction.

❄ ❄ ❄

IT WAS MIDAFTERNOON. RÉAN was in the woods foraging wild greens to add to their soup. Returning to their camp, Réan found Steff sitting on the bluff overlooking the river. Nestled in the shrubbery to avoid detection, he'd sat there since first light observing the town of Zai far below on the opposite side of the river. He'd hardly moved.

After adding the greens and stirring the soup, Réan walked over and sat down next to him. "We've been here most of the day. Why are we waiting? What do you see that I don't?"

"I'm not sure. When we got to this place and looked down on the town, I had the sense something was wrong, but I didn't want to risk going there without understanding what we would encounter."

"Why do you think that? I've only heard stories about Minca. I know you live differently than Carroos, but it looks like I imagined it would."

Steff was silent for a minute. With a deep sigh, he said, "That's the problem. It does look like a normal town. This whole area was once Carroo land. Vestor's army conquered it and burned down the Carroo towns and villages. You *know* what they did to the Carroos they encountered. Vestor rebuilt this town years ago because of its strategic location."

"That makes sense," Réan said.

"Yes, but you have never been to Minca before. Minca is dying. Mincan towns and villages are poor. There's no money for repairs. The Mincans wear old, tattered clothing. The land is dying as well. Farmers can barely grow enough to feed the people. Wells are drying up. Minca isn't surviving like you Carroos on the other side of the Green Mountains. Vestor has stolen the soul of our land. Surely, you've noticed."

"I have noticed. The farther we go from Carroo, the harder it is to forage for food."

"Now look at Zai. What do you see?"

"I see a nice town, well maintained and prosperous. How can that be?" Réan asked.

"That's what I was wondering. Vestor must be sending money and supplies. The question is why?"

"What have you observed?"

"I see many more able-bodied men than would be usual for a town that size. I suspect Zai is less a town and more a base for Vestor's army. But why would he want it to seem like a 'normal' town? That's what I don't understand."

Réan got up and went to the small fire. Returning with two bowls of soup, Réan sat down again and handed one to

Steff. They both ate their soup in silence and watched the town below. After a while, Réan said, "It's a nomiflor."

"A what?"

"A nomiflor. You know those flowers that lure insects into them through their beauty and then eat them?"

"Oh. We call that a nanoflor, but I think you're right. But who or what do you think it's luring?"

"Well, people like us, I imagine, or any Carroo who might venture into Minca. We're not that far from the Dute border to the south, are we? So, maybe unsuspecting Dutes as well."

"And it would be a good location to plan and initiate incursions into lower Carroo and northern Dute," Steff pointed out. "You see beyond the town? It looks like some kind of cave going back into the hill. I've seen a few people going in and out. I bet it's some type of storage facility."

"So what do you suggest we do? We can't go back north to the route you took into Carroo. It's too far and too dangerous. Even if we could avoid the patrols, we'd never get to the Heart Stone on time."

"I agree. Let's think about it."

The friends watched the town until the sun went down and lamps came on in the houses below. They returned to their camp and stirred the coals of their small fire. Steff brought out the last of their bread while Réan added some different herbs to the remaining soup to change the flavor before serving it.

"Could we make the crossing at night and slip past Zai?" Réan asked.

"I don't think that would be easy to do. They have people watching the ford. Not many people cross, but they have stopped everyone. They made a farmer who came through with a wagonload of what looked like vegetables take it all out for inspection. They didn't even help reload it. A couple people from Zai were leaving town, and they were stopped and inspected also."

They resumed eating in silence. Steff said, "It would be nice to get some fresh supplies. I bet we could buy some bread in Zai."

Réan smiled. "I think we should go, but I think we need to have a plan. Knowing it's a trap going in, I can use some Carroo energy to help us."

"What do you mean?"

"Do you remember when you asked about the men who chased you into Carroo? I told you they would be released and that their minds would be muddled so they wouldn't remember where they'd been or what had happened?" Réan said.

"Yes."

"I could do something similar when we go into Zai. I could surround us in just a bit of a blur. No one would get hurt, especially us. The people there would just not totally comprehend who we were or that we didn't belong there."

"Can you do that?"

"I *think* so. I've never actually tried it. But there could be a problem. There might be people there with Carroo energy who could recognize what I'm doing and might even be able to see through it."

Steff thought for a minute and then said, "I think it's worth a try, don't you?"

"Well, we have to keep going forward. So when do we make our move?"

"The town seems busiest in the morning. Do you think going then would work better or going when things are quieter?" Steff asked.

Réan considered for a minute. "When it's busy. We can pass through the crowd more discreetly. Let's go early, get our supplies, and get out of there as quickly as possible."

"We should backtrack a league or so to the bend in the river. We can get onto the Great Road there and look like regular travelers coming into Zai rather than vagabonds from the woods."

"Good idea."

❀　❀　❀

FROM THEIR POSITION ON THE ridge, Steff and Réan watched a patrol of ten soldiers marching north on the Great Road. Réan sent a thank-you to Nesset for warning them. It would have been unfortunate, perhaps even disastrous, to have encountered them on the road. After waiting for a confirmation of clear passage, Steff and Réan made their way onto the Great Road and walked south toward Zai.

Crossing the river was not difficult. The water was knee-deep with a swift current, and Mincan craftsmen had created a solid bridge.

On the town side of the crossing, there was a stone guard-house where soldiers could observe and supervise everyone who came or went. Anxiously, Steff and Réan approached. Two large soldiers came out.

"Who are you? What's your business?" one asked.

Sweat beaded on Steff's forehead. His knife was close at hand, prepared for use if necessary.

"We are simple travelers heading east to visit our aunt," Réan replied with a subtle wave of her hand.

"Pass along, friends," the second man said with a smile.

Steff whispered to Réan as they walked up the road, "That was easier than I thought. Great job, Réan."

"We're not through town yet. Save your praises until later. Look. There are some shops over there. Let's get our supplies and keep going."

They were able to purchase fresh bread, nut butter, and a flask of oil for their lamps. Then they spotted some berry-flavored pastilles.

"I haven't had candy since I was a child," Réan whispered longingly.

"We're on a difficult mission, friend. We deserve a treat," Steff whispered back with assurance. With conspiratorial smiles, they bought some.

Popping a piece of candy in their mouths, they put their purchases into their packs, thanked the shopkeeper, and continued on their way. The townspeople ignored them or smiled as if they vaguely recognized them. They passed another guardhouse on their way out of town, encountering no difficulties there either.

They walked on the Middle Road heading east. When they were a fair distance out of Zai, Steff punched Réan on the arm. "You did it! That was amazing. We got through Zai like water through a sieve," Steff said with excitement.

"I'm afraid not, Steff." Glancing at Steff with trepidation, Réan added, "I could feel someone pushing against my energy."

"Do you think they knew what we were doing?" Steff asked, looking over his shoulder.

"I would assume so. We should know before too long. Nesset is keeping watch on the road behind us."

When Nesset returned, she reported that a man on horseback had left Zai and was following them.

"What shall we do?" Steff asked.

"I think we should stop for some lunch."

"What?" Steff asked, confused.

"Working that energy tired me out. I think we should sit down over there," Réan said, indicating a grassy spot under the trees, "and have some lunch. When the man from Zai comes, we can say hello and offer him some food. If he sits with us, we can assess the situation. If he rides on, we can decide our next steps. He doesn't know we think he's following us. It's also possible that it's a coincidence he left town soon after us. He could be totally innocent."

"That's true. And there are two of us and one of him. Will you be able to tell if it's him? Do you know how strong his Carroo powers are?" Steff asked.

"He was strong enough to pick up on my energetic work, but I don't think he's as strong as a full-blooded Carroo."

"Well, what would you like to eat?" Steff said, shrugging off his pack and walking over to the grass.

"I'd like some bread and nut butter. I'm thoroughly tired of my soup," Réan said with a grin.

"I would never complain about your soup, but bread and nut butter sounds like an excellent plan."

The friends were eating, talking, and laughing when they heard the horseman approaching.

"Greetings, friend," Steff called out when the man came into view.

The man stopped his horse and gave them a nod.

"Would you care to take a break and join us for a bite to eat?" Steff asked.

The man nodded again and dismounted. Tethering his horse to one of the trees, he sat down opposite the two.

"What brings you out today? Where are you headed?" Steff asked jovially.

The man looked at the two. "I'm heading home. And you?"

"We're going to visit our aunt," Steff said.

"Would you like something to eat?" Réan said, extending the bread toward the man.

The man shook his head. Suddenly, the man swayed. His eyes rolled to the back of his head, and he fell back onto the ground.

"Quick!" Réan motioned to Steff. "Bind his hands."

"What happened?" Steff asked while tying the man up.

"It was him. He, too, was assessing the situation. He recognized that you were vulnerable and started putting his energy out toward you. I couldn't let that happen, so I knocked him out."

"Remind me not to annoy you!" Steff said with a smile. They finished their lunch while waiting for the man to regain consciousness.

The man came around with a growl. He pulled against the ropes but couldn't break free. With resignation, he sat back and scowled at them.

"What do you want with me? I mean you no harm."

"I doubt that," Steff said as Réan studied the man intently. "Why were you following us?"

"I wasn't. I told you. I'm headed home. That's all."

"Then why were you attempting to probe our minds, sir?" Réan asked.

"I don't know what you're talking about."

Réan got up and circled the man, mesmerizing him. The man's eyes seemed to glaze over. Quickly, Réan stooped before the man and said, "Tell me!"

"Vestor's orders were to kill anyone suspicious. That means you!"

Réan grabbed the man's head and stared into his eyes for one very long minute. He collapsed in upon himself. When Réan let go, the man fell back onto the ground again.

"We should go," Réan said to Steff.

They gathered up their belongings.

"What about him?"

"We'll untie him. He'll come around in a while but won't remember anything. Don't worry, I did him no lasting harm."

"Would you ask this fine beast if she would like to carry us on our journey?" Steff said, pointing to the horse.

It was a large dapple gray mare. Réan walked over to her, put a hand on the side of her big head, and breathed into her muzzle. They eyed each other for a minute. With a grin, Réan said, "She disliked that man intensely. She would be delighted to take us anywhere we would like to go."

Steff approached the horse. He, too, breathed into her muzzle. The horse in turn pushed her soft nose into his chest. Steff tied their packs to the horse's saddle and mounted. He offered his hand to Réan.

Réan stepped back. "Steff, I've never ridden on a horse before."

"Really? Well, I think you'll enjoy it. We'll make much better time. And she's willing, as you said. Give me your hand."

The horse rotated her head and stared at Réan. She seemed amused at Réan's reluctance. That settled it. Réan reached out for Steff's hand and was pulled up behind him.

Chapter 26

Twelve days had passed since Shree left with Nikka. Cora had been packed since the Autumn Equinox and was eager to leave. Rilda sensed her restlessness and strove to keep her busy. They canned and preserved every fruit and vegetable Rilda could find. Then Rilda sent Cora out to deliver jars of preserves to the neighbors in the valley. Riding in her cart and wrapped up against the chill, she kept her pregnancy hidden. They also brought Cora and Steff's old cradle out of storage, set it up in the ritual space, cleaned it off, and fashioned new linens for it. But it was not enough. Cora was anxious to go to the Heart Stone.

One afternoon, over a cup of tea, Cora blurted out what had been foremost in her mind. "You *have* to let me leave. It's been too long since Shree left. I will go by myself as I had originally planned."

"You most certainly cannot," Rilda said. "We will give Shree a little more time—ten days at most. If she hasn't returned by then, you and I shall both go. Meanwhile, we have our chores to do. You might spend more time meditating. Your constant worry is not good for you and your baby."

"What if—"

"Do not give me any 'what ifs,' sweetest. It will turn out all right."

"How can you be so sure?"

Rilda patted Cora's hand. "Your mother, your mother's mother, and all your foremothers going back to the first Mother Minca lived their lives so that you could be here at this very moment in time. This is your mission. Yours. No one else's. The Goddess and Kameeth have a plan. We do not know what it is, but it will unfold. And that includes Nikka, Shree, and everything else." Rilda heaved a sigh and stood up. "At the moment, your part of the plan is to wait patiently until it's time to leave. This may be the hardest part for you, my dear. Patience was never your strongest virtue." She patted Cora on the shoulder and kissed the top of her head.

Cora smiled. Somehow, Rilda's words made her feel better.

Two nights later, Cora was awakened from her sleep by a tapping at her window. Stepping on her footstool, she looked out. In the pale light of the moons, she saw Shree. Cora waved and motioned for her to come to the front door, her heart pounding with excitement.

Alerting Rilda, Cora went to the door. Shree's caravan sat in the courtyard with a blanket thrown over Pec to ward off the chill. Shree entered, giving both women a strong hug.

"How are you? What happened with Nikka?" they both asked at once.

"May I have a cup of tea to warm these old bones?" Shree said with a smile. "I will tell you all I can."

Rilda prepared tea and biscuits, and Cora went outside

to give Pec some oats while Shree freshened up. When they were seated at the table, Shree said, "Nikka and I traveled quite a ways together. We kept a watchful eye on each other. I was able to send a message to our friends in the Resistance to mark her movements after we went our separate ways. I don't think she had an opportunity to send any messages herself, but I cannot be sure. She was headed toward Merton when I turned south. I looped around and headed back to you. On my way, I got word that Nikka had stopped at an army outpost en route to Merton. We have to assume she was suspicious enough to take precautions." Shree took a long sip of tea and ate a biscuit in two bites before continuing. "I think word may have been sent to the base across the valley. They will come to the house to be sure all is well. We have to leave immediately, Cora. Are you prepared?"

"Yes!" Cora nodded enthusiastically. Then, thinking of Rilda, she turned to the older woman. "Rilda?"

"Don't worry about me, Cora dear. I shall be quite fine here at home. No one would harm an old woman," Rilda insisted, trying to disguise her fears.

With that, Cora felt reassured. She got up at once to change into her warmest tunic, leggings, and cloak and to grab her satchel. Rilda packed food for them to take. Shree had padded Pec's hooves with old blankets and was busy greasing the wheels.

"Sound travels at night. We'll travel as far from the base as we can tonight. I want to be as quiet as possible," Shree said, wiping her hands on an old rag, determination on her face. She had previously removed the wind chime and packed it away. Cora gave Rilda a long, tight hug, whispering her love and prayers into the old woman's ear. Without another glance, she put her satchel and the food in the back of the caravan.

Shree gave Rilda a quick hug and said, "Don't worry about Cora. I will get her safely to the Heart Stone. You might think about going to stay elsewhere in the valley. You're in grave danger if the troops come."

"I must keep up the pretense that all is well here and delay them as long as possible. May the Goddess go with you, Shree," Rilda said.

"And may she hold you in her heart," Shree replied as she climbed onto her seat.

Cora grabbed Rilda tightly again. "Take care of yourself. I will bring your grandchild home as soon as I am able."

"You carry the blessings of the Great Mother with you. Give my love to Steff and Dov. Come home safely."

With a final kiss, Cora climbed up beside Shree, and they left.

Rilda watched until the caravan was no longer visible, whispering prayers and incantations to the Goddess all the while.

❋ ❋ ❋

THE WOMEN TRAVELED THROUGHOUT the night and were far past the base before Shree pulled the caravan into a natural recess in a rock wall large enough to accommodate the caravan. As the sun rose, the women fed Pec and themselves before making up their beds and getting some rest. The effects of stress, excitement, and pregnancy dropped Cora into a deep sleep. In her dreams, she was a girl again, playing with her brother, Steff, and Kip in the garden. They had no worries in the world.

When Cora woke up in the early afternoon, Shree was busy preparing a meal of cooked grains. Cora walked deeper into the recess to perform her morning rituals. When she returned, Shree handed her a bowl. It warmed Cora's hands as she sat beside the small fire. With a nod, Shree pointed at sacks of nuts and dried fruit Cora could add to the grains. They ate in silence. Together they cleaned their dishes and cooking tools and put out the fire. Still in silence, they harnessed Pec and prepared to leave. They traveled down through the foothills of the Iron Mountains and into the lake region of Merton.

Finally, Shree asked, "Cora, dear, are you comfortable enough riding up here? You might be more comfortable inside."

"I suspect I will have to be staying inside before too long. I'd rather be in the fresh air as long as possible."

"Yes. We'll be coming into more populated regions in the next couple days. If we are to get you to the Heart Stone with no one the wiser, you will have to move inside during daylight. There are some safe areas and homes we will visit, but we must err on the side of caution. When is the baby due?"

"She's due at the Winter Solstice."

"She? Are you sure?"

"Yes. I have seen it," Cora said with delight. "I'm going to name her Kippa, after her father."

"Well, well," Shree replied with a grin. "That is the best news for all of us."

"I have also seen that I must be the Mincan at the Heart Stone if we are to set things right," Cora said.

Shree nodded. "Well then, I will get you there." She gave Pec an encouraging *hup*, and they continued on their way. Shree hummed a tune and Cora grinned.

"I know that song. It's the lullaby Rilda used to sing to us when we were little."

Cora sang the words with Shree.

Darling baby, don't you fear.
All is well.
Your mother's near.

Close your eyes and go to sleep.
All is well.
No need to weep.

Tomorrow is another day.
All is well.
I'm here to stay.

When the moons rise high above,
All is well.
You're surrounded by love.

During their journey the following day, Cora climbed inside the caravan. She sat on Shree's bed, quite comfortably, propped up with pillows and a quilt draped across her lap. She had brought her sewing materials with her and planned on adding new panels to her tunics and leggings to accommodate her expanding belly. She could communicate with Shree through a small window in the wall behind the driver's bench.

It was a pleasant day. There was only one occasion when Shree knocked on the wall, a sign they had devised to signal Cora to remain quiet if there were strangers nearby. One knock followed by a second and third was the emergency signal. If Cora heard that, she was to push the peg to move the floor and slide underneath as quickly as possible. Cora would then close the covering back over herself and remain hidden until Shree released her, regardless of how long that might be.

Their first ten days of travel were pleasant and edifying. Cora had not left her mountain valley since Vestor had sent her there as a child. She was fascinated by what she could see through the caravan windows but was also deeply saddened by the barren landscape and impoverished villages.

Along the way, Shree introduced her to women and men who worked for the Resistance. They expressed their excitement at Cora's mission. Word spread throughout their network. Soon, messages arrived for Mother Minca. There were words of encouragement and support but also warnings of troop movements and an increase in attacks on known rebel strongholds. Cora's resolve deepened.

❀ ❀ ❀

RILDA WELCOMED THE BASE commander with a smile. She had been expecting a visit since Cora's departure. She offered him tea and scones, which he accepted. Sitting at the table, they chatted about the weather and Cora's upcoming nuptials.

The commander said, "General Fizor is a distinguished man. I served with him long ago. I am sure he will make an excellent husband for Mother Minca. Where is she, by the way?"

Rilda responded without hesitation. "She's visiting the homesteads across the valley, delivering preserves we have put up. I expect her to return soon."

"Please give her my regards," he said, rising to leave.

Rilda ushered him out of the house with a sense of relief. It had been a cordial visit but clearly an inspection.

The next visit was six days later and not so pleasant. The commander returned with a dozen soldiers. This time he didn't wait to be invited in; he barged through the door without knocking, his saber drawn.

"Bring Mother Minca to me!" he shouted at Rilda.

"She's not returned yet. Won't you put your weapon away and have some tea?" Rilda said, trying to placate him.

"No, madam. I have my orders," he said, pointing the saber directly at her throat. "I am to take Mother Minca to Merton directly."

"I told you. She's visiting the families across the valley," Rilda said with conviction.

"I have been to every homestead in the valley. They have not seen Mother Minca in many days. You will tell me where she is. Now."

"I cannot."

"Sit," he said, indicating a chair. Sheathing his saber, the commander called to his troops. He stayed with Rilda while the men thoroughly searched the house, barn, and grounds. When the men returned empty-handed, the commander scowled at Rilda.

"Madam, if Mother Minca is not able to go with me to Merton, I will take you instead. Perhaps you can explain to Lord Vestor where your charge is."

"I will not leave, sir."

"Yes, you will. And you will come willingly or tied up in the back of the carriage."

Standing up, Rilda cried out, "May the Goddess—"

"Don't come at me with your womanly curses," the commander said roughly. "Vestor has given his orders. I will not defy him, and neither will you."

The commander took a deep breath. He began again with a gentler tone. "Mistress Rilda, we have managed well enough over the years. I have no wish to use force. Please gather your necessities. We leave at once."

Rilda realized there was nothing more to do. With a curt nod, she went to her room. A soldier followed. As he watched, she placed her toiletries into a satchel and put on several more layers of clothes against the cold autumn temperatures. Wrapping up in her warmest cloak, she returned to the commander.

He escorted her outside and into an enclosed carriage. Without another word, the entourage wheeled about and left Mother Minca's homestead.

Chapter 27

Mina woke up to a chilly morning, a light frost covering the ground. She realized Dov had built a canvas lean-to over her. He had wrapped her up in her blanket and placed large, warm stones around her body. *He must have stayed up all night heating these stones,* she thought. She propped herself up and saw him sitting on the riverbank meditating. A layer of her anger fell away. Dov had taken very good care of her. After she went to the nearby shrubs to relieve herself, she walked to the river to splash water on her face and rinse out her mouth.

Dov heard her and ceased meditating. He returned to the campfire and poured some tea into a mug. When she came back from the river, Dov, a stern expression on his face, handed her the mug. She squatted down across from him.

"Are you feeling better?" he asked.

"Yes. I am totally recovered. Thank you for your help," she said with a smile. "What happened?"

"There were only two of them. I killed one and wounded the other. After helping you, I went back to question her. Although she had only a shoulder wound, I found her dead." Dov studied Mina's face. "But she didn't die from her wound. She was poisoned."

"Good Goddess!" Mina said, standing up.

"Yes." Dov hesitated. Then he added angrily, "Was it you? Were your arrow tips poisoned?"

"You think I poisoned her?" she answered curtly.

"I'm asking. In the past, Dutes have used their knowledge of herbs to protect themselves during the war."

"That is true enough, but you have to believe me, if we were carrying poisoned arrows, I would have told you. It wouldn't have been safe for you otherwise."

"Yes, but I'm a Mincan. Maybe it didn't matter to you," Dov said, a harshness to his voice she'd never heard before.

Mina's anger at this Mincan flooded back, and her face hardened into a scowl. She didn't speak for a minute as she got her anger under control. At last, she said through gritted teeth, "I told you I am here working on behalf of the Goddess. I assume that means we are to work together. I would not jeopardize your safety and our mission. Take me to this body."

Together they waded across the river to the place where the two bodies lay. Mina knelt beside the woman. She opened the woman's mouth and looked inside, sniffing closely. She ran her fingers around the gums and sniffed again. Next, she examined the woman's clothing. To Dov's surprise, she also examined the man. When she was done, she motioned Dov over.

"Look at this." She pointed to the neckline of the man's tunic.

"It looks like a stain of some kind."

"Now, look at this," Mina said, pulling up the neck of the woman's tunic.

"I don't see anything."

Mina glared at him. She then proceeded to pick at the thread around the neck of the tunic. In a minute, she had loosened the stitching. Carefully, she pulled the material apart. Several dozen dark, dried berries tumbled out onto the ground next to the lifeless body.

"Do you know what these are?"

"They're dried crickberries."

"Yes. Very poisonous. She was prepared to take her own life rather than be captured. Because her hands were tied, she couldn't get to the berries in her tunic, so she chewed on the berries in his."

"Blessed moons." Dov took a step back.

Mina went to the river to wash her hands. When she came back, she said, "You have commented upon my lack of trust in you, a Mincan. Perhaps you should examine your lack of trust in me."

Dov hesitated for only a second before responding, shamefaced. "You are correct. I assumed you were responsible. I apologize."

She faced the bodies. "We should—"

Dov touched her arm, stopping her midsentence. "Mina, I am truly sorry. Perhaps we could start anew."

She looked at him questioningly.

He extended his arm. "My name is Dov."

He is a very strange person. She clasped his wrist. "My name is Mina. Now, we really have to do something about those bodies. We don't have much time."

"You're right. We have a raft to build."

"I was thinking about these two. They must report to someone. Eventually, someone will show up, looking for them. I hope we are long gone before then."

"Right again. I'll get our packs."

While Dov crossed the river yet again, Mina searched the area until she found the guards' camp.

"Dov!" she called to him on his return. "Come look. They have tools and a cache of food. Even better, they have a boat!"

Dov returned with the packs and examined the small, sturdy boat. He smiled at Mina. "It's in good condition. This will save us a lot of time."

They buried the dead guards and did their best to camouflage the gravesite. By the time they were done, their wet leggings and boots were nearly dry. With a quick prayer of gratitude to the Goddess, they carried the boat and usable supplies to the river and packed the boat.

"It's past noon. We should get going," Mina said.

"I think there's one more thing we should do first. I saw some fallen branches by their campsite. We can attach some of them to the boat for camouflage. It might interfere with your maneuvering, but it could provide us some protection."

"Good thinking," Mina said.

Working together, they secured a number of leafy branches to the sides of the boat. Then they slipped between the leaves, climbed on board, and headed downstream.

Chapter 28

Réan held on tightly as they rode toward the Heart Stone, aware of the strong muscles of Steff's back. They rode swiftly till midafternoon, when Steff left the road to enter deep into the forest. Although most of the leaves had fallen, the woods were thick and little light got through the branches. There was a chill in the air. They dismounted and Steff gave the horse a gentle rubdown, murmuring softly, "Good girl. Atta girl. Sweet girl."

"Ric," Réan said while stretching her thigh muscles.

"What?"

"Her name is Ric. She told me." Réan changed the subject. "Do you get used to using these muscles? I didn't know these particular muscles existed before."

Steff smiled at Réan's discomfort. "You'll get used to it. You might even come to enjoy it. Let me help."

He motioned for Réan to sit down. Kneeling, he gently massaged Réan's thighs. Réan felt the muscles loosen and relaxed, enjoying the sensations.

"This feels so good."

Steff blushed, slightly uncomfortable by the pleasure he got from massaging Réan. "While we're here, let's look at the map," he said, standing up.

Réan grabbed the pack and pulled it out, along with the pastilles. They enjoyed the sweets while checking their route.

"I think we're six or seven days away from the Heart Stone. We'll make better time if Ric will carry us."

"We'll be there ahead of the Solstice, then. Thank the Goddess. I think we might want to stop here to pick up some provisions," he said, pointing west of the Heart Stone to the small town of Ledston. "We don't know how long we'll be staying at the Heart Stone."

"Yes. We can gather edible plants, but foraging grains for Ric and ourselves at this time of year is difficult. We can use the same tactics as we did in Zai. Do you have any idea what will happen when we get to the Heart Stone?" Réan asked.

"No. I'm trusting the Goddess," Steff said. He put a hand on Réan's shoulder. "Réan, if anything should happen to me, promise me you'll get to the Heart Stone without me."

Réan gave Steff a long, hard look. Then nodded once.

A screech pierced the air, startling them both. A warning from Nesset. Réan cocked her head to receive a message.

"There are troops on the road ahead. We should continue through the forest," Réan said.

The friends stored the map and walked Ric through the woods in an easterly direction.

They continued until twilight. With guidance from Nesset, they found a clearing by a creek. Réan built a small fire and prepared supper as Steff settled Ric for the night. They ate in silence, each lost in their own thoughts.

Réan's thoughts returned to the feel of Steff massaging her legs, longing for more of his touch.

❊ ❊ ❊

"QUIT LAUGHING!" STEFF whispered through gritted teeth.

"I'm trying," Réan said while gasping for breath, "but you should see your face."

"They'll hear us," Steff replied in a harsh whisper.

The two were in a ground-floor bedroom in a lodge on the edge of the town of Ledston. They had arrived in the late afternoon in a downpour of rain. After purchasing their supplies, they decided to spend the night at the lodge rather than traveling into the night. One last, warm night before the Winter Solstice seemed like a justifiable indulgence to the two friends. It might have taken all of their remaining money, but they were in agreement.

When they entered the lodge, they saw a number of men drinking and eating around the hearth. They regarded the strangers, paying particular attention to Réan in her Mincan-female guise. Steff, protective of Réan, noticed anger rising in himself. But there was something else that was slightly uncomfortable. *Possessiveness? Jealousy?* He tried to ignore his feelings and negotiated their lodging with the inn-keeper, requesting a simple meal be sent to their room. When they entered the room and closed the door, Réan started to giggle and laugh.

"Shh!" Steff admonished, his face reddening.

"But Steff, you have to admit, it's funny," Réan whispered. "I started out this morning as your sister, and tonight you told the innkeeper I'm your wife! What was that about?"

"Well, I didn't like the way those men were looking at you," Steff admitted grudgingly.

That sent Réan into more gales of laughter. "You are such an idiot!"

Embarrassed, Steff took off his pack and put it on the bed. He tried to focus on the straps to avoid Réan's eyes.

"Steff, I can take care of myself," Réan said, reaching out and touching Steff's arm.

Steff glanced up and was shocked by what he saw. Using a Carroo trick, Réan was a wizened old woman. Steff laughed. Their laughter was interrupted by a knock at the door.

Steff opened the door to see the innkeeper holding a tray of food. She walked into the room with a smile on her face. "Here's a bit of supper for you two lovebirds," she said, placing the tray on the table. She gave Steff a knowing wink on her way out.

The friends grinned at each other. "Let's eat," Steff said.

After their meal, they kept guard for each other while taking turns in the communal privy down the hall, locking their door when they returned. Taking off their boots, they each grabbed a blanket and, fully clothed, wrapped themselves up and lay down beside each other on the bed. Steff fell asleep quickly.

Réan lay awake for quite a while both surprised and confused by her attraction to Steff. Feeling the heat from his body through the blankets didn't help.

※ ※ ※

Just before dawn, Steff shook Réan's shoulder. "Wake up. We have to leave," Steff whispered.

"What's going on?" Réan asked, struggling out of the blanket.

"I heard someone banging on the front door of the lodge. I opened our door a crack to listen. It sounded like a troop of soldiers looking for shelter. I think we should leave now before they know we're here."

Picking up his pack, Steff opened the window quietly and slipped into the night. Réan pulled on her boots and followed. They waited for the last soldier to leave the stable before retrieving Ric. With utmost care—and a little bit of Carroo enhancement—they left town unseen and returned to the woods.

Chapter 29

Rilda sat crumpled in a corner of the small cell. She wasn't entirely sure how many days had passed. Time was malleable when sitting alone in the dark. The stone walls were damp and alive with fungus that hampered her breathing, but she could still distinguish the raw odor of human suffering: blood, sweat, urine, and excrement that permeated the small space.

Her body ached. Her face was bruised, one eye nearly swollen shut. Her back still bled from whippings and burns. Her left arm hung uselessly at her side. She gripped a mug of brackish water in her right hand and sipped the water slowly. Every day or so, maggoty bread or gruel with small chunks of rancid meat floating in it were passed through the door. She didn't care to eat.

When she was brought to Merton, she knew what was in store for her. She just hadn't anticipated how creatively they could induce pain. In the end, she had told Vestor everything. Well, almost everything. She had told him Cora was going to the Heart Stone, but she had not told him she was pregnant.

"Goddess, forgive me. Goddess, take me home," she mumbled repeatedly to herself. The repetition dulled her pain and her guilt.

She heard footsteps. The cell door scraped open.

They are coming for me. It will end now. At last, I will be with the Goddess.

A man entered. Rather than dragging her roughly to her death, he tenderly folded her into a blanket that smelled of strong soap and lavender. He carried her out of the cell.

"Who are you? Where are you taking me?" Rilda whispered hoarsely.

"Shh, mistress. I'm taking you away from here. I will explain when we are free."

He carried her up the stairs. She inhaled fresh air for the first time in days. The man jostled her as they rounded the bend in the stairwell. The movement was too much for Rilda, and she passed out from the pain.

When Rilda came to, she was on the back of a cart hidden in a niche surrounded by wooden boxes and bales of straw. She heard the sounds of Merton's busy market and streets and remained quiet. After a while, the cart stopped moving and a voice called out, "Easy girl. Whoa now. We need to wait for the ferry." The cart shifted as someone got down. Although he was talking to the horse, Rilda realized he was talking to her as well. She remained silent, motionless.

They crossed the river and traveled for a long while before the cart stopped again. The bales of straw were lifted off Rilda. Night had fallen. By lantern light, she saw her rescuer clearly for the first time. He was a short, stocky man who looked to be in his late twenties. Bushy red hair and beard surrounded a friendly face filled with concern.

"Are you all right, mistress? I'm sorry for the rough journey. Here, let me help you down."

They were outside a farmhouse. Several people stood nearby, lanterns in hand. Rilda recognized Ayfer, her neighbor, as he hurried over. She burst into tears.

"Ayfer? You're here?"

"Yes, Rilda. Thank the Goddess you are alive," he said, helping her into the house and to a small bedroom. Rilda lay down, wincing in pain. A tall, thin woman approached. Her smile belied the concern in her warm brown eyes. "This is Cian, a healer," Ayfer explained. "She's here to help you."

Rilda nodded. Ayfer left and Cian carefully undressed the older woman, examining Rilda's bruises and wounds. Rilda's face was badly bruised with a cut above her swollen eye. "It's not deep enough to need stitches, thank the Goddess," Cian said. She washed and dressed the gashes and burns on Rilda's back, her ointment numbing the pain. "Your shoulder is dislocated. I will have to put it back in place." Before Rilda could agree, Cian pulled Rilda's arm, twisting the bones back into place.

Rilda smiled weakly. "Thank you, Cian."

"We will use compresses tonight, but you will need to wear it in a sling for at least seven days. You must exercise it a bit each day so it doesn't stiffen." She found a loose flannel shift in the wardrobe and helped Rilda into it. Helping her into a comfortable seated position, Cian said, "Now, Ayfer wants to talk with you, but not for long. You need to rest."

Ayfer entered the room. He brought hot compresses filled with herbs. Cian secured them to Rilda's shoulder before leaving the room. The aroma soothed her spirit as the heat penetrated her muscles. Ayfer also had a bowl of warm broth for Rilda, which he helped her sip. It was a welcome change from the moldy food of Merton.

She smiled up at Ayfer with gratitude. "How did you manage this?"

"We have been worried about you. The commander and his troops came searching for Cora. We knew she hadn't been in the valley for a long while. After they left, Maji and I decided I should follow them. I watched them enter your homestead. When I saw them leave, I went to check on you. I thought he must have taken you both with him in the enclosed carriage. He was headed for Merton.

"I went home to tell Maji and get some provisions. I came after you. I went directly to my cousin, Dolu, the man who brought you here. He delivers vegetables to Vestor's kitchens. I asked him to find out what he could. He reported that an older woman was brought to Vestor and that she was in the dungeon, but there was no sign of Mother Minca. Why did they take you? Where's Mother Minca? What's going on?" Ayfer asked.

"Cora had a vision of peace. She is traveling in secret to a meeting at the Heart Stone. I'm afraid I gave this information to Vestor." Rilda clutched Ayfer's arm with her good hand, tears coursing down her cheeks.

"That explains something. My cousin was able to get you out because Vestor left with his soldiers and royal guards two days ago. There were very few soldiers left behind. He must be heading to the Heart Stone."

Rilda struggled to get up. "I must go . . ." she said, before collapsing back on the bed.

"Easy now," Ayfer said, gently pulling up the covers. "You'll be going nowhere tonight. Cian added some medicinal herbs to your broth to help you sleep. We can talk about going to the Heart Stone in the morning."

He held her hand gently. After Rilda drifted off to sleep, Ayfer left the room, a concerned expression on his face.

❆ ❆ ❆

IN THE MORNING, CIAN TIED Rilda's arm in a sling before bringing her into the sitting room where Ayfer and Dolu waited for her. When she was seated, Ayfer brought Rilda a cup of tea. She took a sip and then said, "Thank you all so much for your help. Dolu, you are a hero for getting me out of Merton. I am forever in your debt."

Dolu blushed at the acknowledgment. "Glad I could help," was all he said.

Ayfer said, "We have been discussing the situation. Cian says you need at least a couple days of rest before traveling to the Heart Stone. I need to return to Maji, but Dolu says he is willing to take you."

"Oh, Dolu, thank you so very much," Rilda replied, tears in her eyes.

"You will have to travel slowly, mistress," Cian said. "You've been badly treated. And you must wear the sling. Promise me."

Rilda smiled. "I promise."

Chapter 30

Members of Minca's Resistance began to join Shree and Cora on their journey. One woman sat by the side of the road, and when Shree's caravan came along, she got up and ambled alongside, chatting casually with Shree and Cora. The next day, two others joined them. Several days later, a dozen fighters came to their evening encampment and stayed to make the journey. Within days, Shree's caravan was surrounded by three or four dozen well-armed Resistance fighters, men and women, striding toward the Heart Stone, some on horseback and others on foot. They were bedraggled and underfed but filled with spirit. The Mincans in the homes and villages along the way stopped what they were doing to wave, offer food and water, and occasionally join the group. Cora enjoyed the company of these rebels, and they, at last, got to know their Mother Minca.

One evening, a young boy approached Cora. He looked to be about twelve years old, of slight build, with a reserved demeanor. His deep-blue eyes peeked out from a tangle of straw-colored hair.

"Excuse me, Mother Minca, my name is Ebru. I knew your husband, Kip."

"Ebru! Kip told me about you. I hoped to meet you someday. Please come. Let's have some supper," Cora said welcomingly.

They went to the communal campfire and were given bowls of rich bean stew and crusty bread. Finding a quiet spot, they sat together. Over dinner, he told her his story. Orphaned when he was eight years old, he joined the Resistance.

"I could get in and out of any place," he said. "It was Kip who taught me what to look for, how to listen. He didn't mind that I was puny. He said it made me the perfect spy," he explained with pride. "Kip talked a lot about his mother, your brother, and especially you." After a moment's silence, he added softly, "I miss him."

Cora reached out and took his hand. The two talked long into the night about Kip, but they also talked about the parents Ebru could remember only slightly. Ebru discussed his work for the Resistance and what he had learned about Merton, Vestor, and the rest of Minca.

It's a broader knowledge of worry and want than any child should have, Cora thought. Ebru yawned, and Cora put her arm around him and pulled him close. He leaned into the embrace and fell asleep. After that, he rarely left her side.

❀ ❀ ❀

CIAN AND AYFER RETURNED TO their homes. Dolu and Rilda planned to leave in two days. To prevent herself from pacing, Rilda helped Dolu with the cooking and housework as best she could with one arm in a sling. She also plied him with questions. "How far is the Heart Stone from here? How long will it take us to get there? How long did you say? Could we get there any faster?"

Dolu answered as best he could. When her questions started anew, he sighed in exasperation. "Mistress Rilda, you sound like my five-year-old niece. Will your questions never cease?"

Rilda burst into tears, but she knew Dolu was correct. "I'm sorry. I do feel like a five-year-old. I am so anxious, though." She sniffed. "I need to give this over to the Goddess. Forgive me for pestering you. I shall go and meditate. When I come back, I hope to be in a more peaceful place." She smiled weakly and left the room.

She *was* calmer when she returned later and was able to engage Dolu in a real conversation as they worked, without one question about their trip to the Heart Stone. Dolu was a pleasant man with a good sense of humor. A bachelor, he had lived in this cottage all his life. His family were simple farmers. His father had died in the wars, and his mother had died just two years previously. He visited Vestor's kitchens regularly with produce from his and the neighboring farms.

"Mistress Rilda, I haven't tasted anything this good in years. This stew reminds me of my mum's. You knew just the right herbs and spices to enhance it."

"Thank you, Dolu. That's a compliment of the highest order."

"Tomorrow we can prepare our supplies for our trip. I think we can carry enough food and water with us that we won't have to stop along the way, except to sleep. My horses and wagon are steady, but even making the best time possible, I don't think we can be there by the Winter Solstice," Dolu said with regret.

"We can only do our best," Rilda said.

They smiled at each other and continued eating.

A loud knock at the door interrupted their meal. They looked at each other in shock. Quickly, Rilda grabbed a sharp knife in her good hand and backed into a corner out of sight. Dolu went to the door and opened it cautiously.

Much to Dolu's surprise, Cian was standing there, a large leather satchel by her side.

"Please let me in. It's cold out here."

"What are you doing here?" Dolu asked, stepping aside.

"It occurred to me that I should go with you. My apprentice can deal with anything that arises here. So I'm packed and ready to go."

Rilda put the knife down and stepped forward. "Are you sure?"

"Yes. The Goddess came to me in my dream last night and told me so. I'm not one to argue with her," Cian said with a small smile on her face. "So, how's my patient?"

Rilda smiled broadly as she gave Cian a one-armed embrace, clutching her tightly. "I'm feeling even better now. Come, have some stew."

Chapter 31

The Rone River flowed swiftly under a light snowfall. Although the branches were cumbersome and the weight of the boat off-balance, Mina had more than enough experience to compensate. She used one of the oars as a rudder to keep them floating safely through the swift currents. After a few terrifying twists and turns, Dov was able to relax and enjoy the journey. They did occasionally see people on the shore, many of whom were armed, and were grateful to be hidden from view.

Mina steered the boat into a quiet backwater in the late afternoon. Dov jumped out and pulled the boat onto the shore, securing it to a sapling.

"We made good time today. We should be at the confluence in another two days," Mina said, coming ashore.

"We'll be passing Vestor's Southern Fort at the confluence." Dov grabbed the satchel of food out of the boat. Mina sat slumped on a boulder, massaging her neck. Putting the food down, he went to her. "You must be exhausted.

You'd hardly recovered from your injury before commandeering the boat. May I?"

She gave a nod and Dov moved behind her. His strong hands worked through her padded tunic, loosening the muscles as he massaged her neck and shoulders. Mina moaned with pleasure, relaxing even more.

"Thanks. That feels wonderful. There must be a bit of Dute in you," Mina said with a slight laugh.

"My great-grandmother was a full-blood Dute," Dov said. "It will be cold tonight, but I don't think we should risk a fire."

"You're probably right. We'll have to bundle up."

After their cold supper of cheese and dried fish, they constructed a lean-to among the boulders and settled in for the night. Neither acknowledged any awkwardness as they lay side by side for warmth. After a long while, Mina whispered, "Are you awake?"

"Yes."

"I've been thinking about the Southern Fort. I don't think our tree branches will pass close scrutiny."

"I fear you're correct. What are you thinking?"

"The moons will be more than half full. I think we should pass the fort at night. There should be enough light to navigate and enough darkness to keep us safe."

"Can you manage it?" Dov asked.

"I would hope so. The river will widen with fewer rapids as we descend. Although the confluence will be rough, we should move beyond it quickly. I'm comfortable giving it a try, but you're not used to river travel. It's up to you."

"I trust you, Mina, and I trust the Goddess." He shifted into a more comfortable position. "Dream of the Goddess," he whispered, before falling asleep.

Mina remained awake a while longer, assessing her plan and considering the consequences.

She was the first to wake in the morning, slowly coming into consciousness before dawn. Their bodies were entwined. She was surprised by the warmth and security she felt snuggled into Dov. Slowly, she eased her way out of his arms so as not to wake him. As she gazed at her traveling companion, he snorted and rolled onto his side. A strange thought occurred to her; she liked him. Very much.

She walked to the shrubbery for her morning rituals and a quiet moment to meditate and reflect on this discovery. When she returned to the shore, the sun was rising. Dov was awake and packing up the tarp. He smiled at her and wished her a good morning. She smiled back, suddenly feeling shy. That feeling passed as they ate their meager breakfast and prepared to leave. They were, once again, two determined companions heading to the Heart Stone.

❊ ❊ ❊

THE LIGHT OF THE MOONS GUIDED Mina as she steered their boat through the confluence. Dov appraised the fort through the branches. It was lit up as if for a fancy gala. There was a lot of visible activity even at this distance.

"Dov," Mina whispered, "is that normal? Are Mincan soldiers usually up all night?"

"No. They seem to be preparing for something. This does not bode well."

Just before dawn, Mina saw a small tributary and maneuvered the boat up the stream. With Dov's help, she landed the boat in an outcropping of rocks and tree roots, and in silent agreement they secured the boat and disembarked. The woods along the stream provided some protection, but they were not far from a main road.

"Dov," Mina whispered, pointing to the surface of the road.

The road was pockmarked from the hooves of many horses.

"They are heading toward the fort, for the most part," Dov said after inspecting them closely. "Vestor may have discovered our plans and decided to take action." He looked worried.

She touched his arm. "If we travel by night again, we should reach the end of our river journey by dawn tomorrow. It will take several more days to hike to the Heart Stone. With help from the Goddess, we should get there before the Winter Solstice. Let us get some rest and leave at sunset."

"Agreed."

They gathered up more leafy branches to lay over their boat where it was moored. Sliding under the leaves, they made themselves as comfortable as possible. The gentle current rocked the boat and they drifted to sleep, disturbed throughout the night by the sound of horses on the road.

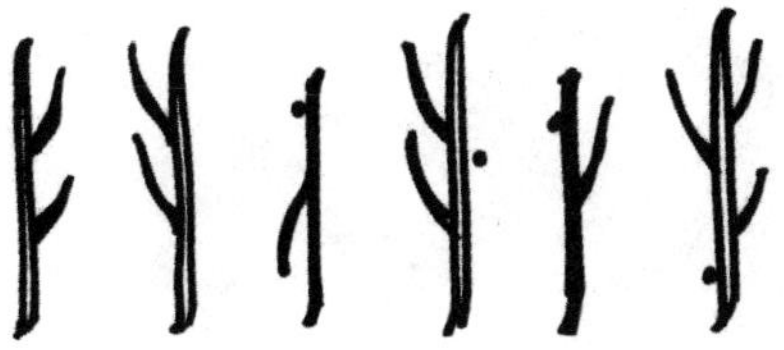

Chapter 32

Nikka walked among the soldiers' tents with General Fizor at her side. Vestor had engaged them both in planning the campaign. Fizor's military strategy was complemented by Nikka's understanding of human frailties and motivations. Initial caution had evolved into mutual appreciation and friendship. They worked together well.

Nikka held Fizor's arm amiably as they walked, speculating in low voices about the battle to come. The soldiers treated Fizor respectfully and cautiously. He was not approachable, but Nikka smiled at the soldiers, often pausing to talk and offer support.

The men were drawn to Nikka. She was beautiful, of course, but she also exuded a seductive charisma. Some soldiers with strong Carroo blood felt a particularly deep connection. They came to her, when possible, and took care of her every need, which she enjoyed with enthusiasm.

She had insisted upon coming with Vestor, but the closer they got to the Heart Stone, the more anxious she felt. Nikka had seen fighting before, had been in battle herself years ago. She understood the usual anxiety before battle, but this was different. There was less camaraderie on this campaign, more fear and aggression. A darkness surrounded the army like a fog. The darkness emanated from the tent that stood on the rise, where Vestor resided.

Nikka shivered and gripped Fizor's arm tightly.

Chapter 33

Steff and Réan stood hidden in the trees. Before them lay the Goddess Way, the road that encircled the Plain of Saund. It stretched for leagues in either direction, but in the center of the plain stood Kameeth's Woods, a vast tangle of ancient trees that reached for the sky. In the middle of the woods was the sacred circle of oaks protecting the Heart Stone. They had arrived. Almost. Vestor's soldiers patrolled the Goddess Way.

"I count at least a dozen," Réan said. "All on horseback."

"Yes," Steff agreed. "Too many of them to fight. I don't know how we're going to get to the Heart Stone."

"We only have to get to Kameeth's Woods."

"What do you mean? Hide up in the trees? Fight them off from there?"

"No," Réan said. "When the war began, Titia wove magic around the woods. Only people aligned with the Goddess can enter safely."

"What happens to the others?"

"They lose their strength. They wouldn't be able to get more than a few steps into the woods before collapsing."

Steff guffawed. "So now we just have to figure out how to get into the woods without getting killed first."

Hearing a call from above, they watched Nesset circling. Réan closed her eyes for a few moments, mind-linking with Nesset.

"The patrol's camp is half a league north. Will they return there at night, do you think?"

"I doubt they would all return. Not if Vestor has ordered them to patrol the perimeter of the woods." Steff dismounted and started to pace.

By now, Réan was used to his ability to work out a puzzle. She dismounted and leaned against Ric to wait. After a long while, Steff glanced at Réan with a conspiratorial smile.

"Maybe there's a way we can trick them into returning to camp while we make a dash for the woods. Didn't I see some fireweed growing a ways back?"

❖ ❖ ❖

DARKNESS CAME EARLY ON THE Plain of Saund. The moons shone faintly through thick clouds as the patrol's camp performed their evening chores. Several men prepared a meal at the cooking fire while others groomed their horses or cleaned their weapons. Suddenly, the men heard a loud screech, then hoofbeats racing around the camp. Startled, the men grabbed their weapons, ready to do battle. A large missile fell from the sky onto the cooking fire. Flames exploded everywhere, catching tents, clothing, and soldiers on fire. The men sprang into action to extinguish the flames. One of them grabbed a horn and let forth a blast of warning, a call for help.

From their sheltered position to the south, Steff and Réan watched the glow of the fire in the night sky. They waited for the rest of the patrol to answer the call from the camp. When the riders had passed, the friends seized the moment. They sprinted across the Goddess Way and the Plain of Saund and into Kameeth's Woods. They ran until they were deep into the woods before they stopped, sagging against the tree trunks in exhaustion.

"We're safe for tonight. Shall we stay here until daylight to find our way to the Heart Stone?" Réan asked, catching her breath.

"Yes. Will Ric find us?"

"I'll let her know where we are."

"Is Nesset safe? That was a perfect delivery," Steff said, grinning in admiration.

"She was able to deposit the bundle of flashweed without getting singed."

The two friends stared at each other in the dim light, then laughed. Steff pulled Réan into a bear hug. They held each other for a long minute. Looking at Réan, he said, "You're the best friend I have ever had."

Réan smiled. "Yes. As you are mine. But there's just one thing."

"What's that?"

"I'm starving."

Steff laughed again and slipped out of his backpack. "Let's eat!"

Ric arrived as they were finishing supper. She was delighted by her reception of a rubdown and oats, along with much cooing and hugs. According to Réan, Nesset was in the branches above feeling very pleased with herself as she feasted on a small rodent plucked from the Plain of Saund.

❀ ❀ ❀

As the first rays of light filtered through the branches, Steff and Réan climbed down from their sleeping perches. They moved through their morning rituals quickly, both anxious to be on their way to the Heart Stone. Suddenly, Réan straightened up. With a laugh and a clap of her hands, Réan twirled in circles. Steff stared in confusion. When Réan stopped, all the enchantments that had turned her into a Mincan woman faded away. Even Réan's hair had returned to its original short crop. She stood there, a pale Carroo in Mincan clothing, grinning.

"Ha! That feels so much better. Let me take these boots off. Then we can get going."

Steff gave Réan a hearty pat on the back. "Nice to see you again, Réan," he said with a smile.

Loading their packs on Ric's back, the friends were on their way. When they arrived at the oaks, the dappled light of the forest gave way to the brightness of morning within the circle. They stood in wonder. All they had known of the Heart Stone had come from stories. Now, they experienced it. In the center were the three standing stones, representing the three tribes. A large, black granite slab, the Heart Stone, lay before the standing stones. Curiously, the grass was not overgrown. Spring flowers bloomed around the Heart Stone, even though it was almost the Winter Solstice. It was as if time stood still within this circle of oaks. Timidly and with reverence, Réan and Steff walked into the clearing. The air smelled of spring.

"This is more than Titia's enchantment, Steff," Réan whispered. "The Goddess herself has been holding this space, ready for this moment."

Chapter 34

Dov and Mina arrived at the landing at dawn. Again, they secured and camouflaged the boat, settling in for a short rest before continuing to the Heart Stone on foot.

They were on the road by midday, traveling quickly and guardedly on the exposed road. By evening, the terrain had altered to rolling hills and deep woods, giving them safe shelter for the night. They worked in companionable silence setting up camp and ate a cold meal rather than risk a fire. As the moons rose, they wrapped themselves in their blankets and settled close to each other for warmth. They awoke early, hurried through their morning rituals, and continued their hike north.

The second night, they lay side by side, wrapped in blankets. The night was clear, the moons and stars bright. In the silence, Dov whispered, "It's a beautiful night."

"Yes." After a minute, Mina said, "If we survive this, will you return to Minca? Do you have a family waiting for you?"

"I suppose I will return. I never married. Cora and Steff are the closest I have to children. I traveled a lot as Mother Minca's Teller, but their mountain exile is home. And you?"

"I had a family once," Mina said, turning her face away from Dov.

"Coren told me. I am so sorry for your loss."

"It was a long time ago."

"I cannot imagine how painful it is for you," he said, touching her shoulder lightly.

Mina trembled and cried silently.

He stroked her arm gently. "I am so sorry."

"But I am ashamed. I have held so much anger for all these years."

"You were right to be angry. What Vestor did was a terrible act against the Goddess and against you."

"But I blamed everyone and everything Mincan for the war. My heart turned to stone. I never allowed for the possibility that there were Mincans in as much pain as the Dutes and Carroos. For that, I am ashamed."

"Ah, Mina, how were you to know?" he said, continuing to stroke her shoulder. "Perhaps that is why the Goddess selected you for this journey."

"You don't despise me?" she asked, turning back to face him.

Dov pulled his hand away. "No, Mina. Far from it. I respect and trust you, and . . ."

"And?" she whispered.

"I have come to care for you."

Mina let out a deep sigh. "I have come to care for you too," she said.

Dov caressed her cheek and wiped away her tears. Tentatively they kissed, gently at first, and then more deeply. But kissing was not enough. They explored each other's bodies slowly, tenderly, awakening desires both had kept repressed for many years.

Later, in the darkness, Mina lay with her head on Dov's chest, folded into his embrace, listening to Dov's beating heart.

❈ ❈ ❈

AWAKENED BY THE SOUND OF shouting and the clash of metal on metal, they scrambled to their feet. Dressing quickly, they grabbed their weapons and raced to the top of the hill. Three of Vestor's soldiers fought with two Mincan civilians on the road below. Swords and knives flashed in the early morning sun. Dov and Mina glanced at each other and, with a nod, took aim with their arrows and felled the soldiers. The Mincans looked toward the hill, startled and cautious, panting from the exertion. They kept their weapons at the ready as Dov and Mina descended to meet them.

"Greetings, friends," Dov said. "Looks like you've had a busy morning."

"Dov? Mother Minca's Teller?" one of the Mincans asked, lowering her sword. She came forward, her arm outstretched. "I'm Vern. We met a year ago. This is my companion, Leif."

"Of course! Pleased to see you," Dov said, clasping her wrist.

"Not as pleased as we are," Leif replied, grabbing Dov's wrist in a strong grip. "Thanks for the help."

"This is Mina," Dov said by way of introduction. "You're in luck, Leif. She's a healer, and you're wounded."

Mina smiled. "Come back to our camp. I can put some salve on that wound. Dov, why don't you and Vern deal with those soldiers and meet us back there?"

Soon, the four were eating breakfast and talking.

"We are heading north to meet our friends," Vern explained between bites. "We hear that Mother Minca is coming. Meeting you here seems like a confirmation."

"I last saw Mother Minca at the Summer Solstice," Dov said. "We can travel together a ways. We're going to the Heart Stone."

"We have also heard that Vestor and his troops are heading south from Merton," Leif said. "The Resistance is rallying in Mother Minca's defense."

"Praise the Goddess and Kameeth," Dov said. "We'd best be on our way."

They packed up and headed out. By late afternoon, they arrived at a narrow gap in the hills, which opened to the Goddess Way. They saw no sign of Vestor's soldiers.

"This is where we part," Dov said. "Safe travels."

With warm embraces and well wishes, the pairs separated. Vern and Leif traveled north on the road, and Dov and Mina jogged across the Plain of Saund and into Kameeth's Woods.

❈ ❈ ❈

THEY ENTERED THE HEART STONE clearing at twilight. Wide-eyed at the springtime they encountered, they shrugged off their backpacks and inhaled deeply. At first, they didn't notice the two figures beyond the standing stones.

"Dov!"

Steff ran across the clearing. He pulled Dov into a strong embrace. When they stepped apart, they both started talking.

"When did you get here?"

"Were you safe on your travels?"

"How did you grow a mustache?"

"You're walking with a limp."

"Are you well?"

"You found Mother Dute?"

They were brought back to the present by Mina lightly touching Dov's arm.

"Dov, there is much to talk about. This must be Steff. Won't you introduce us? And who is this young Carroo?" she asked, indicating Réan, who had approached the group.

Grinning widely, the two men took a breath.

Introductions were made. "Mina was sent by Mother Dute," Dov said, pulling Mina close to his side and kissing her temple.

Steff admired the strong woman with the distinctive scar and streak of white in her hair. "Let me present Réan. Mother Carroo sent him."

Réan stepped forward, extending her arm to both Dov and Mina. "Welcome. I am preparing some food for dinner. There is enough to share."

"Let me help you," Mina said, "and give these two some time together."

As they walked around the standing stones, Mina took Réan's arm roughly and whispered, "He thinks you're a boy! What is this deception?"

Chapter 35

Réan made sure they were out of earshot before turning to Mina. "Please, let me explain."

They sat down at the campfire. "We captured Steff when he crossed into Carroo. He assumed I was a boy. I was with the mountain patrol, the only woman there. I looked like a smaller version of the others. It was an easy mistake. I had never met a Mincan and certainly didn't trust him. As I took him to Cappett, it seemed safer to maintain the illusion," Réan said, flushed. "Then I got to know him and trust him and thought I *should* tell him the truth, but it never seemed like the right moment."

Réan sat for a long moment in meditative silence. Mina stirred the stew, watching the young woman with curiosity.

Réan continued. "When we left for the Heart Stone, I was disguised as a Mincan woman, but he treated me differently. It was as if I had become a strange and delicate creature. I hated it. I missed our easy friendship, so I told him to stop.

But I thought, if he knew I really *was* a woman, he would always treat me like that. So then I *couldn't* tell him." Réan bowed her head. "I hope you won't tell him either."

Mina reached out and squeezed Réan's arm gently. "He clearly cares for you. You have to let him know the truth," she said. Then she laughed. "We see what we expect to see. I won't tell him. The Goddess will sort this out. She has her ways."

"The Goddess has a strange sense of humor," Réan said, grinning wryly.

"Indeed," Mina agreed, returning the smile. "So, you captured Steff? How did you manage that?"

Réan launched into a humorous account of the Mincan's arrival in Carroo. Mina chuckled. Dov and Steff approached them.

"Réan was telling me about your arrival in Carroo, Steff. Trapped by a tree?"

"It was an unexpected ending to an exhilarating run," Steff said with a smile. "And it was the perfect introduction to all things Carroo." He gave Réan a gentle shove as he plopped down next to her.

Réan, blushing, wiped her eyes discreetly and strove to look busy.

"I hear you're a great cook, Réan," Dov said kindly. "What have you prepared?"

"Just a vegetable stew with fresh greens," Réan replied, smiling up at Dov. "Being back in springtime has added some new delicacies."

"There's a clear pool of water just there in the woods," Steff said, pointing into the brush. "There's watercress! We also found some wild strawberries growing nearby."

"Wonderful!" Dov exclaimed, dropping their packs and sitting close to Mina.

Over a leisurely dinner, the four shared stories of their travels to the Heart Stone. Nibbling wild strawberries, Mina described the final installment, the encounter with Vern and Leif, and the gathering of the Resistance fighters.

Energy coursed through Steff's veins. "Cora! And Vestor's army! I need to get to her."

Réan put a restraining hand on his arm. "Not tonight. Tomorrow is soon enough. I will go with you."

"We will go with you as well," Mina stated. "We must ensure her safety."

Dov nodded his agreement. "We detected a lot of activity at the Southern Fort. I suspect they may be on the move north already."

"We are traveling with our friend, Nesset, a hawk. I will ask her to scout the area at first light," Réan said. "Let us get some rest tonight. I can brew some tea to help us sleep deeply and wake refreshed."

❄ ❄ ❄

EARLY THE NEXT MORNING, Nesset returned from her flight and communicated with Réan.

"There's a problem," Réan said.

"What's wrong?" Steff asked.

"The Resistance fighters are coming south on the Great North Road. They have almost two days' journey to the Goddess Way, but Vestor's army is already here, hidden in the hills to the north of the Heart Stone. The army from the Southern Fort is advancing toward the Goddess Way. They are a couple days' march away but could be here before Cora. With Vestor to the north and the army coming from the south, Cora will be trapped."

"The Great North Road goes through the Laurel Valley

to reach the Goddess Way. It's a perfect place for an ambush," Dov said.

"What is our best strategy?" Mina inquired.

"We need to join the Resistance!" Steff exclaimed, standing up.

"That may not be the most effective," Dov said.

"If the Resistance can reach the forest, they will be safe," Réan said with urgency.

"What do you mean?"

"Mother Carroo put an enchantment on the woods. Friends to the Goddess are safe within. Others who enter become debilitated."

Dov and Mina thought for a few seconds. Looking into each other's eyes, they seemed to come to an unspoken agreement.

"We need to stop—or at least slow down—the soldiers coming from the south before we go to Cora," Dov said. He said to Mina with a wry smile, "Well, my love, how do you suggest we stop an army?"

"I think I know a way," Mina replied with a grin.

❈ ❈ ❈

USING THE TOOLS DOV AND Mina had brought, the four managed to dislodge boulders from the hills surrounding the narrow gap leading to the Goddess Way. With Ric's added strength, they maneuvered them into a rough barrier across the roadway almost as tall as Dov. They wedged deadwood and debris amongst the rocks and added flashweed. Réan used Carroo gifts to make it look like a solid wall of stone.

Stepping back, they admired their work. Packing up their tools, Mina said, "Steff and Réan, you need to reach Cora. Let them know about Vestor and how to reach safety."

"Ric will take us," Réan told Steff. "I believe I can get us past Vestor's scouts without them realizing it."

Dov patted Réan on the back. "Mother Titia was wise in her choice of emissary. May your gifts keep you safe. We will wait here. When the army arrives, we will light the wall. Then we will come north to join you," Dov said. He gave Steff a tight hug. "May the Goddess go with you both."

"And with you," Steff said.

Réan informed Nesset of their plan as Steff saddled Ric. Once he was mounted, Steff extended his hand to pull Réan up behind him.

"May the Goddess watch over you," Mina called as they rode away. Réan waved as they rode north on the Goddess Way.

❈ ❈ ❈

SITTING UNDER A TREE AT THE TOP of a hill wrapped in a warm fur cloak, Nikka maintained a meditative silence as she gazed toward the east. She waited for a sign of movement from the Resistance. They would be coming soon, and the battle would begin.

A slight breeze drew Nikka's attention from the far distance to the Goddess Way below. There was movement in the grasses along the road. To a normal Mincan eye, it would seem no more than a gust of wind, but to Nikka it was clearly a Carroo glimmer. She saw a horse with two riders. Her eyes narrowed in recognition, a grim expression marring her beautiful face.

Steff! Well, well, she thought, *I never expected you to get here.*

She watched until the breeze blew onto the Great North Road, confirming her suspicions. She rose and, adjusting her furs, walked quickly down to the encampment concealed on the far side of the hill to Vestor's tent.

Chapter 36

The moons look down from the sky high above,
The eyes of the Goddess, so full of love.
The eyes of the Goddess, so full of love.

The final chorus of the "Goddess Eyes" ballad echoed throughout the Resistance fighters' camp. More than a few eyes were moist with tears.

Cora sat with Ebru, gazing into the embers of the dying campfire. With a sigh, she said, "Dear one, I need some help getting up. Would you be so kind?"

With a smile, Ebru helped Cora rise to her feet. She gave him a hug and said, "She's been enjoying the music tonight, dancing in my belly. I do believe she will be a musician."

A slight commotion caught Cora's attention. One of the sentries approached. Several figures followed in his shadow. When the group came into the firelight, Cora saw her brother.

"Steff!" Cora cried out. They rushed to each other and embraced for a long time, unable to speak. Pulling back,

Cora said, "You look ten years older. When did you grow a mustache?"

Steff grinned at his sister. "It was a 'gift' from Titia, Mother Carroo. And this is Réan," he said, pointing to his companion. "We traveled together from Cappett."

Cora gave Réan a tight hug. "Thank you for coming. And thank you for helping my brother get here. I trust Mother Carroo is well."

"Titia sends her very best to you, Mother Minca."

"No formalities here. I am simply Cora, Steff's sister. You are most welcome to our camp. Are you tired? Hungry?"

"We are both of those things," Steff replied. "But first I want to know how you are. You look beautiful and very, very pregnant."

Cora smiled. "I am well. The gathering of the Resistance has given me strength and hope. Let me introduce you to Ebru. He was Kip's compatriot and is my best support."

Ebru extended his wrist to Steff and then Réan. They shook it solemnly.

"Shree has gone to bed. She will be thrilled to see you in the morning," Cora said. "But tell me, have you been to the Heart Stone? Do you have news?"

"We have. We saw Dov and Mina there. Mina was sent by Mother Dute," Steff explained. "There is much to tell. Vestor and his army are in the hills north of the Heart Stone. We should hold a council before the Resistance goes any farther."

"Ebru, would you spread the word that we'll meet at first light? Then come to Shree's caravan. Let's feed these two and hear their stories," Cora said.

❊ ❊ ❊

Ebru helped Cora climb onto the bed of a farm wagon. Steff and Réan joined her. They faced the crowd of several hundred expectant Resistance fighters. Road-weary and ragged, the men and women looked toward the wagon with hope and determination. Consciously hiding her own trepidation, Cora stood erect, a confident expression on her face.

"Goddess blessings, friends. This is my brother, Steff, and his friend Réan, sent by Mother Carroo. They bring news from the Heart Stone."

Cora surveyed the band of fighters before continuing.

"There are difficulties ahead. Vestor's army is waiting in the hills north of the Heart Stone. Soldiers from the Southern Fort are marching north."

There was an outcry from the crowd, shouts of anger and cries of alarm.

"Do not despair," Cora said, raising her arms in supplication. "The Goddess is with us!"

Steff stepped to her side. He told them about the fire wall built to delay the soldiers from the Southern Fort and the likely attack in the Laurel Valley at the approach to the Goddess Way. He drew Réan forward. Réan explained Mother Carroo's enchantment on the woods surrounding the Heart Stone.

Cora spoke again calmly. "We assume Vestor is aware of Mother Carroo's enchantment. Otherwise, his army would occupy Kameeth's Woods rather than lie in wait for us. We have come a long way together and are almost at our goal. We have to be at the Heart Stone on the Winter Solstice in two days' time," Cora reminded the gathering.

"Knowing what lies ahead, we can make our plans. Let us gather in small groups and consider our options. Send a representative from each group to Shree's caravan to decide our best course of action. And be strong of heart, my friends. We are so close."

❋ ❋ ❋

THE ATMOSPHERE AT SHREE'S caravan was somber. Each group had come to the same conclusion. There was no time to find another route. They had to move forward, straight into the path of Vestor's army.

"Our priority is getting Cora to the Heart Stone," Steff said.

There was a murmur of assent.

"Perhaps, Cora, you could hide in Shree's caravan. It might be safer," someone suggested.

"I won't hide away," Cora protested. "Not anymore."

"Besides," Shree said, "Nikka probably suspects Cora has been traveling with me. My caravan would be the focus of their efforts."

"We could use that to our advantage," Réan said with a gleam in her eye.

The group discussed strategy and then dispersed to prepare. Steff took Cora's hand and led her to the outskirts of the encampment. When they were out of earshot from the others, he squeezed her hand and asked, "How are you doing? Honestly."

She embraced him, and he held her close. "Don't tell anyone, but I'm terrified," Cora confessed. Her eyes brimmed with unshed tears. "When we made our plans, everything seemed possible. Traveling all this way, I have come to know these people, their passion and commitment. And Ebru. And the baby!" Cora sobbed, her tears flowing freely now.

Steff stroked her back.

After a moment, she said, "They look to me as Mother Minca. Strong, wise, courageous. I don't feel like Mother Minca. I feel like little Cora who wants to hide under the covers in her bed."

Steff laughed gently and kissed the top of her head. "Ah, Cora. You have always been Mother Minca. Your strength lies in your empathy. And your stubbornness."

She pulled back. Wiping her tears, she asked, "Stubborn?"

"Absolutely," he said with a grin. "If you weren't stubborn, you would have succumbed to Vestor long ago. You would be in Merton preparing to marry that general. I would be preening in front of Vestor's cronies. What a horrible thought! Yes, absolutely stubborn. And I love you for it."

She managed a smile. "Well," she said in a childlike voice, "maybe a little stubborn."

Steff hugged her tightly once more before letting her go. "We should get back. We have a lot to do."

There was a flurry of activity in the camp as they prepared for the march to the Heart Stone. Weapons were cleaned and blades were sharpened. Steff was given a sword and Réan a set of daggers. One older fighter gave Cora a large, padded leather vest studded with metal. It managed to cover most of her belly when tied, the armholes loose enough so her movement was unrestricted.

"Cora, love," Shree said, giving the vest an adjustment, "I've brought you this far. I *will* get you to the Heart Stone."

Cora smiled and kissed her on the cheek. Then Shree helped her into the back of a farm wagon.

The men and women of Cora's fighting force set off in the afternoon with grim determination, timing their arrival at the Laurel Valley for dawn on the Winter Solstice.

❈ ❈ ❈

THE LAUREL VALLEY WAS SHROUDED in a heavy mist, muffling the sounds of their movement. Shree drove the wagon on the outer flank of the fighting force, as far from Vestor's troops as possible. Her own caravan was strategically placed behind the outriders at the front of the force. Steff rode Ric alongside the wagon, his blade drawn. Cora crouched in the back with Ebru at her side. They gripped their swords, alert. Réan sat beside Cora, tucked between two bales of hay, her eyes closed, clutching her daggers and using her skills to shroud the wagon. She also enhanced Shree's caravan to subtly attract Vestor's soldiers.

"Blessed moons," whispered Cora. "This mist may serve as camouflage."

"I'm not so sure," Réan whispered in response. "Nesset tells me there's a woman on the hill with Vestor. She has strong Carroo—"

Before Réan could finish her sentence, a wave of arrows pierced the mist, felling many of the fighters. Screams and cries filled the air. Those that were able surged forward to reach the Goddess Way, where they encountered Vestor's foot soldiers blockading the Great North Road. The battle commenced in full. As the heat of the fighting dissipated the mist, Vestor's soldiers swarmed toward Shree's caravan.

❈ ❈ ❈

HIGH ABOVE THE FIGHTING, VESTOR, Fizor, and Nikka watched the battle. Vestor's soldiers greatly outnumbered the Resistance fighters. Victory seemed inevitable.

"They think Cora is in the caravan. A Carroo trick," Nikka remarked to Vestor. "Can you see beyond the caravan?" she said.

"I see nothing," Vestor said with a snarl.

"As I thought. We are not meant to see. Cora is shrouded in Carroo energy. Your soldiers don't know she's there."

"Can you do something?"

"I believe I can," Nikka replied, closing her eyes and raising her arms. She took a deep breath and concentrated, sending a message to the soldiers below. Those with enough Carroo blood picked up her call. As one, they fought their way to the farm cart where Cora was traveling.

"Nicely done, Nikka," Vestor said. "Let's see if they can kill the ingrate."

❈ ❈ ❈

SHREE DROVE HER HORSE AS FAST as possible on the flank of the fighting, and Steff rode alongside. Six soldiers converged upon them. Shree focused on driving while Cora, Ebru, Réan, and Steff fended off the attack. As the wagon pulled away, one of the soldiers took lethal aim at Ebru with his sword. Cora, seeing a blade descending, lurched in front of Ebru wielding her own sword in defense. As she sliced the soldier's neck, his blade entered through the armhole of her vest, deep into her chest. Ebru was saved, the attacker fatally wounded. Cora collapsed onto the wagon bed.

"Shree! We must get to the Heart Stone! Cora has been wounded!" Réan screamed as she and Ebru tried to staunch the bleeding.

Shree urged the horse forward, breaking through the fighters. Réan enhanced the wagon's shielding. They moved like an invisible wind through the battle with Steff following close behind.

❈ ❈ ❈

"Vestor, they are getting away!" Nikka cursed as she watched the wagon and outrider take off across the Plain of Saund.

Although Vestor could not be sure what he was seeing, he trusted this woman, as did Fizor. On Fizor's signal, the archers delivered a volley of flaming arrows aimed at Kameeth's Woods itself. The archers raced to the west and let loose another volley of flaming arrows, igniting another section of Kameeth's Woods. They continued on, determined to burn the woods down.

❃ ❃ ❃

SHREE STOPPED ABRUPTLY WHEN they reached the woods. The tops of the trees were aflame. Steff scooped Cora up onto Ric's back and entered the woods, heading to the Heart Stone. Cora moved in and out of consciousness, bleeding profusely. The others scrambled off the wagon and followed as quickly as they could.

❃ ❃ ❃

DOV AND MINA RACED TOWARD the battle. They had set the barricade on fire and left before the soldiers from the Southern Fort broke through. Dov saw the wagon and rider breaking away from the fighting and heading for the woods. Knowing in his heart it was Steff and Cora, Dov called to Mina and motioned that they should go directly into the woods.

They arrived to find a desperate tableau. Cora lay on the ground in front of the Heart Stone. Steff knelt beside her, applying pressure to the wound. Réan was tearing the bottom of her tunic for wadding. Shree held Ebru tightly.

The boy was near hysteria, crying, "It's my fault! My fault!"

Assessing the situation, Mina ran for her pack and medical supplies, calling out, "Keep pressure on the wound, Steff!"

Dov stood in shocked stillness, his heart breaking.

Returning, Mina lifted Steff's hand to look at Cora's chest. Without speaking, she pulled a pouch out of her medicine bag and sprinkled powder onto the wound. She repacked the wadding and secured it in place.

"That should help stop the blood flow," she said to the group. "The wound is very deep, and she's lost a lot of blood. The shock has also brought on labor, and I fear the child is in as much danger as Cora."

Cora's eyes fluttered open. With surprising strength, she grabbed Mina's arm. "You must save this child," she said, breathing deeply. "Promise me!"

Mina looked deep into Cora's eyes before giving her a curt nod of agreement. Steff wept silently as Ebru's cries became wails.

Hearing Ebru, Cora reached out for him. He came to her side. She lovingly whispered, "Ebru, my sweetest, you must not blame yourself. We are all in the hands of the Goddess."

Ebru took her hand and kissed it. "Cora, Mother Minca, I live to serve you and the Goddess."

Mina opened a small vial and said, "Cora, I'm Mina. Mother Dute sent me. I am going to rub this on your gums. It will help with the pain."

Cora nodded assent. Almost immediately after Mina applied the salve, Cora's body relaxed, and she drifted off.

Smoke from the burning forest filled the clearing. Dov spoke up. "This smoke is not helping. If only there were some shelter."

Mina said to Réan, "I saw some Spirit Writing on the Heart Stone. See what it says."

Réan ran to the stone and brushed off the leaves and twigs scattered on top. Finding the Spirit Writing, she read the words quickly.

The Goddess has been waiting for you.
To go within, call out Dedrum Daru.

Stepping back, Réan called out, "Dedrum Daru."

To everyone's surprise, the black granite slab slid noise-lessly aside, revealing steps leading into the earth.

Chapter 37

Réan glanced at the others, then scampered down the
stairs. She found a lantern, lit it, and called out, "It's
safe. Bring her down."

Steff lifted Cora gently and brought her into the under-
ground chamber. The others followed and the granite slab
slid back into place. Réan found other lanterns and lit them.
They were in a large space untouched by time. In the center,
there was a fire circle surrounded by cushions and wood
arranged, ready to light. A pallet was laid before a shelf,
which was clearly an altar that held a beautiful crystal globe
and fetishes representing earth, air, fire, and water. They laid
Cora on the pallet beside a stack of clean linens.

Could the ancestors have known we would need these? Mina
wondered.

Mina inspected Cora's wound more thoroughly. Then
she spoke sharply and with authority. "Réan, please start the
fire. We need to boil some water. Shree, there are some containers." She nodded toward some cooking pots near the fire
circle. "There's a pool beyond our campsite near the standing
stones. You and Ebru, bring some water. Quickly!"

Taking the containers and Ebru's hand, Shree called out, "Dedrum Daru." When the granite slid back, she pulled a reluctant Ebru up the stairs.

Once they were gone, Mina addressed the others. "This is worse than I feared. From the coloration of Cora's wound, it's clear there was poison on the blade. There's no time for natural labor. The poison is in Cora's blood. I must save the baby before it's too late. That was Cora's wish. I don't know if it's possible to save both of them. Steff, Dov, I need your consent."

After a moment's hesitation, the two men nodded solemnly and asked how they could help.

"Steff, please hold Cora and keep her from moving. She won't feel any pain, I promise you, but there may be some muscle response to what I need to do. On a deep level, she will know you are there and feel comfort.

"Dov, would you be able to help me with the birthing? It will not be easy."

"Of course. Just tell me what to do."

"I will help too," Réan said, "but what about Ebru?"

"I will take care of him," Dov said.

The granite slid open. Shree and Ebru returned with water. Dov met them on the stairs. Taking the containers, he said, "Shree and Ebru, the Resistance fighters who are able will make their way to the Heart Stone. Many will be injured. Will you ensure their wounds are tended to and that they are comfortable and fed?"

Ebru glanced behind Dov to Cora's prone figure. "I will do my best, Dov, to serve the Mother," he said.

Shree nodded. They went back up. The granite slid back into place as Mina's work began in earnest.

Cora lay still. She knew she was dying but felt no pain or sorrow, only warmth and deep lethargy. She saw her beloved brother, who held her, tears running down his cheeks. She smiled up at him, wanting him to know that everything was all right.

Her eyes were drawn to the fire across the chamber. Beams of light shone through the small air holes in the ceiling, lighting tendrils of smoke as they rose and twirled about the room. An old woman sat still and quiet beyond the fire, wrapped in a beautifully embroidered blanket, her long gray hair cascading over her shoulders. She smiled at Cora, her eyes filled with love. She extended her hands in welcome.

Kameeth! Cora thought.

Kameeth communicated to Cora silently, mind to mind, heart to heart. "*Mother Minca, my beloved, you have brought the tribes back together at the Heart Stone. At last, the Goddess can set things right.*"

❀ ❀ ❀

THE BATTLE RAGED ON. SOLDIERS from the Southern Fort joined the melee. Although they were greatly outnumbered, the Resistance fighters fought with a vengeance. The Laurel Valley filled with sound of blades clashing and fighters screaming. The acrid smell of blood was strong as the wounded and dying covered the ground.

The perimeter of Kameeth's Woods was in flames. Then the rain started. Dark clouds gathered over the woods, raining droplets down on the burning trees. Yet the clearing in the center of the woods, the Heart Stone, remained warm and dry. The intensity of the rain increased, battling for supremacy over the flames.

From her position on the crest of the hill, Nikka observed the storm over the woods. This was no ordinary rainstorm. This was the Goddess at work. For the first time, Nikka felt fear. Wrapping herself tightly in her fur cape, she stepped back into the shelter of the trees, cowering.

Vestor, caught up in observing the battle, was not concerned with the weather until he realized the fire was going out.

"More arrows, Fizor! Burn the woods!" he yelled.

Fizor shouted instructions to the archers. They did their best, but their arrows were extinguished by the rain as they flew through the air.

The storm expanded to encompass the battlefield. The ground, already wet with blood, became a muddy morass. And still the rain came down. Weapons slipped and missed their mark. Visibility in the deluge was next to impossible. And still the rain came down. The weight of the fighters' clothing and battle gear hampered their movement, making fighting impossible. Men from both sides crawled off the battlefield seeking shelter. And still the rain came down.

As Vestor watched his army succumb to this force of nature, he grabbed Fizor's arm in a viselike grip. "Do something!" he yelled through the wind and the rain. "I cannot lose. I *will not lose!*" He flung Fizor to the ground.

Fizor crawled away from Vestor, through the mud, shouting orders to his men.

His hands clenched, rain running over him in rivulets, Vestor stood defiantly on the crest of the hill. He turned his face toward the sky and roared curses at the rain, Kameeth, and the Goddess.

❊ ❊ ❊

"It's a baby girl!" Mina exclaimed. "She is healthy, praise the Goddess."

Cora heard her baby cry and thought with relief, *My work is done.* Looking toward Kameeth, she smiled and released her final breath.

❊ ❊ ❊

THE CLOUDS ROILED OVERHEAD, spewing torrents of rain. And then, for an instant, the rain ceased and the sun shone through the clouds. A baby's cry echoed through the air—a new Mother Minca born.

In that moment of brightness, a glimmer of hope sparked in Vestor's heart. "Fizor, to arms!" he bellowed.

Before Vestor's army could be roused, the rain began again. Out of the storm clouds multiple bolts of lightning erupted, a fierce celebration of the new life. Vestor's soldiers quaked in terror. The battle was over. Vestor roared defiantly at his defeat at the hands of the Goddess.

One last bolt of lightning flashed from the sky, striking Vestor as he stood on the hill.

The ensuing shock wave sent Nikka reeling. She lost her footing and fell, hitting her head on a stone.

Through the rain and mud, Fizor staggered to Vestor's side. Vestor was dead. Fizor let out a howl of pain and anguish and crawled to Nikka, who still lived. Lifting her gently, he carried her body back to Vestor's camp and the healers.

With a final roll of thunder, the storm ended as quickly as it began.

❊ ❊ ❊

THE RESISTANCE FIGHTERS STUMBLED into the clearing, bloody, wet, and muddy. Shree and Ebru saw to their needs as best they could. Of the many men and women who came with Cora, less than half had survived. The warmth of springtime, the strong tea that Shree had prepared, and the cleansing of wounds restored the spirit of those who lived.

In the early afternoon, the granite slab opened. Dov came out of the ground. He announced to the gathering, "Cora, our beloved Mother Minca, died from her wounds today."

There were gasps and howls of sorrow. Shree held Ebru in a tight embrace as he cried.

Dov raised his arms to regain their attention. He spoke again. "Before she died, her daughter was born. We are blessed with a new Mother Minca."

Steff appeared before the crowd carrying Cora's daughter. He raised the tiny infant high into the air for all to see.

Voices called out, "Blessings on Mother Minca! Long live Mother Minca!"

Then another voice was heard. "Dov! Dov!" Leif and Vern came running through the woods. "Vestor is dead! His army gone! The battle is won!"

Chapter 38

Fizor carried Nikka back to camp. Vestor's healer, Micol, took Nikka from his arms and carried her into the healer's tent. Laying her on a cot, he examined her in silence.

"She has a concussion, but she will recover." Reaching for his trunk of medicinals, he selected an ointment, poured some onto a cloth, and gently dabbed at the wound on the back of her head. Glancing at Fizor, he asked, "Vestor?"

Fizor blanched, swaying slightly. "Vestor's dead. Struck by lightning."

Nikka muttered something, and the men looked to her. She was unconscious but struggling.

Hearing a commotion outside, Fizor left. About twenty bedraggled soldiers staggered into camp.

"The others?" Fizor asked.

"They wouldn't come back," one of the men said. "They ran off."

"Well," Fizor said, "so be it." Taking a breath, he addressed the soldiers. "Tend to the wounded and break camp. Quickly."

Fizor returned to the tent. "We must leave as soon as possible. Is Nikka able to travel?"

"Yes," Micol said. "We can make her a bed in the healer's wagon."

"Make haste. We must be gone. Take only what's necessary."

Micol nodded, closed up his trunk, and left the tent.

Fizor sat on the cot next to Nikka, his head in his hands. The tension that had been holding him together released, and his body sagged.

Nikka twisted and muttered. Fizor stroked her forehead and whispered, "Easy, Nikka. Shh."

"Parul? Is that you?" Nikka asked, delirious.

"Hush now, hush."

Nikka's eyes opened wide. Recognizing Fizor, she clutched his sleeve. "Vestor?"

"He's dead."

She started to cry. "What are we to do now?"

"Calm yourself. Those of us who returned will leave here and go north. My brother has a farm. He will take us in." Then Fizor asked, "Who is Parul?"

"Parul?" she asked, jerking away.

"You called out his name."

"He was my mentor, and Vestor's teacher. He is long dead," she whispered.

"I'm sorry," Fizor said. Before he could say anything more, Micol returned.

"We're ready to leave, General."

Patting Nikka's shoulder, Fizor rose, his face impassive and his jaw set. "Let's get on with it, then."

❈ ❈ ❈

FIZOR AWOKE BEFORE DAWN. Nikka, wrapped in her furs, sat by the dying fire. "Could you not sleep, my dear?"

She turned toward the general, a haunted look in her eyes.

"Last night . . . in the dark . . . he was reaching for me."

"Who?" he asked.

"At first I thought it was Vestor, then I recognized Parul." She shuddered, pulling her furs tightly around her.

"It was a bad dream. That's all."

"It was real."

"Vestor is dead. So is Parul. They cannot reach you."

"But—"

"Enough, Nikka. We must be strong for the others," Fizor said.

She nodded, facing the fire so he wouldn't see the fear and worry in her eyes.

Chapter 39

The moons rose high over the clearing. Torches were placed around the perimeter, and a fire burned on the center of the Heart Stone. Cora's shrouded body lay on the granite, a garland of spring flowers outlining her form. She would be buried in the Mincan tradition in the morning.

Once again, Dov stood on the Heart Stone. In the firelight, he raised his arms. "Friends, this has been the hardest of days." He moved in a circle as he talked so all could see. His hands moved gracefully, inviting connection. "The story of this battle will be told to our children and grandchildren.

"But it is not over yet. It is the Winter Solstice, the element of air and the time of quiescence. As is our tradition, we will take some time, breathe deeply, and meditate. Please make yourself as comfortable as possible, close your eyes, and let us take three deep breaths together."

They began the Winter Solstice meditation. Sitting in silence, each person continued to breathe deeply. They relaxed into a deep meditative state to connect with the

Goddess. They contemplated their blessings, the victory over Vestor's army, and their gratitude for surviving the battle. They wept for Cora's sacrifice and the death of their compatriots. They gave thanks for their family and friends, the new Mother of their tribe, for Kameeth, and for the Goddess of all. Each person took as long as they wanted and needed.

When Dov intuited that everyone was complete, he said, "As it was, in the time before time, the Goddess danced the dance of creation among the stars . . ."

❀ ❀ ❀

RILDA ARRIVED WITH DOLU AND Cian three days later. Steff was shocked at her appearance. Rilda was gaunt with a troubled expression, carrying physical and emotional scars from her time in Merton. Hearing of Cora's death brought her to her knees, weeping.

Steff presented her with her granddaughter, which brought a bit of light back to her eyes. Holding the little bundle, she said, "She is so beautiful! She looks just like Kip!"

"Cora told me she wanted her to be called Kippa in his honor," Shree said, putting her arm around Rilda's shoulder.

Rilda looked at her cousin. "And so it shall be," she confirmed, smiling through tears.

That evening after supper, Dov again stepped onto the Heart Stone. Illuminated by torch and moonlight, he helped Rilda step up. Steff handed Rilda Cora's baby. Then he and Ebru joined her. With a smile, Dov began the blessing of the child.

We come together in celebration.
A birth. A new beginning.
Kippa.

We call upon the Goddess to be with us.
We call upon Kameeth to be with us.
And Minca, Mother of us all.

We invite the Nature Spirits to join us,
and the angels as well.

We honor the four directions and the four seasons.
We honor Cora, the mother, and Kip, the father,
We honor Rilda, Steff, and Ebru, who have pledged to raise
this child.
And we share their joy.

Dov smiled and lifted the baby out of Rilda's arms. Holding her up for all to see, he continued.

Who will stand with Rilda, Steff, and Ebru?
Who will love Kippa and teach her the ways of the world,
teach her to honor her family, her community, and all
of nature?
Who will cherish this child in darkness and in light?"

Everyone in the clearing shouted out, "We will! We will!" Dov continued.

In the eyes and heart of the Goddess, this child is truly blessed.
She is bound by love to her parents and all who are
gathered here.

Everyone joined in for the completion.

So be it. So be it. So be it.

❊ ❊ ❊

CIAN WORKED WITH MINA and the healers while Dolu worked with Steff, Réan, and some of the others to repair the wagons and Shree's caravan and bury the dead from both sides.

They discovered where Vestor's encampment had been but could find no trace of any of Vestor's soldiers who might have survived the battle. The camp was deserted, torn asunder by hurried flight.

One morning after breakfast, Steff and Réan sat on the Heart Stone sipping tea. Leaning back, Steff looked at Réan. "I didn't realize that all Carroos could read Spirit Writing. In Minca, it's only the women."

Réan blushed and stared into her tea mug, avoiding his eyes. "Yes . . . well . . . um . . . in Carroo, it's only the women as well."

Steff thought for a minute. "But you were able to read the Spirit Writing on the Heart Stone," he said, confused.

"Yes, I could."

Steff lurched off the Heart Stone and stared at Réan as if for the first time. "Are you telling me you're a woman?" he asked, shocked.

Réan's blush deepened. "I am."

Steff searched for the womanly features she had kept hidden. "We've been traveling together for all this time, and you hid this from me? What is wrong with you? I thought we were friends," he said with a scowl, slamming down his mug and walking away.

Réan got up to follow him. Dov, who had overheard this exchange, reached out an arm to stop her. "Let him go."

"But he's so angry," Réan said miserably. "I need to make things better between us."

Dov gave her a small smile. "I've known Steff all his life. He can be quick to anger, but it will pass soon enough."

"But I have to make him understand. I *wanted* to tell him, but—"

Dov gave her a quick hug. "I understand. Mina explained the situation to me."

Réan sagged in despair.

"Drink your tea. I'll talk to him. It will be all right."

❊ ❊ ❊

STEFF WANDERED THROUGH the woods grumbling to himself, kicking at sticks and stones. *A woman! How dare he— she—lie to me all this time. Krickers! She made a fool of me. A real fool. Probably laughing all the while. How could I have been so stupid? I should . . . I should . . .*

In frustration, he slumped under a tree where Dov found him.

"Go away, Dov. I don't want to talk to anybody right now."

"I just saw Réan. She's very upset."

"She? You know he's a she?"

"Mina told me."

"Krickers. Am I the only one who was too stupid not to have known it?"

"No. You're not. I wouldn't have known if Mina hadn't told me," Dov explained. "Mina said you assumed Réan was a boy when you arrived in Carroo."

"Well, I did. She looked like the rest of them."

"Hmm. I wonder why she didn't tell you she was a girl?" Dov asked.

"Well, she wouldn't, would she. She didn't know me. I was just some Mincan who wanted to see Mother Carroo."

"So, you're saying she was taking precautions—staying safe?"

"Yeah, I am. But we became friends on that trip to Carroo. At least I thought we did."

"But you were still a Mincan and maybe not to be trusted?"

"Probably," Steff said grudgingly.

After a moment, Dov said, "Hmm. I wonder why she didn't tell you she was a girl when you left Carroo for the Heart Stone?"

"She was dressed as a Mincan woman, posing as my sister."

"Yes, and?"

"She got mad at me. Said I treated her differently."

"Did you?"

"I guess so, but—"

"But what?"

"It was hard. She was very attractive as a woman, and I—"

"What?"

"I was uncomfortable."

"Hmm. So you found her attractive and were uncomfortable, so you made *her* feel uncomfortable?"

"When you put it like that—"

"Yes?"

"Well, it almost makes sense. But she *should* have told me," Steff said.

"Hmm. And when exactly should she have told you?"

"I don't know, but she should have."

"Maybe. Let me know when you figure out when she should have done that. On the other hand, the two of you worked very well together. You got through some difficult situations and made it to the Heart Stone. That's important to remember," Dov said, patting Steff's thigh before standing up. "Take your time. See you back at the circle."

❈ ❈ ❈

IN THE LATE AFTERNOON, STEFF returned to the Heart Stone. He found Réan standing alone at the fire circle.

"I thought you trusted me."

"I do trust you," Réan insisted. "With my life. It's just that . . . I was afraid."

"Afraid? Of what?"

"When you arrived in Carroo, I used my gifts to keep the truth from you. I didn't know you and didn't trust you. The longer I deceived you, the harder it became to tell the truth." She struggled with her next words. "I was afraid that if you found out I was a woman, you would stop being my friend."

"Why would I stop being your friend? Blessed moons! That's ridiculous. I thought you knew me better than that."

"I'm sorry. Can you forgive me?"

"I guess I have to." He gave her a friendly shove. "Boy or girl, man or woman, you're still my best friend."

Réan shoved him back. "As you are mine."

❈ ❈ ❈

AS THE FIGHTERS RECOVERED their strength, they made their farewells and headed to their homes. Dolu transported a few of them in his wagon when he and Cian left.

On a clear evening, several days after the battle, Réan and Steff prepared a stew over the fire, chatting amiably as they worked. Mina and Dov walked around the clearing, talking softly. Ebru sang to Kippa as he fed her the brew Mina had made to sustain her. Rilda and Shree gazed dotingly on the baby.

As they gathered for dinner, Rilda said, "Friends, Shree and I have been talking about returning to the mountains. It's time to take Kippa home. Ebru will be coming with us. How about you, Steff? Dov?"

"Mina and I will return to Dute to let Bejla know her vision was true," Dov said.

Steff looked at Réan before speaking. "I would like to go back to Carroo with Réan. We want to tell Titia the news together. I will come home after that."

Réan smiled.

"Would it be possible for all of us to meet at the Heart Stone for the Spring Equinox?" Mina asked.

"Of course, we can," Rilda said. "It would be good to gather the tribes again."

Dov smiled shyly and said, "There's another reason as well. Mina and I wish to wed. We will ask Marna to come to the Heart Stone with us to perform the ceremony. We'd like to be married here."

"Wonderful! We'll all be here!" Everyone agreed with delight.

Steff punched Dov affectionately on the shoulder. "Congratulations, my friend," he said, before humming "The Traveler's Lament," much to Dov's amusement.

In the morning, they packed up and prepared to leave the Heart Stone. They placed flowers on Cora's grave. Then, after many hugs and kisses, they parted ways.

"May the Goddess protect you!"

"Till we meet again!"

"Farewell!"

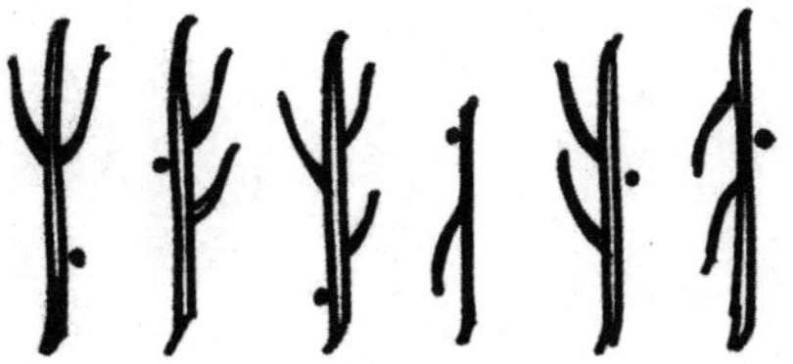

Chapter 40

For the first time in many years, a true spring appeared across the land. The fields sprouted, trees budded, and flowers bloomed. Even the birds' songs sounded happier.

Spring Equinox at the Heart Stone was the first gathering of the tribes in thirty years. There was a sense of jubilation and anticipation.

Mother Carroo came with Réan, along with Réan's friends from the mountain patrol. Mother Dute, Bejla, Coren, and his daughter's family came with Marna, Dov, and Mina. Shree, Steff, Ebru, Rilda, and Kippa were joined by Maji and Ayfer and their children. They all brought brightly colored tents and plenty of supplies, as they planned to stay for many days of celebration.

Just after dawn on the Spring Equinox morning, Marna married not one couple but two. On the journey back to Carroo, Steff *did* treat Réan differently, knowing she was a woman. Free of the constraints of disguise, Réan treated Steff differently as well. Their deep friendship blossomed into passionate love.

There was great happiness when their friends and families sang the wedding song.

Oh, joy of joys.
True love is found.
The vows are made; their wrists are bound.

Let's celebrate.
Gather all around.
The vows are made; their hearts are bound.

Goddess blessings.
The two are crowned.
The vows are made; their lives are bound.

Following the midday feast, it was time for the Spring Equinox ritual. Kippa, in her baby basket, was placed upon the Heart Stone. Titia sat on the edge of the granite beside her, rocking the basket gently. A large bouquet of spring flowers, a basket of fresh-picked wild strawberries, and a bowl of clear water were placed nearby while the others formed a circle around the stone.

Marna stood in the center of the Heart Stone to tell the creation story. Her graceful movements and melodic voice engaged the listeners anew with the wonder of the tale.

Marna stepped down from the Heart Stone to stand with Tasha and the Dutes. Titia, as the eldest mother, led the ritual, picking up the basket of strawberries. The circle moved slowly as each person stepped up to Titia before moving on. Titia offered everyone a strawberry, saying, "May you never hunger." When all in the circle had eaten a strawberry, she turned to Kippa, whose eyes were wide in wonder. Titia squeezed a little strawberry juice into her open mouth. "And may you never hunger, dear one," Titia said. Kippa smiled and cooed.

Titia picked up the bowl of water. Again, each person stepped forward. Titia offered each one a sip of water, saying, "May you never thirst." After serving the others, she turned to Kippa again. "And may you never thirst, Kippa," she said while pouring a tiny drop of water into Kippa's mouth.

Sliding off the Heart Stone, Titia joined the circle. Holding hands, they danced around the Heart Stone. Three steps to the left, a small hop, and reverse for one step to the right. They repeated the pattern while chanting the Spring Equinox canticle.

Water, earth, fire, air
We live under the Goddess's care.

Earth, fire, air, water
And the blessings of the Goddess's daughter.

Fire, air, water, earth
Spring reminds us of our rebirth.

Air, water, earth, fire
The Goddess provides all we desire.

Water, earth, fire, air
We all live under the Goddess's care.

Following the ritual, they relaxed in the sunshine talking, playing games, telling stories, and singing songs. At twilight, Steff and Réan, their wrists still bound, picked up the bouquet of flowers from the Heart Stone. Joined by the wrist-bound Dov and Mina, they walked to Cora's grave. Placing the flowers on the ground gently, Steff whispered, "I miss you so much, Cora. Réan and I pledge to cherish Kippa. We will tell her about your vision and the love, strength, and courage you needed to carry it out. We will tell her how you set this healing in motion."

Dov put his hand on Steff's shoulder. "She is with the Goddess, Steff."

The four friends stood together at Cora's grave for a long time before returning to the festivities.

Beneath the Heart Stone, Cora's spirit sat with Kameeth's. They smiled at each other, knowing that they had done their part to set the world right.

Acknowledgments

According to the proverb, "It takes a village to raise a child." It took a big village to help me get this book to the finish line.

Thank you to my early readers, Tara, Gayatri, Aaron, Pam, Katie, and Lenore.

Thank you to the Roving Writers and my Pittsburgh and Reykjavik writing friends.

Thank you to my teachers, Erica, Gail, and Kathy.

Thank you to my editors, Nic and Lorraine.

Thank you to Hedgebrook, Iceland Writers Retreat, and SparkPress.

Thank you to my family, friends, and my women's group.

And my thanks to you, dear reader.

About the Author

Catherine Raphael grew up in a suburb of Pittsburgh, Pennsylvania, and has a bachelor's degree in fine arts/metalsmithing from Syracuse University. She worked as a jeweler for sixteen years and did construction work on Arcosanti, Paolo Soleri's "City of the Future." Raphael has performed as a storyteller and an improv actor. She is one of the founding mothers of the Women and Girls Foundation of Southwest Pennsylvania. She has served on the boards of the Ms. Foundation for Women, the Women Donors Network, and volunteered with other progressive women's rights organizations. In 2014 she attended a master class at Hedgebrook—the friendships she made there coalesced into the Roving Writers, her writing group. Her stories have won prizes in Writer's Advice and the Ageless Authors competitions. Her work has been short-listed in Women on Writing and long-listed in Bumble Bee. This is her first novel. Raphael resides in Pittsburgh, PA.

Author photo © Ilana Ransom Toeplitz

SELECTED TITLES FROM SPARKPRESS

SparkPress is an independent boutique publisher delivering high-quality, entertaining, and engaging content that enhances readers' lives, with a special focus on female-driven work. www.gosparkpress.com

Gatekeeper: Book One in the Daemon Collecting Series, Alison Levy, $16.95, 978-1-68463-057-8. Rachel Wilde—sent from another dimension to bring defective daemons in for repair—needs to locate two people: a woman whose ancestors held a destructive daemon at bay and a criminal trying to break dimensional barriers. Helped by a homeless man with unusual powers, she uncovers a rising shadow organization that's changing her world forever.

Ocean's Fire: Book One in the Equal Night Trilogy, Stacey L. Tucker. $16.95, 978-1-943006-28-1. Once the Greeks forced their male gods upon the world, the belief in the power of women was severed. For centuries it has been thought that the wisdom of the high priestesses perished at the hand of the patriarchs—but now the ancient Book of Sophia has surfaced. Its pages contain the truths hidden by history, and the sacred knowledge for the coming age. And it is looking for Skylar Southmartin.

Alchemy's Air: Book Two of the Equal Night Trilogy, Stacey L. Tucker. $16.95, 978-1-943006-84-7.Now that she's passed her trial by fire, Skylar Southmartin has been entrusted with the ancient secrets of the Book of Sophia. Ahead is her greatest mission to date: a journey to the Underworld to restore a vital memory to the Akashic Library that will bring her face to face with the darkness within.

The Infinite Now: A Novel, Mindy Tarquini. $16.95, 978-1-943006-34-2. In flu-ravaged 1918 Philadelphia, the newly-orphaned daughter of the local fortune teller panics and casts her entire neighborhood into a bubble of stagnant time in order to save the life of the mysterious shoemaker who has taken her in. As the complications of the time bubble multiply, this forward-thinking young woman must find the courage to face an uncertain future, so she can find a way to break the spell.